THE FIFTH GATE
THE COMPLETE CASES OF
TUG NORTON, VOLUME 1

THE FIFTH GATE
THE COMPLETE CASES OF TUG NORTON, VOLUME 1

EDWARD PARRISH WARE

ILLUSTRATIONS BY
F.M. FOLLETT

COVER BY
LEJAREN HILLER

POPULAR PUBLICATIONS · 2022

TABLE OF CONTENTS

THE TREE-TOP TRAIL

Around a Cache of Fresh-Water Pearls
Revolve Actions and Emotions of Greed
and Hate and Murderous Lust

1

THERE WERE NOT enough night-watch and special police jobs to meet the demand, after the new commissioners got through shaking things down. Even if there had been, I doubt that I would have been content with one.

I had for some time past treasured the notion of starting a little investigation bureau of my own, and it looked as if the time had come to start it, when the chief called me in and said:

"Tug, you're fired. Commissioners think some new blood, of a different political strain, will pep the detective department up. Sorry to lose you. So long."

I might have put the bureau over then, had it not been for two things. First and foremost, there occurred directly afterward a scandal in connection with the Tri-State Detective Agency that nearly shook Kansas City off its hills—and folks developed a strong prejudice against any kind of detectives not connected with their own police force. That was bad.

Add to that hurdle the fact that men who have capital to invest in such ventures invariably think that brains don't develop only under frosted thatches, and you will know exactly why I failed.

Six of my thirty years had been spent on the force, and my record was good—but that didn't seem to spell

anything with the business men who had high-paid posi-
tions to assign, when I went after 'em.

Queer, but the average business man thinks that a few
years' service either as a patrolman or a detective spoils a
man for any other kind of work. Maybe it does. I don't
know, for I haven't tried it out. I'm still in the detecting
business, and expect to have that kind of harness on when
I die.

Yes, I put the bureau over, all on my own, and this is how
it happened.

I was reflecting over an after-supper pipe in my room
at Mrs. Reese's boarding house in Charlotte Street, where
I had lived for three years, when a soft knock on my door
informed me that the lady herself was outside. I got up
without a tremor, for I wasn't so near the cloth that I had
to stall my landlady—besides, Mrs. Reese wasn't that kind.
So, without trepidation, I switched on my light, opened the
door and invited her in.

I could tell that she was troubled, and before she had
spoken a dozen words knew further that the matter was
an unusual one.

"It's about Miss Carleton," she began, sitting down. "Her
father died last week, as you know, and since that time I
have been very uneasy about her. At first I put her unusual
conduct down to her father's death, as I naturally would,
but the fact that she has not been outside of the house since
the funeral, has had her meals sent to her room, and keeps
her door locked even in the daytime, convinced me there
was something the matter, other than a daughter's grief
over the death of a father.

"I am not nosey, Mr. Norton, but I have liked the girl

Rutter was still absorbed by his preparations,
when my hands came free

ever since she came to live here, three months ago, and I stood it as long as I could. Yesterday, I went to her room and begged her to make a confidante of me, if there was anything troubling her. Well, there is something troubling her, and that's why I've come to you. She needs help, and badly. And I thought that, since you are foot-loose right now, you might do something for her, poor girl. At least, you can hear her story."

I nodded assent. True, I had never posed as a first-aid to distressed young women, but Mrs. Reese's interest in her quickened mine. Besides, I had seen Miss Carleton at table a few times, and rather liked the look of her. Maybe I could be of some assistance—if the job happened to be in my line.

"Suppose we go down and talk matters over with her," I suggested. "I take it that the trouble is something my peculiar talents recommend me for, else you would not have called me in. I'm ready, any time."

Mrs. Reese led the way to a back room on the ground

floor of the big house, and knocked lightly on the door. Frankly, I was just a bit bored by the whole thing and, only for Mrs. Reese, wouldn't have been in it at all.

I had interviewed weepy young women before—women who felt they had a deep grievance against somebody, and who desired a husky young chap to do something to that somebody. I was in for it, though, and waited while a key turned in the lock, and the door opened a crack.

"Oh!" The exclamation came in a soft, relieved tone, and the door opened wider. "Come in, Mrs. Reese."

We walked in, and Mrs. Reese introduced me to her boarder.

"This is Mr. Norton, of whom I spoke, Miss Carleton. You've seen each other at table several times, I know."

I bowed to a slim, brown-haired, gray-eyed girl of about twenty, who, contrary to what I expected, flashed me a look from eyes that were not dim with tears. Her face was pale, and there was a weary look upon it which almost spoiled its prettiness. Tiny lines about the eyes, too, which showed strain—fear, I took it.

She smiled briefly, and with an entire lack of spirit which was significant. It was clear to me that she was a party to the interview, only because Mrs. Reese insisted, and that she was not hoping for much out of it. Well, neither was I. Which only goes to show how badly fooled we both were.

"Mrs. Reese tells me that you are in need of some advice, assistance perhaps, and thinks I should be able to aid you," I said, opening the way as I sat down.

The girl looked me over quite frankly, before speaking, then sat down also. Her expression gave me no hint as to whether I had passed muster. She appeared to consider her problem, with lids lowered, then:

"It can do no harm to tell you the circumstances," she said. "But I fear there is little chance of you doing anything for me. I can end the whole matter myself, with a few words, and be free from what I believe to be a real personal danger. I should, I believe, like your advice upon that particular point. Whether to end it or not. It is not right that I should yield to certain demands urged upon me, but when one's life is in danger, it is hard to resist taking the easiest way out—the safe way."

She looked at me, seeking, I felt sure, to determine how I felt about it. I was keeping my thoughts for possible use later, and my face would have been a real asset to me, had I elected to be a gambler. She saw nothing, and went on talking.

2

THE GIRL'S STORY, reduced to the salient points and set down here, may strike you as it did me, as a plain steal from fabric dreams are made of. Had it not had a convincing finale, I would have shied off, then and there. As it was— well, I didn't shy off. That finale wouldn't let me.

Peter Carleton, the girl's father, had, it appeared, spent some time in the Black River section of Northern Arkansas, fishing for pearls. He had had the good sense to credit the report that pearls had been discovered in fresh-water oysters—mussels, that is—and followed a hunch that he'd be lucky if he gave himself a chance.

The section he selected for his operations lay below the little inland town of Powhattan, about ten miles distant from that place and some fifteen or sixteen miles away from what might be termed civilization. Wild and rugged, as to its physical character, and wild and lawless in its social aspect, was that bit of Ozark hills on Lower Black River.

Carleton, working alone, made a find early in the game, and kept right on making them. For good and sufficient reasons, he kept the news of his good luck to himself. A lot of men had gone to the river country after pearls, and many of them were not at all particular how they got them.

In the vicinity of the log shack Carleton had built on the river bank, and occupied alone, was the camp of four men whom he regarded with suspicion, and whom he avoided in so far as he was able. They were a bit wilder and less law-abiding than any of the others about—and all were bad enough.

Peter Carleton kept his rough pearls in a belt about his middle, gave it out that he had been playing in hard luck. But he couldn't resist the impulse to take his gems out, every once in awhile and, in the fancied safety of his locked cabin, gloat over them. One night, while gloating, he heard a noise outside the shack's one window and, glancing fearfully toward it, discovered that he had not quite covered the opening with the blanket blind.

He spent the rest of that night sitting up, a rifle across his lap. Next morning he discovered tracks beneath the window—fresh ones. He had been spied upon, and his possession of the pearls discovered. No question about it. His fifty-thousand dollar horde was in danger.

It did not surprise him in the least to find himself watched by his four neighbors, after that night. Sometimes it would be Chilton, who appeared to be the leading spirit of his camp; sometimes Red Rutter would be on the job, or Doc Burns or Pete Crump. No matter which one trailed him, the job was expertly done.

Carleton had hidden the pearls, it goes without saying, and outside his cabin at that. The gang realized that, and watched him accordingly. It was Carleton's cue to move, and take his pearls with him. It would have been difficult to do, as a matter of fact, with no law within ten miles, and those miles made longer than the statute calls for, by hills and hollows, rock-clad and matted with thickets. The river was not regarded by Peter as a possible avenue of escape. It could be too well guarded.

Of course, he could have gone to Powhattan and brought the sheriff and a posse back with him and retrieved the cache, but he didn't.

Peter Carleton, in trying to cheat, did what a lot of men do. He overlooked the inescapable fact that the way of the transgressor—a double-crosser in his case—is hard. Frank Jaggard, a lunger who had gone to Powhattan in search of health, had not much strength but he did possess a little money. Two hundred dollars of his little store had been furnished Peter Carleton at a time when he needed it— before he began making his finds.

Jaggard had grub-staked Peter—and Peter was afraid to let even the sheriff know that he had made good, because, then, he'd have to split with Jaggard. Sounds hard, that, and it is hard—black, even. But, as Peter figured it, what was the sense of handing over about twenty-five thousand dollars to Jaggard, in return for the loan of two hundred? Some men are that way, and Peter Carleton was.

Before hiding his fortune, Peter had selected two fine specimens which he secreted in the toes of his boots, and one morning he set out for Powhattan after supplies. The Chilton crew intercepted and searched him. They, in look-ing for a lot of loot, never gave a thought to the old man's boot toes. He couldn't have much there.

They turned the whole thing off as a joke, and allowed him to proceed on his way—accompanied by one of their number, who claimed to be going into town for the same purpose as Carleton. Peter understood that move, of course. There was a possibility that he meant to circle back and get the pearls.

In town, the old man easily eluded his companion,

no longer suspicious, and the next day he was in Kansas City. There he settled down, after selling his two pearls, to await a favorable time in which to return and bring out his fortune. Chilton and his crew would soon get tired of watching an empty cabin, and vamose.

They got tired of watching the cabin, all right, and they searched it with care. Through a letter which Peter had received from his daughter, Beth, and forgot to destroy, they located his own hiding place. Henry Chilton was the first member of the gang to appear in Kansas City. He made Peter a proposition.

He would be satisfied with half the pearls, and guarantee to see that the old man got back home with his half all safe. Peter turned it down. Henry had him right where the wool was short, however. Jaggard had kicked up a fuss when he found his partner had skipped, and Chilton had figured out the real reason behind Carleton's actions. He knew that Peter would not appeal to the law, and he knew that he could not return for the pearls and get away with them—he was too closely watched for that.

Chilton went away, and Burns took his place, watching the old man and taking care to let him know about it. One after the other, they took turns in keeping cases on Carleton—and the upshot of the matter was, the old man couldn't stand the pressure. He had died in the night, heart disease it was called by the examining physician, and I guess it was, all right.

Since then Red Rutter had been on the job, trying to get information out of the girl. They figured that Carleton had undoubtedly told her where the pearls were hidden. Rutter had even appeared at Mrs. Reese's dining table, she taking transient mealers too, and had frightened the girl on other occasions. He felt safe, of course, since no one would believe such a story as she would tell, if, contrary to what he believed, she spoke at all.

Finally, two days before, Rutter had called Miss Carleton on the phone, and told her that unless she told him what he wanted to know, she'd be sent along to join Peter. The gang had grown tired of waiting, and would take no more fooling. Maybe he was bluffing, and maybe not. At any rate, he thoroughly frightened his victim.

When the girl had related her story up to that point, she ceased speaking and eyed me closely. I was still playing poker. Didn't want her to know what I thought of her tale—because I didn't think much of it, in fine. Didn't believe it. It was altogether too improbable.

"Had your father disclosed the hiding place to you?" I asked.

She nodded. "I know exactly where the pearls are," she assured me. "They are safe enough, and easily got at—except for the hazard of Chilton and his gang."

I was asking myself this question, rather than listening to her:

What was she playing for? What kind of a skin game was she up to? Looked like a straight enough girl, too. Well, the straight appearing ones are the really dangerous ones after all.

"Well," I said, "you might let me have that, too, and then I'll be able to give you my advice—if you want it."

Miss Carleton hesitated for a moment, then decided to let me have it.

3

—

"**A MILE BELOW** my father's cabin on the Black," she said, "is a place called Rock Point. It extends out in the river and is the only one in that section. Ninety yards, stepped yards, father said, back of the place where point and shore meet, is a small donnick in the midst of heavy timber.

"One day while he was hunting along there, he discovered a squirrel's den in a pecan tree on the donnick—the only such tree there. Where the tree forked about twenty feet from the ground was a hollow. It was not perceptible from the ground, and father knew about it only for having seen a squirrel come out of it.

"Thinking it a safe place, he filled a baking-powder can with the pearls and dropped them into that hollow. It was not deep, and he filled it with small stones which he carried in his pocket for that purpose. That was done the night he heard the man at the window, before they had time to set close watch upon him. That is the story father told me, just before he died," she said, simply. "They are there, and there they will stay, in all probability—unless—"

"Unless you yield to the demands of Rutter, eh?" I finished for her. "Well, are you going to?" I was stalling for time until I could decently go back to my room and finish my pipe.

"Would you?" she countered, her great eyes unflinchingly upon me. Darn it! The girl did look the part of a straight one, and there could be no denying it!

"Well, now—as for that," I stalled, "I wouldn't. Still, you know, I'm a man, and better able to—"

What I said doesn't matter, since from the first word I was merely talking to cover something else. Miss Carleton was sitting with her back to a window which was partly open from the bottom, and I sat where that window was in the range of my vision.

Just when the listener showed up outside the window, I don't know. He was there when I started to frame my answer to the girl's question. A red-headed, pinched-face man, who might be Rutter—granting, of course, that he existed.

Slowly, I felt for the gun on my hip, keeping my tongue going all the time. No, I didn't mean to shoot the fellow. I'm not given to such fool tricks. He might be just an ordinary eavesdropper, and then what? I merely meant to get a bead on him and make him come through. I failed, though.

Miss Carleton, noting my action with the gun, turned toward the window.

"Rutter!" she gasped, all a-tremble. "It is he—Rutter!"

I covered the distance to the window in a leap—but what was the use? The man was gone. I didn't follow, either. He would be away in the darkness, and to find him would be difficult, not to say impossible. I looked at my watch, instead.

"Sit down, Miss Carleton," I told her calmly. "While it's on my mind," I said to Mrs. Reese, who also had seen the man at the window, "please give Miss Carleton my room on the upper floor—she won't be accessible there."

"Why—why," stammered my landlady, "are you giving it up?"

I nodded. "Temporarily, at least. Now, Miss Carleton," I went on, "I am going to make you a business proposition, and Mrs. Reese shall witness it. Until that fellow appeared and corroborated your story, I, frankly, did not believe it. Sorry, but it just wouldn't go down. It's different now."

"Oh, I'm glad!" Beth Carleton exclaimed. "I could hardly believe it myself, until the Chilton gang materialized, and then I could not doubt. Since father's death, their persistence has confirmed all he said."

"Exactly. Now, about the business proposition. I need a bit of money myself, to start—well, to start up in business. I'll take this job on, bring the pearls to Kansas City, and Frank Jaggard with them—if I can find him. When the gems are sold, my fee shall be twenty per cent of the whole—if the amount reaches fifty thousand, or goes over. If it's under that amount, then my percentage will have to be larger. I'm not a hog, but the job is going to be a nasty one."

"Oh, that will be satisfactory!" the girl exclaimed, her eyes lighting. "Even more—"

"No. Just as I've put it—and Mrs. Reese will remember, thereby protecting all concerned. Now," I said, looking at my watch again, "I've got to make a certain train at the Union Station in just thirty minutes—"

"But the money for the trip," Miss Carleton interrupted. "I haven't it in the house, and can't get it until the bank opens to-morrow. I attended to money matters for father and there is a small balance."

"I'm not broke either," I told her. "And I guess I'm up to

risking a bit on a sporting proposition. Besides I can't wait for you to draw. Here's what I want you to do: Stay close until I get back. You won't be in any further danger from Rutter, or, likely enough, anybody else. Still it will be as well not to show yourself. I'll be back when you see me." I took my hat and started for the door.

"Are you going right now?" Mrs. Reese demanded. "Without a bag or anything?"

"Sure," I told her. "I'm going to try and beat Rutter to Powhattan, else get there along with him. You see, that window is partly open and, ten to one, he now knows where those pearls are as well as I do!"

With that I left them. That train would depart in about twenty minutes.

I got a good seat in the smoker, and when the southbound Frisco Flier pulled out I sauntered through the entire train, except the Pullman section, to learn if Rutter was a fellow passenger. I failed to find him, but I knew that he was on the train. Knew it for two reasons.

In the first place, if he had reached the window in time to hear Miss Carleton tell me where the pearls were hidden, he'd catch the Flier, or break his neck trying. It was the only fast train south for twelve hours. Secondly, if he had not heard enough of the conversation to tell him where the cache was, he'd know that I was in possession of the information. Having been smart enough to put over what he had on the old man and the girl, he'd figure right now that I'd been called in on the case.

Therefore I was careful to give him plenty of chances to trail me to the train. Yes, I was fairly certain Rutter was among us.

There were a number of men reclining in chairs in the smoker, hats or newspapers over their faces, like there always are in the smoker of a night train. One of those sleepers was doubtless Rutter. On that assumption, I got a pillow from the porter and settled back where I could watch.

I had never been on a case that promised as much and, at the same time, as little as this tree-top trail I'd taken up. If the pearls were there and I succeeded in getting away with them, I'd have the capital I needed to set up the little sleuthing parlor. But—

I was about to tell myself that the story the girl told was just a bit of word-cooking; that old man Carleton would have been a nut to go away and leave those pearls. I knew darn good and well that, in his place, I'd have got them out of the river country, the Chilton outfit to the contrary notwithstanding. I was just about to give myself a good cussing for the fool I'd been, when that little word "old" sort of hung in my mind. That word explained a lot.

Carleton, while not by any means decrepit, was, nevertheless, an old man, and his mind not keened up to scheming things and doing a good job of it. He couldn't figure a good way to get out of the river country with the pearls, and he did the best he could. Where he fell down was in underestimating the sagacity and the stick-to-it-iveness of the gang he was up against.

After all, I concluded, had I been in Carleton's place, carrying his years and his inexperience in the ways of crooks, I'd likely have done just what he did—maybe worse.

Now my experience has taught me that it is a pretty bad thing to go after something that you only half believe exists. You are apt to leave just enough of yourself out of the search to cause you to fall down on it. And when I finally opened up and gave full credence to Peter Carleton's tale, I couldn't have been bought off the case for twice the amount of the cache. The thing became real, and that changed its complexion entirely.

4

I SETTLED BACK, hat over my eyes, while the train reeled off the miles. I made no plans, because I didn't know enough about what I'd be called on to face. I knew this only: About three hundred and fifty miles distant was the little town of Black Rock, to which place I had bought a ticket. I'd reach there shortly before daylight the next morning and I'd have to take a stage over three miles of hill road to Powhattan. Ten miles down the river from Powhattan lay the scene of my operations. I'd do my planning when I got there.

"Springfield! Springfield! Twenty minutes stop at Springfield!"

I glanced at my watch and found that it was two o'clock—and two hundred and twenty-five of those miles were behind me. I hadn't slept any, of course, and no redheaded man had rewarded my wakefulness. I began to grow a bit uneasy about Rutter. It was absolutely necessary for me to know where he was and what he was up to. Then I got an idea.

The train stopped and numbers of passengers hurried out to a restaurant near by, for an early morning cup of coffee. I got up and followed—but I didn't go directly to the restaurant. I slipped inside the waiting room and watched the crowd.

Rutter came down the steps of the smoker, looked about him for an instant, then hurried over to the restaurant. He'd been under one of those spread newspapers, all right. I sauntered along in his wake and while we ate our sandwiches and drank our coffee across the horseshoe from each other, I studied him and he studied me.

It was the face I had seen at the window, and no mistake. Rutter was a heavy-built six-footer, topping me about an inch, and looked to be about forty. As for the rest, he would probably stack up as a pretty useful crook, with somebody to do the scheming for him. Not much intelligence, but the jaw of a doer.

I ate leisurely, and pretty soon the other passengers began to leave. Rutter grew a bit restive. At length we were the only ones left, and he got up, walked to the door, looked toward the train then back at me again.

"Gimme another cup of coffee," I ordered. "And a piece of—say, what kind of pie you got?"

The hasher turned to fill my order.

"Al-l-l-l Ab-o-o-a-a-r-r-d-d-d-d!" yelled the conductor.

I don't know whether it was the engineer of the passenger releasing the air, or a gasp from Rutter that I heard. I glanced under my hat-brim and saw him hesitate in the doorway. If he sprinted for the train, I'd sprint too, for the question in my mind would be answered.

He didn't—and the question was no longer one. I knew for a certainty now.

Rutter stood in the doorway watching the Flier's tail lights fade out down the track, then he stepped out. I finished my apple pie, paid up and followed—cautiously.

He stood outside, rather disconsolate looking, hands in his side coat pockets.

"Got a match?" I asked, strolling up to him.

He fished one out and I lit up. "Well, we both got left, didn't we?" I commented. "Suppose we stroll along a ways," I went on. "It's a bit too public here for what I want to say."

Eying me warily, Rutter walked beside me toward the station. About halfway there I stopped. "This will do," I told him. "You took the bait, all right. Swallowed it down."

"What the hell do you mean?" he demanded truculently.

"Just this, Red-head: I wanted to know where you were and how much of Miss Carleton's conversation you had overheard. I found out. You don't know any more now than you did a week ago—except that you've got a man to fight instead of a woman."

"Say, are you a nut? Wadda you mean, anyhow—"

"Can it, Rutter, can it," I told him. "You're not dealing with old man Carleton now. All of your cards are on the table, face up—you just don't know it. You gave yourself away when you failed to take that train just now. If you'd known what I thought you might know, you'd be on it.

"Take your hand off your gun," I went on, eying his right-hand pocket. "I'm not going to hurt you—not right now, and you can't afford to bump me, because then you lose your chance to find out what I know. Get that? Well, get this: I haven't got any restraint whatever on my actions. I can afford to bump you—and I will, understand, if you tail me a bit farther!"

I walked off without waiting for his answer. The freight

yards were just below the depot and I found a switch-shanty close by.

"What's the chance for a freight south, old-timer?" I queried a switchman there.

The words were hardly out of my mouth when the "toot-toot" of a road-engine, at some distance down the track, answered the question. I ran across to where a red-ball was getting under way for Memphis. Glancing over my shoulder, I saw that Rutter was making for the train, some fifteen car-lengths below.

"All right," I reflected, as I swung myself to the roof of a car, "you're doing just what I thought you would, and as I'd do if the shoe was on my foot—but one of us is not going to get to Black Rock, and that's certain!"

The drag picked up rapidly, and I flattened out—not on the running-board, but alongside it, my face toward the caboose. Shortly after the engine whistled out of town, the fireman opened the fire-box door, and a glare lit the train-top.

Red-head was crawling along the running-board toward me, about ten car-lengths away. Being flat on the roof, he couldn't see me—that's where I had the advantage. The fireman closed the door, and Rutter faded out.

Here was my position, now. Rutter had one valuable bit of information. He knew that I was on the job, that I knew where the pearls were hidden, and that I was going for them. But that was the extent of his knowledge. Chilton and the rest of them were in the river country, on the watch, and Rutter had to get the word to them, and at the same time keep cases on me, on the chance that I might lead him to the cache.

Well, he was going to earn his money; for I meant to make him work for it.

5

I DIDN'T LOSE sight of Rutter for long. The fire-box was opened again, shortly afterward, and in its lurid light he showed about five cars away.

I had time to catch him in the act of opening a hatch-door in the roof, above the icebox of a refrigerator car, and then it was dark again.

That didn't make any difference. I knew where he was locating himself, and that was enough. Giving him about five minutes more, I started crawling toward where he had been.

I maintain that a sleuth who goes about killing folks when there is any other way out, doesn't remain a sleuth long. It isn't being done, nowadays—if ever it was. I didn't want to kill Rutter, and at the same time I knew I would do it, if that was the only way in which I could drop him out for a couple of days. Besides, I was acting in my private character—the only one I had, since the commissioners got busy—and it behooved me to walk easy.

I got to the end of the car where I had spotted Rutter, and found just what I thought I would. He had slipped the plug out of the opening to the icebox, dropped it inside the empty and himself down on it. Then he had closed the hatch-door on top of all. A snug place to ride, and there he meant to stay until Black Rock was reached.

Well, that suited me. I, too, meant for him to stay there. Crossing heavily to his car, I opened the hatch-door, keeping back where he couldn't see my face if the firebox should open again.

"Where ya goin', bo?" I bellowed down, gruffly, dazzling him with my flash. "What ya ridin' on?"

"Down the line," came the answer. "I've got four-bits—here!"

He stood up to hand the supposed brake-man a coin, and I had a fair swing at his head with my clubbed six-gun. He crumpled up, and dropped.

I shut the hatch-door over him, found the hasp and fastened it. Rutter would be there when Black Rock was reached, all right—and a good ways beyond it. Of course there was a chance that he might come back strong enough to make somebody hear him, at some stop or other, and get out, but it was a mighty small one. He'd be too sick after that clout I gave him to stir about much this side of Memphis.

In that case, I'd have that two-day lead I wanted. Anyhow, I had to take the chance—else kill Rutter, and, as I said before, that isn't my way, if I can help it.

I got to Black Rock about ten o'clock that morning, and to Powhattan two hours later. The inland town was small, but lively. A lot of pearlers outfitted there, and the saloons seemed to be having a good trade. A merchant who did an outfitting business sold me a bateau, tent, a pair of pearling-tongs, and other truck I needed to stall with. A few questions along the river front assured me that I was headed in the right direction—Rock Point—and, about

three in the afternoon, after I'd changed to a pair of over-
alls and jumper, I pointed my boat down-river.

I couldn't figure where I was due to have trouble, since
I looked about like any other pearler in the country, and
Rutter hadn't got word through to Chilton. I'd locate the
tree, hang around my camp, which would be close by, then
get the pearls after dark. By daylight I'd be on my way back
to Kansas City.

That is how I figured it, but I had a hunch that things
were not going to be quite that easy. It wouldn't be natural for them to be. There was one thing against me at the
start. I didn't know Henry Chilton, or his two pals, from
anybody else in the river country. On the other hand, and
in my favor, neither did Henry and his pals know me.

I drifted on down. Many boats were anchored on the
bars, of which there were plenty in the Black, their occu-
pants pearling along, more or less dexterously.

"How far to Rock Point?" I inquired of a pearler, swinging in beside him after I had been afloat about an hour.

"Three miles," he told me. "You can't miss it. First you
come to old man Carleton's cabin on the right bank, then,
one mile below, the Point sticks out in the water, big as a
house. You'll know when you get there."

Things were developing too favorably. I began to get a
trifle uneasy, and to expect the break against me I felt sure
would show somewhere. Up to the present moment it
hadn't required any special use of what brains I possessed
to follow this trail. Anybody might have followed it.

Miss Carleton might as well have hired a husky out of
any crowd, and sent him after her property. I don't mean
that I wasn't perfectly satisfied to have things run smoothly.

You bet I was—and hoped they'd continue to. But—my experience with crooks had not been of a nature to warrant me in getting careless just because everything seemed quiet and peaceful.

Pretty soon Rock Point loomed up ahead, and I steered for it. After drawing the bow of the bateau well up from the water, I climbed the ridge of the point, and gained the bank. Night was coming on, and the heavy timber beyond was gloomy. Walking westward, I counted my steps. Ninety yards would be about ninety of my strides.

"—twenty-four, twenty-five, twenty-six—"

I broke off, staring incredulously. The donnick was there ahead of me—and it was bare. Not a tree on it. Moreover, beyond the donnick stood a one-room log cabin, its newness testifying to its recent construction!

That break had come—and the tree-top trail had seemingly reached a sudden and highly unsuccessful termination.

I didn't stand there gawping long. There was no fence about the place, and I walked along a path to the door. Just as I got there it opened and a beefy man of about forty stood on the sill.

"Well?" His tone was anything but friendly.

I grinned. "Done a darn fool thing," I explained. "Forgot to bring matches along from Powhattan, where I outfitted. Don't know how come me to overlook—"

"It don't matter how you come to do it," said the man in the door. "If you ain't got any, do like we do when we are out—go to town and get some!"

He slammed the door in my face. But that didn't bother me, because I'd found what I went to the shack to look for.

Above the door was a pecan log—and the only one, so far as I could see, in the structure.

"It's the place, all right," I reflected, as I made my way to the boat. "Somebody has built a camp on the very spot Carleton chose for his cache. That argues that whoever cut the pecan tree, found the can, and that's that!"

I paddled the bateau back upstream for a couple of miles, noted that Carleton's old place was occupied, went ashore at the first camp I saw, and asked a few questions.

"Who's camped in the second cabin below here—the one above Rock Point?" I asked of a pearler who was steaming his catch of mussels in a big boiler.

"Henry Chilton," he replied. "Him and two or three others."

"How long since they built that shack?"

"Couple of months ago," the pearler answered, straightening and eying me. "Say, why don't you go down there and ask them what you want to know?"

"They're not the ones I'm looking for," I replied. "Trying to find a friend of mine who came on ahead of me. Wasn't anybody at the cabin, awhile ago, to ask. Much obliged."

I did some thinking while I dropped down stream again, and then made camp at a point half way between Carleton's old shack and the one on the donnick. The way it looked to me, things stacked up about as follows:

Chilton and his gang had made a permanent camp on the donnick, and had used the logs from the place in the building. That was natural. The pecan log was there in the structure, and it was a cinch that the can of pearls was not in the log—couldn't be, because whoever handled the log would surely have discovered them. All right. The pearls had been discovered by one—no, two members of the gang. Two, because they'd naturally work in pairs while cutting and trimming the logs. Two members of the bunch had those pearls.

Which two?

"Rutter," I reflected, "is out of the reckoning. If he had them he'd never have wasted any time in Kansas City. Chilton? No. He'd not be likely to do much of the hard work of the building; being the leader, he'd leave that to the others. Besides, he is the brains of the gang, and would have figured a way out if he'd come across the loot and wanted to do a bit of doublecrossing on his own hook.

"That leaves it up to the other two—Burns and Crump. Yes, they're the ones, and they've been waiting for a favorable time to get away. Probably for Henry to go to Kansas City to relieve Rutter. That would give them all the chance needed. I'm doing a bit of guessing, of course, but I'll wager I'm right."

6

FURTHER REFLECTION IN my blanket that night strengthened my belief that I was right. I didn't want to believe it, either, for if it proved to be correct it just about finished my chance to get the pearls. I'd have to watch Burns and Crump until one or both betrayed the hiding place, and that would doubtless take time. Rutter would appear, sooner or later, and when he came the country would be too hot to hold me. When I got up in the morning I felt pretty hopeless, and no mistake.

After breakfast I slipped through the woods and hid beside the clearing around Chilton's cabin. The place looked like somebody had swept it with a broom, it was that free from trees and undergrowth. Pretty soon two men came out and went toward the river, both carrying tongs. One was the beefy man whom I had seen the day before, and the other was a heavy-set fellow, some years younger than his companion.

I went back to camp, got into my bateau, and anchored on a bar where I could pretend to pearl, but in reality watch for Rutter's coming. It was a lonely spot, and I meant to give myself some time by catching Rutter before he reached camp. He failed to show up, however, and when night came I went ashore.

Maybe it was because I was too deep in thought, or

perhaps because I had no reason to think myself under suspicion—anyway, I did not see the beefy man and his companion until I was almost to my tent. When they stepped from behind trees, both handling their guns in a businesslike manner, I saw them right enough.

"It's our turn to do a little questioning," the beefy man said sneeringly, as he relieved me of my gun. "I didn't like your looks when you was stalling about them matches last night. When you went to the trouble to row up river and ask questions about us, I figgered it was time to take you in. Now walk on ahead, and keep going!"

There wasn't anything for me to do but obey. When we reached the cabin, the third member of the crew let us in. He was about the general size and build of Rutter, and proved to be Crump. The beefy man turned out to be Chilton, as I had sensed all along.

"Now," the latter began, when I had taken the chair pointed out, "who are you, and what is your business here?"

"I'm Joe Hinton, and I'm here to pearl," I replied. "Who are you, and what the hell do you mean, treating me this way?"

"Where did you come from?" Chilton went on, ignoring my counter question.

"Walnut Ridge—"

"That's a lie!"

The door was pushed open suddenly, and Rutter stood there, his eyes glaring hotly at me.

"It's the fellow the Carleton gal sent down—after you know what!" he added; and, while the others listened, their faces glowering, he detailed the happenings of the past two days. "I got out of the ice box at Jonesboro, the subdivision, and got here as soon as I could. Now, here's what: that guy knows where the cache is, and it's up to us to make him tell."

I knew there was no use stalling any longer about myself, so answered up before I was spoken to.

"You fellows are too many for me!" I said ruefully. "Suppose I do know what you want to find out, and do tell? What then? Do I go free, and get a cut?"

Chilton grew thoughtful.

"Reckon that's the cheapest way out," he opined. "Put us next, and you get a one-fifth share. It's a good thing for you that you ain't inclined to be stubborn, because I've got a way to make folks talk. Come through, if you're going to, and let's be done with it."

I stole a look out of the corner of my eye at Burns and Crump, to see how they were taking things. If I had figured things right, they must be getting darned uneasy.

Strangely enough, they seemed as eager to hear my revelation as Chilton and Rutter were. Had I been mistaken? It looked like it.

"If it wasn't for them fellows camped up at old Carleton's place, I'd have them pearls now and be on my way," I told them. "I ain't sure which log it is, and the girl didn't remember, either; but one of the logs in the back of that old cabin holds what you're looking for."

There was a silence in the cabin, and I could hear all four men breathing.

"What do you mean, inside one of the logs?" Henry demanded, after a bit.

"I mean that Carleton scooped out a hole in one of the logs, hid the pearls there, then closed the hole with bark and clay—chinked it up, the girl said, so it wouldn't look any different from the other chinking. That's all I know."

What happened then was not altogether unexpected. The whole crowd made a grand rush for me, and before I hardly knew what was happening I was stretched on a bunk and roped tight.

"We'll see whether you've been telling the truth or not!" Henry leered. "God help you if you've lied! Rutter, you stay here until we get back. Burns, you and Pete had both better come with me! Might have trouble getting them two pearlers out of the way. We'll be back in about an hour," he said, turning to me, "and if we've got the pearls we'll get rid of you nice and gentle like. If not—well, you'll wish you hadn't lied, that's all!"

7

I DIDN'T FIGURE on being there when they got back, but of course I didn't mention that. It takes a good hand at the business to rope a man so he'll stay, provided that man is in full possession of all his faculties and knows a bit about that game too.

If Henry and the others stayed away an hour, or even half that long, I'd be gone—granting, of course, that Rutter wasn't a lot keener than I had reason to think him to be.

They didn't waste any time getting away, and when they had gone Rutter stood by the bunk and cussed me whole-heartedly for about three minutes. I didn't blame him much for that. After a bit he went outdoors and returned with a big stone, about fifty pounds, I judged. He placed it on the floor about ten feet from my bunk, then procured a ball of baling wire and sat down beside the stone.

"They tell me drowning ain't so bad, after all!" he remarked pleasantly, as he began to wrap the rock in a net of wire. "Never tried it myself, so can't say positive."

While he worked with his wire, becoming more and more absorbed in the task, I worked at the rope. The bunk being against the back wall, and in the shadow, it was easy enough to do, if I used caution.

"This doubled wire, now," the worker went on to explain,

"goes round the neck, and the rock kind of drags the person which is attached to the neck, down close to the bottom of the river—and there he stays!"

Rutter was getting a lot of malicious pleasure out of that line of talk. I knew, of course, that while he was making a joke of it, the rock was intended for me—and no mistake about that. Then my hands came free and I set to work on my legs and ankles.

Rutter continued his pleasantries anent the rock.

"Anybody which has a rock fixed to their neck, and is then throwed into a deep hole of water," he explained, "never tells about what's happened to him—nor who done it."

I made a noose in the fifteen-foot length of half-inch rope and coiled the free end. Rutter was still absorbed by his preparations.

"I'm going to ask Henry to let me tie this rock on yore—"

The noose sailed through the air and settled over his shoulders, dropping down around his arms. He came up with an oath of astonishment, wheeled, and reached for his hip.

By that time I was on the floor and putting my weight on the rope with a jerk. He managed to get the gun out, but went down at the same time. Before he could use it I was on top of him and the gun was mine.

Rutter took my place in the bunk—only he was tied right, and the gag in his mouth would stay there until somebody would take it out.

My gun was on a table, and I pocketed it along with Rutter's.

Outside, I took my bearings and started off north across

the clearing. I was running, and fast at that. The pearls would have to go over until another time. As far as Joe Hinton was concerned, he was a blown-up proposition in that section. My bateau lay at anchor between the Carleton cabin and the clearing, and I went for it. I was free, and had two good guns. If I met with that outfit on the way, well—

I didn't. I crossed a patch of moonlight above the clearing, and something caught my eye that made me forget Chilton and the others for a time at least.

When I had entered that cabin I wore a pair of stout, black shoes. Now they were gray. That is what attracted my attention and brought me to a full stop. A minute later I was back-tracking toward the clearing.

I was on the right trail at last!

Whoever had cut that pecan tree afterward sawed off about sixteen feet of the trunk for a log, leaving the top. The rocks old man Carleton had filled the hole with, in order to make sure the squirrels wouldn't use it again, had kept the can in place for awhile at least.

What do they do with tree tops and brush, after clearing? Why, they stack them up and burn them, of course! What I had seen on my shoes was a thin layer of gray wood-ashes—and a minute later I found the pile which I had run through in my flight.

I dug like a chipmunk in that ash heap, for my time was short. I never stopped to think what effect fire might have on pearls. Several old cans were unearthed, refuse from the camp, but that was all. I'd almost given up when—wonder of wonders—I thrust my arm down a gopher hole square in the bed of the fire. I brought up a heavy can. It was rusty, black, and open at the seams—but the pearls were there!

As far as a glance could tell, they had not suffered in the least while the fire raged above.

I shoved the can inside my shirt bosom and turned to the woods again. Then things broke—and broke fast.

Chilton entered the clearing from the north, and on the run. Burns and Crump were right behind him. Being in plain view, they saw me instantly.

Chilton reached for his gun—but his fingers never touched it. He dropped in a heap, and my next shot got Crump and doubled him up. The next minute I gained the cover of the timber, and Burns, who had ducked for the trees at my first shot, missed me so far I never even heard the bullet sing.

THE KAW VALLEY DETECTIVE AGENCY—you will probably hear of it if you come to Kansas City—is my place, and it's going strong, thanks to my cut of the pearls.

Jaggard, the innocent cause of all the trouble, never has been located, but if he or his heirs ever get wind of what's happened they'll be richer for some twenty-odd thousand dollars which Miss Carleton insists belongs to them, and which she's keeping for them.

THE FIFTH GATE

*The Ruggles "Boys" They Were Known
as, But They Stopped at Little Short of
Murder to Carry Out Their Plan*

1

WHEN THE GATEWAY INSURANCE COMPANY sent along its fat retainer, and then let two months pass without calling on the Kaw Valley Agency to do anything to earn the money, I began to think my sleuthing bureau had acquired a strip of pure velvet. At the end of the third month I began to worry a bit; corporations do not customarily pay for something they don't get, and, as the Gateway company was a flourishing concern and liberal, I wanted to do something to earn my money and keep the officials in good humor.

I need not have worried. On the first day of May, three months after our connection had been established, Asa B. Howard, general Manager of Gateway, walked into my private office, laid his hat and gloves on the table, and started me out on a case which, in some respects, rivals anything my bureau records hold—and they are not blank books by a long shot.

"My company must pay, in a very short time, a ten thousand dollar policy which we have cause to suspect should not be paid," Mr. Howard began. "I will acquaint you with the history of the case and get your views upon it, Norton."

He went straight to the point and, reduced a bit more, the facts ran about as follows:

Abner Ruggles, a bachelor of fifty years, residing in

southwest Missouri, near the Arkansas line, had, two years previously, taken out a five thousand dollar straight life policy. A year later he took out a second policy for a like amount, paying the premiums in advance on each. Investigation, at the time disclosed the fact that Ruggles was a large holder of unimproved lands in his own and adjoining counties, regarded as wealthy by his neighbors, and, while of a taciturn, reserved disposition, was nevertheless thought of as a good citizen; progressive in real estate matters, and a booster for his community.

It was not, in view of his extensive realty holdings, regarded as odd that he should take out rather heavy policies at his time of life, though it would have been looked upon as a suspicious circumstance in one of less substance. The policies were issued, the beneficiaries being two younger brothers, Brack and Melville Ruggles, both of whom lived on a farm near the home of Abner.

A month prior to Mr. Howard's visit to my office the company had been informed of the death of Abner Ruggles. His cabin, located off the main road in the country near Pineville, had burned in the night, catching, so the information read, from a woods fire which swept that section. The tragedy had not been discovered until late the following morning, owing to the cabin's isolated location, and Abner Ruggles's remains had been so nearly destroyed as to render positive identification impossible.

Usually there is some peculiar mark by which even a partially destroyed body can be recognized, but in Ruggles's case there was none. He had never had any dental work of a lasting nature done, and there was nothing to dispute the supposition that the man found in the ashes of the

An instant later I was swept over the lower falls

burned cabin was its owner. He had never been known
to entertain guests overnight, and a check of the sparsely
settled community disclosed no one missing. There was
nothing, in fine, to suggest that all was not above board in
tire matter.

Gateway sent a man down, as is usual in such cases, and
it was his findings that caused the officials to decide to go
slow about paying the policies. It seems that the large real
estate holdings of Abner Ruggles, carefully scrutinized,
were large in point of volume only. He had bought lavishly
at a time when it was his belief that much lead and zinc
ore lay under the rocky soil of that section of the Ozarks,
only to find later that his belief had been a delusion only.
He had retained the land because no purchaser could be
found for it, and the taxes had taken some, while small
mortgages claimed other portions. The land was, it developed, a liability rather than an asset.

In short, Abner Ruggles, at the time of insuring, was a

poor man, and in no sense justified in taking out such large policies on his life. There was no good reason for his doing so, since he had no immediate family to benefit by it. His two brothers, both bachelors, were all his kin, and, so far as was known, he had had no very great liking for them.

"Why, then, the large policies?" Mr. Howard asked, and I pondered the answer.

"Looks like there might be something crooked, for a fact," I told him. "Still—a life insurance policy provides ready money for the heirs only. Would a man insure himself in favor of persons whom he does not care a great deal about, then get himself killed in order to make them rich? Hardly."

"We learned something else," Mr. Howard went on. "It appears that at about the time the insurance was issued Abner Ruggles had become a pretty hard drinker. That did not develop in the rather superficial investigation into his personal habits before the risk was taken. Such inquiries never go very deep; the risk's word as to alcoholic indulgence is usually regarded as sufficient, except, of course, when a physician's examination shows conclusively that he has impaired his health by drinking liquor.

"I don't know that Ruggles imbibed to that extent during the past two years, but report has it that his mind became affected during the latter part of his life. Not greatly, it seems, but noticeably. He spent more time with his brothers than had been his wont, and consulted them about business matters, taking their advice about running the little farm he cultivated."

"I see. You think that he might have insured himself at their suggestion."

"Exactly. Add that Brack and Mel Ruggles are quarrelsome, grasping—hard to get along with, I think covers it— and you will perhaps find yourself thinking along the same lines as myself. Both the young Ruggleses have narrowly escaped penitentiary sentences for cattle stealing and other like offenses. Lack of positive evidence, and the laxity of country juries, contributed to their acquittal. They are hard citizens, if our man's information is reliable. We think it is."

"Hum. If I get it right, you are almost committed to the theory that Brack and Mel Ruggles persuaded the elder brother to take out insurance in their favor and then killed him. That's putting it straight. Am I right?"

"I won't go quite that far," Howard replied thoughtfully. "Still, ten thousand dollars is a large sum, and we want to look into the case before we pay it. There is a lack of reason for the taking out of such heavy policies under such conditions. That is in itself sufficient to warrant a thorough investigation. We expect you to take hold of the thing at once, and give us your report as soon as possible."

"I'll do that very thing," was my assurance. "You'll hear from me when I have anything to report. Of course, if I find something that looks suspicious your company can refuse to pay the policies—stand suit if it is instituted."

That closed the conference, and two hours later I left Kansas City *en route* to the Missouri hills.

I left the train at Neosho, for reasons which will develop as I go along, instead of continuing to Anderson and thence over a seven mile drive to the part of the country for which I was headed.

The Far West Mining Company had its headquarters in Neosho, and the company owned a lot of worthless land close to Pineville. Some of it lay back of the Ruggles farm; that information was picked up by the insurance investigator and passed on to me. One hour after reaching Neosho I had an option on a section of land lying in the hills above the farm of Brack and Mel Ruggles.

That was not my only reason for detraining at Neosho, however. When I left the town in the late afternoon I drove a rig which would have landed me in jail had I driven it along a city street—granting I came in contact with an officer of the Humane Society.

My two bony nags were snails for fair, and when I stopped them in the road they leaned against each other for support. The wagon, on the rickety seat of which I bumped, was about the most dilapidated vehicle the junk yards of Neosho could produce—and the driver was in keeping with the whole outfit.

While I am tall and what is termed well developed, Nature did not outdo herself in fashioning my features. A few smears of dirt, a chew of tobacco in my jaw, a sad-brimmed felt hat on top of my sandy hair—and, presto! I am most anything I claim to be. Certainly my daily associates would have had difficulty in reconciling the Tug Norton they know with the proprietor of the sorry outfit.

A few articles of household furniture—cook stove, antiquated bedstead, mattress, chairs, together with a cross-cut saw and a double-bitted ax were loaded into the wagon bed, thus dubbing me a "branch-water man" of the rankest breed.

The road from Neosho to Pineville, a distance of twenty-five miles, follows the valleys between rock-clad slopes of the Ozarks, without encountering a railway track the entire distance. At intervals there are crossroads stores and settlements about them—each store being designated by the name of the community it centers. The valley from Neosho is not known by any particular name; it is not called a valley by the natives, but is subdivided into "hollows," and each hollow has its name. There is Thief Hollow, Dry Hollow, Wet Hollow, and so on.

2

—

FOUR MILES NORTH of Pineville the road climbs over Bunker Hill and drops into Dog Hollow. It winds on past the Sunnybrook Store, clinging to the base of the ridge on the west, leaving a broad strip of table-land on the east. The table-land extends back a quarter of a mile to the first rise of the wooded hills which lie between the road and Big Sugar Creek, and is occupied by fairly prosperous farms.

Back of the farms, the hills remain just as Nature created them—plus the tangled havoc of decay, and the erosion of many centuries which has transformed almost every hollow into a creek bed. Those hollows, whether dry or full of water, are moats for the protection of the timbered, precipitous slopes; because of them logging is a well-nigh impossible operation. Trees, there, simply attain their growth, decay, and fall. They litter the landscape, and, combined with the wild tangle of undergrowth, make passage difficult.

At noon on the second day after I left Neosho my snails staggered to a stop before the Sunnybrook Store, a small, weatherbeaten, box house at a crossroad in Dog Hollow, and I lowered myself stiffly to the ground in full view of half a dozen natives which were engaged, all and singular, in whittling away the front veranda posts. They eyed me silently as I approached.

"Howdy," I greeted them.

"Howdy. Come fur to-day?"

"Camped up above Erie las' night," I answered. "On my way to some land I'm buyin' offen the Far West folks. Lays behind a farm that belongs to a man named Ragsdale, or Raggles, or something or other like that. It's called the Pauley Section. Mebbe some of you-all knows where it is?"

There was a short silence, then an old fellow spoke: up.

"Reckon you-all mean Ruggles, 'stid of Raggles," he offered. "Brack an' Mel Ruggles. They lives 'bout a mile on south, first white house, and their east fence line borders on the Pauley Section. Thar's a gate givin' onto your place from Brack's. Reckon you-all can find it."

"Yeah, I reckon. I heered they was a house of some kind on the land, lessen the woods fire got it?"

"It didn't. The fire, I mean," the old man said. "Reckon you won't call it a house, though, after you've seed it. A body can live in it, mebbe—if they ain't too particular."

"Reckon I'll git along up there. Much obleeged."

I climbed aboard, stirred my snails out of a doze and started them shuffling along. As I departed I heard a chorus of snickers and a subdued reference to "another branch-water man."

A branch-water man, be it said, is a type quite well known to all timbered countries, particularly hilly, inaccessible regions. He is a rover, preferring to dwell for a time on a worn out farm in the wilds back of some other fellow's place, and, as the saying goes, drink out of a branch rather than spend time and energy in digging a well. The branch-water man generally fools somebody into thinking he means to buy a place, makes a small payment down, then cuts enough ties and cord wood off the premises to make the small payment back and a living besides. When the spirit moves, he moves.

I wanted to be taken for a branch-water man, and it seems I had been. Well and good. I drove on down the road, around a turn, and came to a white house on the left hand side. A gate gave ingress from the road to the barn-lot, and, after trying for a spell to raise somebody and failing, I opened the gate and drove in. At the bottom of a hill below the barnyard I found a faintly traced road which led across a bit of meadow and up a long hill into some brush-land. Following it, I came to a gate which gave onto what I rightly judged to be the Pauley Section.

Beyond the gate a grass-grown trail led off east between the trees, and I followed it for a quarter of a mile, coming at length to a tumble-down log cabin which stood in the midst of a small clearing. One room had a floor of puncheons, and a fair roof of clap-boards, and into it I moved my worldly goods. Then I turned my team loose and made myself at home.

The easy part of the job was done. I was on the ground, and in a character calculated to arouse derision rather than suspicion. Just what my next move would be depended solely upon circumstances.

This much I knew: If Brack and Mel Ruggles had killed Abner for sake of his insurance, then I had to establish that fact beyond a doubt. To do that it would be necessary to watch their movements, find out where they forgathered, and listen in on them when they were alone. If they had committed such a crime they would probably talk of it to each other when they fancied themselves out of earshot from others. A slight chance there, I'll admit. It was, however, a chance.

Also, I counted upon catching them outside the law on some other matter—cattle or timber stealing, or maybe a bit of moonshining. Once in the clutch of the law I'd find a way to make one or both come through. There are ways, you know.

Anyhow, I was on the ground, and ready for whatever should arise.

The next day I drove into Pineville, ostensibly after supplies, but in reality in the hope of getting a look at Brack and Mel Ruggles. I made the trip, however, without laying eyes on them. An elderly woman, who kept house for them, was visible when I drove in on my return. She nodded distantly in reply to my "good evenin', ma'am," and went inside.

The next day I sawed up some down timber and split some wood, keeping an eye out for my neighbors. About noon I received a passing call from a native who was hunting squirrels and who gave me some information without knowing it.

"Did the fire git many places?" I asked, while he sat for a spell on a stump. "Do much damage?"

"It got Ab Ruggles's place—an' him 'long with it," was the reply. "Burned him to a cinder. He musta been drunk. That's how he come to git caught."

"Did he live hereabouts?"

"A mile east," the native replied, pointing. "Across Shelf Creek and over th' hill from here."

"That's right bad," I said. "Leave any fambly?"

"No. Jist Brack an' Mel, brothers. They git all his land, an' th' insurance money. They're damn lucky, if you ask me."

"Reckon them's my neighbors—Brack and Mel," I offered. "Them the ones you refers to?"

"Yeah," said the native, rising. "Though I don't know if they're neighbors or not—except that they're close to you. I ain't saying nothing ag'in''em, you understand, but they're good folks to let alone."

With that, he departed.

Ten minutes later I was on my way through the timber toward Ab Ruggles's burned cabin. When I reached the fire area, I found only one thing to interest me—and that important.

The square of black earth upon which the cabin had stood was enclosed by a cleared patch of ground of twenty acres, no trees or undergrowth on it. The woods fire had come in from the south, as the distant hills in that direction clearly showed by their burned-over condition. In order to reach Ab Ruggles's place the fire must first burn down the side of a steep hill, leap across a small brook, creep to the edge of the clearing and ignite the grass and cornstalks about the house. That would not have been improbable, granting there had been no one at home to fight its progress, or in case Ruggles was lying in a drunken stupor at the time. That part seemed all right.

What caught my eye, and challenged my interest, was this:

A fireguard, eight rows wide, had been plowed around the clearing about two hundred feet distant from the cabin—and it had been done before the woods fire came. The turned earth of the guard had been burned over too; such small sprouts as had grown since the plowing were consumed. That was queer.

Consider this also:

Between the fire guard and the timber the ground was covered with deep ashes, fluffy before the rains had beaten them down, but discernible nevertheless. That indicated that much grass and short brush had been growing in the field when the fire laid it waste. Between the fire guard and the house, however, there was a total absence of such ash—proving to my mind, that Ab Ruggles had back-fired between the house and the fire guard. In other words, he had burned off that portion of the land between the plowed strip and the cabin—thus making a safety zone for the protection of the buildings.

How, then, had the fire reached the house?

A strong wind might have carried sparks to the roof. Yes, it might—and then it might not. If it did not, then the Ruggles cabin burned from some other cause than the woods fire. That was certain.

Another thing. Would it be likely that a man who was so cognizant of the hazard of forest fires that he plowed a guard and back-fired against them, to lie down and permit himself to take chances on a windy night? Would such a careful man fill up on hooch and go to sleep, when he could have seen from his door log that the woods fire was raging beyond him in the hills?

It had an unnatural look, to say the least.

I went back to my shack, pondering things, meaning to find out later whether there was a strong wind blowing the night of the disaster to Ruggles. I didn't dare ask too many questions, of course, but there would be ways of getting the information without seeming to seek it.

3

THE NEXT MORNING I drove my nags down the steep hill, across the brook, up past the Ruggles barn, and onto the highway through the barnyard gate. I drove slowly, keeping my eyes peeled, but saw nothing of the Ruggles boys. They seemed, whether purposely or not, to vanish at my approach.

In Pineville I learned, while discussing fires with the natives at the swapping yard, that the night of the Ruggles tragedy had been still—absolutely windless.

"Had thar been a strong wind, that whole section would of went," a native told me.

I drove back, feeling that I was making progress. Nothing proven, of course, but cause for question of that fire well established.

It was late in the afternoon when I headed my snails off the road at the Ruggles place. Getting down, I approached the gate—to find it secured by a chain and a new padlock.

Evidently Brack and Mel had stayed home long enough to bar me from access to my section. Well, I'd see about that.

I climbed the fence, went up to the rear door of the farm house, and my call was responded to by Aunt Jane, the housekeeper.

"I reckon Brack meant to leave a key for you, Mr. Kane,"

she said in reply to my question, "but he went down to the store, and tuck both of 'em along with him."

Kane was the name I had given as my own.

"When will he be back?" I asked.

"Wouldn't be surprised to see him any time now," was the rather indefinite answer. "Won't you-all come in and wait?"

"I'll wait outside," I replied sourly.

It was nearly dark when Brack and Mel came along the road from the Sunnybrook Store—a mile distant.

"You've got me locked out, Ruggles!" I said, irritation sharpening my voice. "What's the idea?"

Brack Ruggles came up to the wagon where I sat. "Sho, now!" he exclaimed. "I meant to leave a key for you, and plumb forgot it!"

He fished a key from his pocket and tendered it.

"I still don't get the idee for locking the gate!" I told him.

"It's my gate," Brack Ruggles replied slowly, "and I got the right to lock it if I want to."

"But the law says you ain't the right to bar me from my farm!" I remonstrated.

"Ain't barring you. You got a key, ain't you?"

It dawned upon me that Brack Ruggles was well within his rights, legally speaking; that he was acting in a very unneighborly manner was true, but he had a right to do that, too. In any case, his position was sound, and must be submitted to.

I opened the gate, drove through and locked it again, the two Ruggles, big, rangy men, watching me through the twilight.

Brack, the elder, was about forty, and Mel was three years

younger. Neither man was very prepossessing in appearance, and I was not surprised to find them surly.

I drove homeward, pleased to have at last come in
contact with my men. That they objected to me using a
roadway across their property was clear. Why? Did they
suspect my true character, or were they acting so in keeping
with their surly, unneighborly dispositions?

As to the roadway, I had the law on them. They could
not legally refuse me a right of way to my property. The
Missouri Legislature had enacted a statute which made it
incumbent upon owners of ground along the public high-
ways to allow privileges to property lying behind them.
Otherwise such property, isolated by reason of its inacces-
sibility, would be just so much waste land. Brack and Mel
were on the wrong side of the law, though, only in case they
fenced me off and refused to allow me to pass.

That night I slipped down the hill and approached the
Ruggles house—only to be turned back by two big dogs
which disputed further advance.

"They're protected from eavesdroppers, anyway," I
reflected ruefully, as I scouted homeward through the
timber. "Yet I've got to figure out a way in which to establish surveillance over them. I've got enough, I believe, to
warrant the Gateway people in contesting the collection
of the policies—but I'm a long way from home at that!"

During the next two days I stuck around my place,
cutting wood and making a start at getting out a few ties.
I did not want to be caught spying around the Ruggles
place, preferring to let them make all the moves, as I felt
sure they would. I had only to wait.

Though two days passed without incident, and on the

morning of the third I set out, astride one of my snails, for Pineville. I didn't have any business there, but I wanted to connect with Brack and Mel again, if possible. The more I thought about the pair, the more convinced I became that they would, in making it hard for me in my character of humble landholder, betray themselves in the insurance matter—granting there was something to betray.

At the gate giving onto the Ruggles farm, at the west line of my section, I found another lock. It secured the gate by means of a piece of log chain. Attached to a length of dog chain, secured to the post by a staple, was the key.

That key told its own story. The Ruggles boys were bent upon annoying me. Had they given the key to me, with the request that I lock the gate after using it, they might have been actuated by fear of intruders—cattle thieves, possibly. But to leave the key chained to the post where all who chose might use it, was merely serving notice on me that they would comply with the law—in the most annoying manner possible. That lock made it impossible for me to open the gate without getting down from my horse.

I opened the gate, mounted and rode down the hill—to be stopped by a new wire fence, and another gate. This gate was not quite at the bottom of the hill, and it would make a halt on the incline dangerous in slick weather.

I got down and found that this gate had no lock; but when I opened it the thing collapsed on the ground and occasioned a good deal of trouble. I had to drag it out of the way of my horse, straighten it up, and fasten it again. A "gap gate," the natives term such.

"Three gates!" I exclaimed aloud, for I had suddenly become aware that Mel Ruggles was standing across the branch from me, evidently enjoying what he thought to be my discomfiture. "Two of them locked, and the other a regular devil—"

Mel laughed loudly, slapping his lank legs with his hands.

"What's the idee for a gate here?" I demanded, letting my anger blaze.

"Brack an' me wanted it there!"

"You fellers seem to have got a craze for gates, since I come into the country!" I charged. "Why don't you-all come right out and say you don't want me passing through your place, and be done with it?"

"We ain't got no objections," Mel replied. "We just needs the fences and the gates, that's all!"

"You are lying, Mel Ruggles!" I charged, shaking my fist. "You-all want me offen the hill, and you aim to make me all the trouble you can—"

"I'm aiming to make you some, right now!" Mel gritted, leaping across the branch, his heavy face flushed. "You-all can't call me a liar!"

He couldn't have acted more to my taste, had he been rehearsed in the scene.

"Come on!" I shouted, flourishing my arms. "I need action, and plenty of it!"

"You air going to git it!"

Mel Ruggles was half a head taller, and twenty-five pounds heavier, than me; his muscles were hard from swinging an ax, pulling a saw, and a lifetime of outdoor activity. But I had the advantage of athletic training, and was tough and sinewy; above all, I was skilled in the use of my fists. He had strength and awkwardness; I had strength and skill.

Mel came on with a snarl and a vicious swing at my head—but I was not there to meet it. The level strip of ground bordering the branch afforded room for good foot-work and I made the best of it. Before Mel recovered I stepped in and rattled his teeth with a stiff punch to the chin, followed it with a jolt in the pit of the stomach, and had the glee of seeing him drop to his knees. I stepped back, waiting.

Mel took his time getting up—and when he did so he rushed suddenly, and I caught the gleam of steel in his hand.

"Knife, eh?" I thought. "Can't fight fair! All right—I'll show you a bit of sure enough rough work!"

I side-stepped Mel's knife swing, thrust out my left foot, caught him squarely on the ankle with a heavy boot and sent him sprawling. The next instant I kicked the knife from the hillsman's grasp, and planted my heel with crush-ing force in the palm of his outflung left hand.

With a howl of pain, Mel gave up—but there was some-thing else also coming to him.

The branch was running about three feet of water, and the sprawling man lay just on the edge. With a thrust of my foot, I tumbled him over the rim, stood for a moment watching his floundering efforts to climb the slippery bank, then mounted and rode on.

I felt much better—even sang a little song along the road to Pineville. Things would break now, in a hurry.

4

I KILLED A lot of time in Pineville, purposely delaying my departure until after nightfall, and when I turned in at the Ruggles place it was as dark as a stack of crows. I opened the gate quietly, and walked beside my horse toward the barn, covering myself. That Brack and Mel might be laying for me, I knew, and my chances in the darkness would be better than in the daylight. I did not think it very likely that they would choose their own farm upon which to commit a really serious assault, even though Mel had, in the bitterness of defeat, drawn his knife. Except for that break, the campaign had so far been conducted with a certain degree of subtlety.

My horse suddenly swerved to one side, and I advanced cautiously, coming up against another obstruction.

A few strands of wire supporting another "gap gate," had been strung from the barn to the yard fence during my absence—another bar to my right of way!

Evidently the Ruggleses were content to retaliate for Mel's drubbing, with another gate nuisance.

"Four gates!" I muttered thoughtfully—and continued to think of them as I went on to my shack.

"I'll prowl around in the woods toward Sugar Creek, in the morning," I resolved, as I prepared to turn in to bed. "Brack and Mel have a kettle of some kind on the fire hereabouts, and they don't want anybody in its vicinity. It may be a moonshine operation, or, perhaps, a corral hidden away in some wooded hollow where stolen cattle are harbored, preparatory to butchering them and peddling them to the markets in the neighboring villages. There's something, at any rate, else why the gates?"

All the other residents of the community treated me with a sort of good-natured tolerance when they met me; treated me pretty much as such folks invariably do children and persons of unsound mind. Their attitude made that of Brack and Mel stand out as noticeable as a bear in a snow storm.

When I stepped to my door log next morning I found Brack Ruggles sitting on a stump in the clearing, a thirty-thirty rifle in the crook of his arm.

"Morning, Ruggles," I greeted, standing in the doorway. "Out kind of early, ain't you?"

"Yeah. I figgered to git me some squir'ls, this morning, over in the hills," the native answered.

I eyed the thirty-thirty.

"You fellers shoot squirrels with a rifle, in this country?" I queried.

"Sho'. Scatter-guns spile 'em," I was told.

"A feller needs to be a mighty good shot to git a squirrel with a rifle, though," I commented. "I ain't good enough."

Ruggles swung around and eyed a distant tree where a woodpecker was at work.

"See that pecker-wood, yonder?" he asked. "Well—watch!"

He raised the rifle, and fired. The woodpecker leaped

away from the tree trunk, somersaulted, folded its wings and dropped straight to the earth—minus its head.

"Good shot!" I applauded. "But you-all has something in mind to talk to me about this morning—what is it?"

"You and Mel fit, yistiddy, down by the branch."

"Yes. What about it? Didn't Mel git enough?"

Brack's tobacco-stained mustache lifted in what might pass for a grin. "Yeah. That boy, now, is right mean tempered, though; don't never forgive nobody that bests him. He worries me. Mel's a lot better shot than even me, and when he's full of hate—well, it worries me, that's what!"

"Why don't you lock him up somewhere—insane asylum, mebbe?" I queried helpfully. "If he's that dangerous he ought'n to be allowed to run loose!"

Brack eyed me from under drawn brows, and when he spoke his words were slow and pointed.

"A good shot, like Mel, is handy to have around," he said. "Hawks, after chickens, and things like that. He don't never miss."

"I reckon I git you, Ruggles—and you're not gitting anywhere with me," I said calmly. "Spit it out—why don't you want me up here?"

"Wa-al," Brack replied, "we-all have been used to graze our stock on the hills up here, and we git our winter wood here, too. Naturally, we'd ruther not have anybody stop us."

"You can graze your cattle here, as usual, and as for wood, there's more down on the ground right now than I'd use in a lifetime. You're welcome to as much of it as you want," I offered, knowing that Brack Ruggles did not graze stock there, and that he had plenty of woodland on his own place to supply him with fuel.

"Reckon, now, you wouldn't take what you paid down on this land, and twenty-five dollars beside, and move on?" The question was put suddenly.

"No!" I was equally as abrupt.

Brack got up.

"Going to stay, whether or no, huh?" he asked, his face ugly.

"Whether or no—you bet!"

"All right! I'd be careful, though, prowling about the woods. A rock might turn under your foot, and you might git your neck broke!"

With the warning, which I understood was meant for a threat, Ruggles shouldered his gun and stalked off toward Big Sugar.

I watched the tall, heavy figure until it disappeared in the underbrush, then went inside and carefully examined my guns. I'd be needing 'em soon, I knew. Through a window, I picked out the figure of the native on the side of a hill across Shelf Creek. There was a clear spot above one of the falls, from which "shelves" the creek took its name, and Brack Ruggles stood there a moment, looking back. Then he plunged into the brush, toward his own place. The squirrel-hunting was over.

Shortly afterward I set off toward Sugar Creek, on the scouting trip I had decided to make the night before, keeping on the north side of the stream.

Shelf Creek tumbled down from the hills to the west in a series of falls, found easy going in the hollow below my cabin, and roared away down it in the direction of Big Sugar. A mile from my place, I came to where a second hollow took off from the first, in the shape of a "Y," the stem being the creek's course from its source to that spot. The stream dropped down over a shelf and formed a pool where the hollows divided, then continued on over a second shelf and followed the left-hand hollow. Below the second shelf, or falls, was a second deep pool—and I distinctly saw bass leaping in it.

"I'd fish in that pool," I thought, "only—a rock might turn under my foot, and I might get my neck broke!"

I prowled on toward Big Sugar, finding about the wildest, most rugged and difficult a body of land as I had ever seen. Occasionally I took a shot with my "scatter gun," and scared a squirrel out of its wits every time. I wasn't aiming to hit. I kept my eyes out for anything of an unusual nature, or that hinted of the recent presence of man. Exploring the choked hollows which intersected the main one, and, taking my bearings from each high peak I encountered, I finally reached Big Sugar—and had drawn a blank.

About five o'clock I climbed out of a hollow already holding the shadows of evening, and reached a narrow bit of bench land on the side of a laurel-clad hill. There the sunlight still lingered. I was on the homeward track, and I looked about me to make sure of my direction.

P-i-i-n-n-g-g-g!

A bullet whined past my head, clipping the leaves from a laurel bush beside me, and I dropped to the rocks and laid flat.

"Brack!" I thought. "Mel, maybe! Anyhow, whoever it was, he missed! Too far away, and bad light at that! Hell, this is getting too hot to be funny!"

Lying low, I scanned the sides of the hill from which the shot must have been fired, far up the hollow, but the marksman was doubtless using smokeless powder, and his position could not be determined. A distant report, like the tap of a hammer on a barrel head, had followed the whine of the bullet; that was all.

I wormed my way back into the brush, skirted the peak and came out on the west side of the hill, keeping in the cover. The sun sank, and darkness came swiftly into the hills, rendering the going, bad at best, infinitely worse. Just when I had begun to question whether or not my instinct for direction could be trusted in the darkness, I came out on the south side of Shelf Creek, above the pool where the valley divided. I had only to cross the stream, and walk the mile between it and my cabin.

I followed upward, seeking a shallow place for crossing, and as I walked on through the twilight I found that I was following a dim path which skirted the bank.

"A calf path, probably," I thought—then stopped, head bent in a listening attitude. "And a calf, or something, coming along it behind me!"

I whirled, peering through the gathering gloom—and found Brack Ruggles not five feet from me.

5

—

WITH AN OATH of surprise, Brack attempted to swing his rifle up, but I was upon him before he could use it. The footing was bad, and we went down together—slipping, sliding and rolling toward the creek. I had no time to use my fists, it requiring all my strength to hold my wiry adversary. Brack was likewise occupied, you can bet.

The finish came just above the deep pool where the valley divided. Brack, as we rolled over with first one and then the other on top, seized a heavy rock with his right hand and brought it down sharply upon my hatless head. I relaxed instantly, gasped out a groan I could not restrain—and toppled over the bank into the pool.

I sank to the bottom, and came to the top, spouting water. The cold plunge bad, however, revived me and I struck out to swim as noiselessly as possible to the shore at the far side.

Suddenly I came up against an obstacle, and found that I had reached the rock ledge which turned the stream from the right-hand hollow into the left. I seized a projecting rock; it came away, and I reached out again—and felt the rough, splintery edge of a board in my fingers.

Though it was too dark to see, my fingers could, and did, investigate. I felt along the top of the board, drawing myself up silently to the rim of the ledge—and a moment later found that the ledge, on both sides of the narrow gorge where the hollow cleft the hill, was not a ledge at all, but a carefully placed camouflage of rocks. Between the two layers of rocks was a solid wall of heavy boards.

"Another gate!" I exclaimed under my breath. "A water-gate this time, made to turn the creek back down the left-hand hollow! Somebody didn't want any water in the hollow below—and so they stopped it from coming! That would be Brack and Mel, of course!"

I got to my feet, confident that I was safe from Brack's rifle in the darkness, and found that I could wade shore-ward along the inner side of the gate, the water being barely up to my chin. I was proceeding slowly, cautiously, when a rock turned underfoot and I saved myself from going down by a wild thrust of a hand for the ledge—making a splash in the water like a huge fish leaping.

There was a roar from the bank above, a long stream of fire split the darkness and a bullet sang by my ears. I ducked, slipped, felt myself caught in the swirl of the current and struggled to regain my footing.

It sounds like a lot of hokum for me to be saying it, but it is none the less true that in that moment of peril I laughed—laughed because it came to me with the sudden-ness of a flash of lightning what that fifth gate meant. Its discovery gave the whole snap away, and it was so simple, after I'd caught it, that I couldn't help chuckling at my own dumb-headedness.

I didn't chuckle long, though, for I was out farther than I had thought and, an instant later, scrambling and clutch-ing for something to hold to, I was swept over the lower falls, and down a twenty-foot drop to the rocks of the pool.

The pool had considerable depth, fortunately for me, and I took the drop with no worse results than a few bruises. Lying low until I recovered my breath, I crawled over the rocks toward the sheet of water through which I had just fallen—and walked through it into the entrance of the cavern it masked.

That was the secret of the fifth gate. In the face of the rock shelf was a deep, narrow crevasse—snugly hidden by the waterfall. I followed the crevasse back, going carefully and with my gun—fortunately, or rather foresightedly protected by its waterproof holster—in hand. Presently the passage widened a bit, and I made out a dim light farther on. A second later I crouched at the entry of a cavern, a room measuring about ten feet by twenty, the roof shored up with props.

When my eyes became accustomed to the poorly lighted interior I made out that the place was crudely furnished with a cot, chair, a hanging lamp and a barrel or two which served for tables.

Something stirred in the shadows beyond the circle of light, and a man suddenly came into view. He was big, although stooped of shoulders, and his long gray hair was matted and neglected. His whole face, emaciated and pale, seemed covered with beard, and his rough clothing was wrinkled and soiled. He sat on a box beside one of the barrels, uncovered a basket and began eating the food which it contained.

"Well, Abner," I said, stepping swiftly into the circle of light, "don't be a hog. I'm hungry, too!"

He leaped to his feet, terror spreading his eyes, and a cry of astonishment on his lips.

"Who—who are you?" he gasped.

"A guest, for the time being," I answered easily, sitting on a box across the barrel from him. "How long before Brack will be back?"

"I—I don't know what you-all air talking about!" the old scare-crow stammered, looking about him like a wild animal seeking some avenue of escape.

"Cut that out with me!" I ordered sternly. "The game's up, and you might as well come through. You are Abner Ruggles, and you have been hiding out here since the night you were supposed to perish in the fire. Going to own up?"

The old man simply stared, his mouth shut in a tight line.

"All right!"

I moved so swiftly he had no chance to defend himself or to make the least move to avoid me. A minute later he was stretched on the floor of the cavern, and another minute sufficed for me to tie him with his belt and mine. Then I picked him up and placed him on his cot.

"See this knife?" I queried, sitting down beside him, and taking out a keen hunting knife. "Its point is sharp, and you are already supposed to be dead. Nobody would ever know that I put you out, save Brack and Mel—and they wouldn't dare tell. Now—are you going to talk?"

I must have looked vicious, what with the soaked garments I wore and the dim light shining upon my none too handsome features, for the old boy suddenly decided to spill it all.

"I'm Ab Ruggles, yes—and I ain't denying it," he cried out. "This doings is mostly Brack's and Mel's, but I reckon I'm to blame for letting them do it. What do you want to know?"

"Nothing much," I answered. "I already know most of it. Tell me this—and tell the truth, else I won't answer for what happens. When will Brack be back? I know he has just left, because the food in the basket is still warm. What time will he bring breakfast?"

"Just a-fore daylight," was the answer.

"Will he be alone?"

"Mel is coming with him to-morrow," Abner told me. "We-all aims to talk matters over then. Seems like the insurance company don't want to pay the money. That's what we been waiting on. Soon as that was paid, and things quieted down, I meant to git clear of the country. Reckon I won't, now!" he finished mournfully.

"No, you won't, and that's a fact," I replied. "No, whose body did you fellows steal—or did you kill somebody, and burn the corpse in your cabin?"

"It was the corpse of Wiley Bennett, which died two days afore I did—I mean, afore—"

"I know what you mean. You dug him up from his grave, put your clothes on him, your knife and watch in his pocket, then—say, who set the woods afire?" I slipped that question over on him unexpectedly and he didn't have time to think up a lie.

"Brack and Mel," he answered. "They set the cabin, too."

"Guess that's all I want to know," I told him. "Now you can go to sleep, if you are in the humor for it, and we'll have a little reunion of the Ruggles brothers in the morning."

To my amazement, the old chap breathed a long sigh and said:

"I aim to sleep! Ain't slept to do no good since I come here! Now it's all over, I'm too wore out to even care!"

A few minutes later he was snoring.

It was a long wait, there in that moist room so carefully prepared for the big fraud. The food in the basket was good, however, and I found some tobacco in a box on the barrel. Lighting up, I sat back and waited.

There wasn't much to think about. The case was as clear as spring water. Brack and Mel had contrived to turn the water of Shelf Creek out of its course and used it to conceal their cave, after which they had only to wait until somebody in the neighborhood died and was laid to rest in the isolated little cemetery. No risk about stealing the corpse, of course, since no one in the community would even dream of the place being plundered by ghouls. In fact, the whole matter was commonplace—up to a certain point.

The gates! I had to laugh over the gates!

"They constructed one too many," I reflected, as I noted that my watch marked the hour of four. "The fifth one was their—er—Waterloo, so to speak!"

I woke Abner quietly, about four o'clock, and gagged him good and tight. Then I arranged the lamp so its rays would not penetrate that part of the room nearest the entrance. After which, with my gun clubbed and ready, I took my stand just inside.

I didn't have long to wait. A swishing sound, made by a body slithering through the falls, announced the arrival of my quarry.

Mel came first—and I dropped him with a swing of my gun-butt, then covered Brack before he even knew what was happening.

"Hell! I mighta knowed you-all was a damned, sneakin'

detective!" was all he could think of to say, after I had disarmed him.

"But you didn't," I gibed. "Else you'd have shot me out of hand!"

"I shore would! Anyhow, you ain't got nothing on us— we didn't collect no money!"

"Not a thing," I replied, "except—now let me see. Grave-robbery, arson, false pretense and conspiracy to defraud."

With that, I walked over and released old man Abner.

"You're batty, Ab," I told him. "That's plain. Clear out, and stick around where I can get you when I want you. About all you lose is your insurance premiums. As for you two—"

I let the judge tell it to Brack and Mel for me.

Ten years is a mighty long time!

ROCK SALT

*It Seemed the Job Was Done With
the Utmost Care, But the Blunders
Were Legion to Tug Norton's Eye*

1

THE DARKER THINGS are, the harder they are to keep dark.

The above is a positive statement of a no less positive belief of my own, I having criminal matters in mind when I make it. The penitentiaries of the land are filled with men who will agree with me.

There is something about a brutal crime—wanton murder, like killing a man in pursuit of plunder—that arouses the ire of a real sleuth to the point where he'd sooner quit the business than drop the killer's trail before landing him where he belongs. That's one reason why I say the darker a thing is, the harder it is to keep dark.

I might not have been so keen about the express company case, seeing that I was called in only to help an old partner out in a tight, except for this one thing:

Every time I thought of Stanley Jefferson lying there on the express car floor with a bullet in his brain, where he had fallen in the line of duty, I visualized a wholly imaginary monster in the act of firing that fatal shot and, in spite of the fact that I'm as cold-blooded and cool-headed as a good sleuth ought to be, I saw red.

Quit that case? Why, I couldn't, once I saw Jefferson, until I clamped my hand on the substance of that vision— and clamped it hard.

It was on a night in August, and hotter than usual in the Middle West, when my telephone rang a long, loud, imperative peal. I had just got into bed, with my electric fan going full speed, and settled down for the night. I reached for the receiver.

"Tug Norton talking," I called into the mouthpiece.

"Good!" ejaculated a well known voice. "This is Jim Warren, Tug—and I'm in a hell of a hole! Just in from Memphis, with a handful of hot leads in that Springfield explosion case—you've read about it, of course—and not a man available for anything but that. I've hardly stepped off the train when I'm called back to the express car of Number Four, find the safe looted, one express messenger dead and the other on the floor with handcuffs on wrists and legs. To make matters worse, I'm out of commission physically—temporarily at least! If you've got a heart in you—"

"I'll be right down!" I broke in. "Track number three? Train four?"

"Right! I'll wait."

Jim Warren was my partner when we both worked out of headquarters, here in Kansas City. We were subtracted from our jobs on the same day, and for the same reason: our blood wasn't of the right political tinge. I opened the Kaw Valley Detective Agency, and prospered. Jim got taken on as chief special officer for the express company, Frisco division, and a better man for the job couldn't have been picked.

As it turned out, they needed good men and lots of them, right afterward. It seemed as though every crook in the

I got down and peered at the deposit of ashes

country had turned his attention to the express company, concentrating on the Frisco division. Jim earned his money.

Naturally he would call on his old pal, in a tight, and quite as naturally I would get right up on my toes and answer on the run.

Train Number Four had been in about an hour when I boarded the express car, ten minutes after the call came. Warren sat on a box beside the door, one eye heavily bandaged, his face drawn with pain. He got up and shook hands.

"Who blacked your eye?" I queried, letting my glance rove about the car's interior.

Except for one thing, the car appeared pretty much as it naturally would at the end of a run. Each end, from the doors back, was stored with packages, boxes, suit cases, trunks, and other commercial articles. Between the doors—two to a side—and against the walls, were the stationary desks where the messengers wrote up their trip sheets, made out bills, and did such clerical work as the job imposed. Beneath the desk on the right was an oblong iron box—the ordinary sort of chest express companies transport valuable packages in. This one was open.

The object in that car which had the effect of altering the whole aspect of its interior, then intruded itself upon my vision, and I walked over to where Stanley Jefferson's dead body lay almost under a desk, across the aisle from the one under which the chest was situated.

He was lying on his back, arms thrown outward, face bathed in blood from a wound in the right temple. On the floor, almost under his right hand, was a forty-five revolver.

McFee, division manager of the company, and four others—including one of Jim's assistants, a deputy coroner, and an agent from the Terminal Company—were grouped about the second messenger, who sat at the far end of the car, his face white as ever it will be in death, eyes seeming never to shift from the bloody figure on the floor.

"There's some mighty unusual features about the whole thing, Tug," Jim was saying. "I want help bad. Coming in on this same train, sitting forward on the lefthand side of the smoker, I got an eye full of chat, you know we call it that, blown in through an open window just as we left Paola. One piece got under the lid and nearly knocked my eyeball out. I'm almost nutty with the pain of it now. Craymer and Bausworth, either of whom I might rely on, are both away in Birmingham. If you will give things a going over—"

"That's what I came for," I answered. "When was this discovered?"

"We pulled in at ten thirty sharp, and ten minutes later;

while I was inside the station getting this eye looked after, a platform man came for me. When Number Four stopped, on track three, half a dozen trucks were lined up as usual to receive the express. The doors remained closed, in spite of repeated hammering on them.

"One was broken open, and this layout, practically as it remains, discovered—except that Paul Ducret, the other messenger, was on the floor, about where McFee is standing now, with his hands secured behind him by a pair of handcuffs, and his legs likewise fastened. He was all but dead from suffocation caused by a gag in his mouth. You can get the story from him whenever you're ready."

I went forward, speaking to McFee, who was known to me, and Jim said:

"Norton is going to sub for me. Mack; I'm not fit for anything, with this eye raising merry hell, to say nothing of other matters—"

"Get the doctor hold of that eye, Jim," McFee told him. "Norton has my authority to take hold here."

Warren, only waiting for me to get on the job, hustled off, and I turned to Ducret, a tall chap, with good features, albeit he was still pale and badly shaken up.

"As briefly as possible, without overlooking anything, tell me what happened," I said, sitting down on a box near by.

"We were about ten minutes out of Fort Scott, this side, and I was in this end of the car, checking over the goods we had taken on at the last stop, when I heard an explosion, turned and saw my partner, Jefferson, reeling to the floor. A man, his face masked with a handkerchief, stood about fifteen feet distant, at the other end of the car.

He had a pistol in his right hand, the barrel smoking. Jeff

crashed down, the revolver he had evidently snatched from the desk before him, clattering on the floor. As I turned round, the masked man swung the gun on me and ordered me to put my hands up.

"I was twenty feet away from my gun, which was in a pigeonhole of my desk, and there was nothing for me to do but obey. He approached, ordered me to lie down, and when I complied he fastened handcuffs, which he took from a coat pocket, about my hands and ankles. Then he leisurely proceeded to search me, remove my keys, and loot the box.

"After that, he examined Jeff closely and turned to me with the remark:

" 'He's dead—and you will be, too, if you don't talk up, and give me straight answers to my questions."

"I asked him what he wanted to know.

" 'How many stops between here and Kansas City?'

" 'Two,' I replied.

" 'What are they?'

" 'Paola and Olathe.'

" 'Any express to put off or take on there?'

" 'We're a fast train,' I told him. 'Don't handle any express except what is billed straight through for the entire trip, or from one railway division to the other.'

" 'I thought so,' he replied. 'Just wanted to make sure.'

"Then he gagged me, and covered me with a tarpaulin. From that time until the boys broke in here at Kansas City, I saw nothing, and heard nothing. Don't even know when he left the train. We slow down just before we get into Rosedale, where the Katy Shops are, and I think I heard a door shoved back then; but I can't even be sure of that. All I know is that he was not here when the boys got in."

He ceased speaking, eyes going again, to the form of his partner on the floor.

2

"**ANY IDEA WHERE** the bandit came from?" I asked.

"I hadn't then, but of course I know now," he answered, pointing to the opposite end of the car.

I went over, and McFee indicated a long trunk, such as some commercial travelers use. It told its own story, without need of words from Mack.

The trunk was long enough and, without a tray, sufficiently deep to contain a man of medium size, and it evidently had done so. The lid had been raised and detached from the body, and I noted that the rivets in the top part of the hinges were in reality small bolts, their nuts inside. It was easy to see how the trunk had been opened by the bandit. It had been delivered to the express company securely locked, and seals had been attached to the catches at each end. When the hidden man desired to step out of concealment, he removed the nuts from the hinge bolts and tipped the lid forward. The small wrench he had used lay inside.

That trunk was unusual in more ways than one. It had been lined, sides, ends, and bottom, with a heavy, cotton-padded comforter, to prevent injury to its occupant, and a close examination divulged the fact that it was in reality a "knock-down" affair. The occupant could, by using the little wrench, remove the front, the back, or the ends—thereby making it fairly certain that he would not be trapped in case other express of heavy character should be piled on top. It happened that none was, but it might have been otherwise. That contingency had been prepared against.

Nor was that all. Holes had been bored from the inside, two in each end, and corresponding holes had been made in the lining. When the trunk was received by the express company, large commercial stickers on each end concealed the holes. After the trunk was safely stowed aboard the car, the bandit had only to thrust a finger through the holes, puncture the paper and get all the ventilation needed. That had been done. A bit of earth in one end of the queer box showed where the bandit's feet had reposed, and the cotton of the bottom section of the comforter was compressed by his weight.

I took a look at the address sticker on the lid. The name was Avery Benton, and the address 7642 Wyandotte Street, Kansas City, Missouri. The shipper's name and address also appeared. It was L.P. Norris, 1824 Jefferson Street, Memphis, Tennessee.

"All faked, of course," I commented to McFee. "No need to look 'em up. Wire Memphis for all the information they can give you about this trunk. Time received at their office; who brought it; any details they may have. Get somebody started tracing its origin. It is practically new, and ought not to be very difficult to trace back to the first purchaser. Haven't much hope of anything in that quarter, as a clever crook could easily cover it up. Still, there is a bare chance that he didn't. Have you checked over the parcels in the car?"

"We waited for that until such time as you could make your examination," McFee replied.

"Now," I went on, "how much was taken?"

"I was wondering when you'd come to that," Mack said, good naturedly sarcastic. "The company lost one hundred thousand dollars—seventy-five in one package, and twenty-five in another. The larger amount was sent by the Southern Bank and Trust Company to its branch here, and the other was express company funds."

"Humph! A stake worth taking chances for!"

Warren had taken such action as is customary in such cases. Telegraph and telephone had spread the news far and wide, together with a meager description of the bandit. A squad of Terminal men, and the Rosedale authorities, had been set to search in that vicinity. Not a thing would come of it, of course, but Jim knew that a certain amount of activity was expected of him and he had performed accordingly. He knew, as did I, that the crook would be harder to find in such fashion, than a needle in all the hay in Kansas.

The proper place to start hunting for that killer was right there in the car where the job was done.

"Get an ambulance to take the body away," I told McFee, "then clear out. Give me two good men to check over the plunder in here, and instruct the platform men to take it away. Ducret's story is mighty straight sounding. How long has he been with the company?"

"About two years in his present position. Before that, three years' service as a delivery man for the company in Birmingham. The fact that he has this job is proof that he is trusted."

"Fair enough. But hold him for the present. He shouldn't

kick at spending a night or two in the station's detention room, knowing himself innocent. The facts will probably show that this was a one-man job, and that Ducret was not implicated. No reason to think he was. Still, he might be. Have one of your men take him along."

"If you think it necessary, I'll do it, of course," McFee agreed reluctantly.

"I do think so, merely as a precautionary measure. Do it now, too, will you?"

Ten minutes later I had the car to myself, save for the two company men who were to check over the packages under my eyes. It was a long job, requiring an hour, and when it was finished we had done nothing except prove that, so far as the express was concerned, everything was regular; each article accounted for on waybill and trip sheet. That was what I had expected.

The express gone, I had the car alone. Shutting the doors, I sat down opposite the trunk, which I had retained, and gave myself a few minutes in which to study that feature of the robbery.

It took nerve to get inside that box for the purpose it had served. True, the thing was arranged so as to almost exclude the possibility of being unable to get out of it— yet there was one chance that it would be so placed in the car as to render it impossible. It might have been wedged in the center of other trunks and boxes, with two or three heavy articles on top. What then?

Failure to the scheme, of course, and probable discovery at the end of the run when the express was unloaded. If things broke favorably to him after the trunk was placed in the receiving room at the station, the bandit might have effected an escape, it is true.

But in the receiving room trunks and boxes are always piled up, space demanding it. As I saw it, there was a good chance that the bandit, in getting into that trunk, was springing a trap on himself which would release him only into the clutches of a cop. He must have been well aware of the chance against him. Yet he took it.

One hundred thousand dollars! Crooks take chances just as desperate, more so even, every day—and for far less. I concluded that a hard-boiled thief, knowing the amount of the stake he played for, would not have let a little thing like possible capture in that box deter him for a minute. Those fellows play hunches anyhow, and believe in the thing called luck.

I considered the probability of a confederate in Memphis, the point of shipment. Surely one would have simplified matters greatly. Still, it was quite possible to work the racket alone. The crook had only to tag the box properly, summons a drayman, pay him for the hauling, and provide him with the money for the express charges, and tell him to call for the article at such and such a time. When the drayman showed up the crook would be safely inside.

The trick could easily have been turned that way.

As to prior knowledge of a large shipment of currency on that particular run, involving a leak in the express company's office, that did not necessarily follow. Number Four was the only through train from Memphis to Kansas City each day; it might safely be counted on to carry rich freight every trip. A crook could hardly miss out in plundering the strong box, no matter what run he happened to choose.

The more I thought about the matter the more convinced I became that it was a one man job. Still, I wasn't overlooking any bets on account of that idea. Memphis was being combed for information covering the situation. The trunk probably would be traced to the original seller; possibly to the latest owner in a roundabout way. The drayman ought to be easily located, and the house from which he took the trunk surely should give up something of value. I should begin getting reports from Memphis by morning. In the meantime I wasn't counting at all on what those reports brought me.

3

—

I GOT UP, feeling that while the cleverly contrived box looked like a mighty good lead, the crook would have figured it that way also—and he'd be keen enough to cover up all traces of it. The past history of that box would not enlighten us much.

I've heard of crooked jobs being pulled without leaving any clues behind, but I don't take any stock in such. There are always clues—and usually they are plentiful enough and big enough to lead to the undoing of the party who left them. This particular case was no different, in that respect, from all others I had handled. I had only to look in the right place—and then correctly construe what I found. Looking, and construing, being, of course, about all there is to sleuthing.

I stood in the spot where Jefferson presumably was when he met his end. He had probably been writing up waybills at the desk. He heard a noise in the end of the car on his right—maybe a command—turned, saw the intruder, reached for his gun and got it, only to be stopped by a bullet in his temple. I could visualize that well enough.

Ducret, in the opposite end of the car, his back turned to the scene, would naturally not be aware of what happened in those few seconds which elapsed between the instant of the bandit's discovery and the report of his gun. He would not have been in a position to defend the company's property, having no gun on him; there was nothing for him to do but submit. From the moment Ducret saw the bandit, until the latter threw the tarpaulin over him, everything was clear.

The tarpaulin was used in order to keep the second messenger from seeing the bandit in the act of leaving the car, how he carried the loot, and all that. Naturally, the less the messenger knew about the actions and appearance of the robber, the less he'd be able to tell. It was a long run from the point where the killing took place to Kansas City; probably the crook did not want to keep his face muffled up during all that time.

At any rate, the things which constituted my task were the things which occurred while Ducret lay under that cover. What did the bandit do? How did he carry the loot? In what manner did he pass the time before dropping from the express car just outside Kansas City?

For some time I had been standing near the squat, cast stove which is part of the equipment of every express car, my eyes drawn particularly to an object which lay on its flat top. The object was not in itself interesting; it had a right to be in the car. A stick of sealing wax, about half consumed, was the thing my glance fixed, and, without reason, held upon.

I approached the stove and took the stick in my hand, and knew immediately why it had been noticed: it had melted on the under side, and was considerably thinner than it should have been also, it was misshapen from having laid on top of a hot stove.

I suddenly took thought of the terrific heat of that August night. Why should any one want a hot fire in that stove? Messengers sometimes burn trash in their stoves, even in summer weather, but that makes at best but a momentary blaze—certainly not sufficient to heat the top and melt a stick of sealing wax which lay there.

I got down on my knees in front of the stove, opened the door, and played the rays of my flash light inside it. The moment my face came close to the opening, my nose told me that cloth had been recently burned there, and the heavy, unbroken ash in the bottom corroborated it.

Spreading a paper on the floor, I took the ashes out and placed them on it; there is no mistaking the ash of cloth for that of paper; the two are as distinctly different in ash as they are in substance. Somebody had burned a considerable bundle of cloth in that stove not long before.

I dug deeper, cleaning the inside of that bowl thoroughly.

Beneath the cloth-ash was a lot of paper-ash. That was to be expected. What puzzled me, though, was three strips of unconsumed paper, each strip consisting of numerous layers riveted together, which came out last. I wasn't puzzled long over them, though.

Somebody had burned three magazines, without separating the leaves, and the fire had not been hot enough to do more than char the riveted edges—commonly referred to as the "back."

Maybe the magazines had been used to start a fire in order to burn the cloth?

Second thought told me that was not true. Ever try to burn a magazine, or kindle a fire with a folded newspaper? It can't be done.

Those magazines had been thrown in the stove in order to destroy them. Why? In the name of common sense, why?

At that moment Jim Warren returned. I slid a door back in answer to his pounding and gave him something to do.

"Ducret is over in the Union Depot's detention room," I told him. "Go over and find out whether he or Jefferson built a fire in the car stove on the trip, and, if so, what was burned. Ask him if he knows anything about any magazines—newsprint type—being aboard."

Jim hustled off, and was back in a few minutes.

"Neither he nor Jefferson built a fire in the stove," he reported. "As for the magazines, he knows nothing about there being any in the car. There could have been, he says, and he not know it. He can't imagine where they could have come from; though, unless Jefferson had them. Jeff never was a hand to read, and had no time to do so on the run. Ducret thinks it safe to assume that there were no magazines brought aboard by him. What's the idea, Tug?"

"Somebody built a bonfire in the stove," I answered. "I'm a bit curious about it."

Right then my glance rested on Jim's bandage, and I began to wonder about the eye under it.

"Chat. Humph! Must have been a pretty strong wind blowing, to lift a handful of the roadbed and slam it through the window of the smoker. How come, Jim? There was no wind in Kansas City at that time; not even a zephyr teasing the air."

Chat is nothing more or less than stone crushed into small bits; the same being useful in smoothing up the surface of roadbeds. Action of the elements soon fuses the particles into a more or less solid mass—a crust, in fine.

"Why—"

Jim broke off, growing thoughtful.

"Yeah," I ridiculed, "think it over. Even a strong wind would not have lifted chat from the roadbed and hurled it into a car window, even if the stuff had only just been laid. Some fine particles, disturbed by the passing wheels, might ride that high and sift in—does do it, I know. But you say there was a lot of it—"

"Yes. Other passengers, sitting behind me, complained about it."

"A man on top of the car ahead—this car, as it happens— might have dropped a few handfuls of chat down, and the suction undoubtedly would have drawn the particles against the side of the car directly behind. The fireman or the engineer might have got some amusement out of toss-ing chat off the engine, or it might have been thrown out of the left hand door of the mail or express car. But who the devil would do that, and where would they come by the chat in the first place?"

"Sounds damned foolish, I'll admit, Tug," Jim conceded.

"Lead me to that smoker," I ordered. "Has this train been broken up and the coaches set out?"

"No. Orders were to leave it as it was when it came in, until officers had a chance to look it over."

"Good! Let's go."

Jim led the way to the car behind and opened the door with his pass-key, pointing out the seat he had occupied.

"Can't see what bearing my accident could possibly have on the case," he complained, watching me search about on the floor between the seats and down behind the upholstery.

"I'm just curious," I replied.

Next I went over the woodwork of the window, scraping the crevices of the sill with my knife blade.

"Let's go outside," I suggested, and led the way to the platform.

Jim followed, and stood by while I made an examination of the sills of each window on the left side of the smoker. Then I did the same to the door sills on that side of the express car.

Inside the smoker, on the upholstery of the seat Jim had sat in, as well as from the sills of several of the windows, I had collected several small bits of gray mineral. In a corner of the express car door, nearest the smoker, I had found a number of like particles.

"Your curiosity satisfied?" Jim demanded irritably, staring with his good eye at the bits which lay exposed in my palm.

"No," I answered. "It's increased. What I want to know now is this: When did the Frisco begin surfacing its road-bed with rock salt?"

The lids of Jim's single optic widened slowly to their fullest extent, while he eyed the gray fragments which I held out to him.

"Taste one," I invited, enjoying his discomfiture. "Maybe you'll then understand why the slug that swatted you in the eye stung so infernally."

Jim placed one of the particles on his tongue, made a wry face then spat it out.

"By George!" he exclaimed. "Rock salt it is!"

"Yeah, just common old rock salt—but not quite so common, considering where it came from, as that chat you thought it was. Looks like it, I'll admit. So you are exonerated—"

4

"BUT WHERE IN blazes did it come from?" Jim wondered with emphasis.

"Somebody might have stood beside the track and hurled handfuls at the train when it passed," I explained. "Granting some sort of idiot could enjoy doing so. That's one way."

"Don't blame you for being sarcastic," Jim said. "The truth is, knowing that the roadbed was surfaced with chat, I never once thought the stuff could be anything else."

"I'm not being sarcastic, Jim," I assured him. "The fact is I'm wondering. The stuff, in all probability, was thrown from a car ahead of the smoker—the express or mail car. Maybe from the engine. Suction would account for it coming in at the windows. I figure that if it had come from the mail car, above the express, none would have reached the smoker; as for the engine, we can just about eliminate it."

"There might have been a shipment of rock salt in the express car, though that's an odd thing to send so expensively, and it might have spilled on the floor and been swept out."

"Would the bandit have been likely to sweep it out?" I queried. "Remember, that stuff came in at the windows after you left Paola, and at that time Jefferson was dead and Ducret helpless."

"Of course! Who, then, could have thrown it? And, even so, what possible bearing can it have on the express car robbery?"

"That's what I'm wondering—what bearing," I replied. "You told me that there were some queer features about this case, Jim, and I agree. Several that are damned queer. The trunk is one. That fire in the stove, the cloth ashes, the partly destroyed magazines are others. But most curious of all is that charge of rock salt which peppered the side of the smoker, sprinkled the passengers and nearly knocked your eye out—"

"Charge?" Jim interrupted. "There were several of them! The stuff rattled on the glass in the upper sash of my window, and peppered the seats inside, three or four times."

I made no comment on that, but studied things over for a few minutes in silence. Then I went back inside the express car.

"Look for rock salt," I told Jim shortly. He did, and I did, but none could we find. There was not one single fragment of the stuff to be seen. I was about to give up, when I remembered the stove. It had proven fruitful before, maybe it would again. I did not examine the inside of the bowl this time, though, but got down and peered at the deposit of ashes in the receptacle beneath the grate. There I found what I was looking for.

The ashes in the pan were speckled with fine bits of stuff which was unmistakably rock salt.

"Well!" Jim declared when I imparted the news to him. "I'm damned!"

"So am I," was my response. "But I'm hoping to win redemption. In the meantime, I'm going to take this problem to bed with me. It's nearly my getting-up time now, granting I was in position to do it. A few hours' snooze may make things clearer."

"Right!" Jim agreed. "I'll put a man inside the car to watch it. What about the rest of the train?"

"Let 'em have it," I told him. "Set the express car off to itself somewhere, and keep it watched. I think I've learned all I can from it—but you never can tell. The trunk is still in it, too, you know."

Jim was about to depart, when I called him back. A notion had struck me between the eyes, and I acted on it.

"How is express delivered—I mean, does it all go through a sort of general clearing house before the trucks get it?"

"Sure."

"Then have every item in this car's shipment weighed before it is sent out in the morning and retain every one that is either overweight or under. Get me? Weigh it up carefully, see it done yourself, and keep everything that does not tally with the weight stamped upon it at the point of shipment. Now I'm going to get some sleep."

I did just that—slept—and I recommend a like course to all who are brain-weary from fruitless conjecturing. Next morning I went to my own office, the Kaw Valley Bureau, and attended to a few important matters there, dismissing the express case from my thoughts. I'd get back to it later.

At nine o'clock McFee called up and asked if I thought it necessary to continue to hold Ducret.

"Yes," I answered. "I shall probably release him some

time this afternoon, but certainly not until the Memphis report is in. He's not suffering greatly, I imagine. Hold him."

Mack asked a few questions anent the case, then hung up. An hour later Jim arrived with the report of the investigations made at Memphis.

We drew an absolute blank. No merchant in the Tennessee city had sold such a trunk, nor could any trace of the drayman who delivered it to the express company be found. The latter circumstance was easily accounted for: a confederate, possibly; more likely, the fellow had been fixed with a juicy tip, and would not allow himself to be found easily. In any case, I was no longer interested in the Memphis end; the whole thing could, and likely would, be solved right here in Kansas City.

"How about the weight on those express packages?" I asked Jim.

"They will be brought up from the station right away," he informed me, "and they will be weighed."

"Good enough. Now I'm going to do a bit of work in another quarter. I'll call about the weight matter later."

Jim left. His eye was still giving him the devil, and he was due at the doctor's.

I phoned the express company, got Ducret's Kansas City address and drove to it. He lived at a private rooming place in East Tenth Street, close in.

The landlady made no objection to me having a look at Ducret's room, she knowing me as a man from headquarters in the old days. I went up and spent half an hour digging into the messenger's things. Wasn't looking for anything in particular just giving things a shakedown because, for one thing, Ducret was a possible suspect; another, I was at a standstill, and then was nothing more important to do just then.

I found nothing at all unusual, at first, but one thing I discovered in a vest pocket of a suit he had evidently worn recently puzzled me for a few minutes—but only for a few. It was an unused, one-way ticket from Kansas City to Memphis, via the Frisco.

What the devil was he doing with the thing in his pocket? I glanced at the date, and learned that it had been issued two weeks before, and concluded that he had probably picked it up—the hard luck of some passenger.

But there was something to oppose to such a conclusion. If he found the ticket, why had he kept it? He couldn't use it—hadn't done so, in fact, and the thing was now long out of date. Had he simply forgotten it? Maybe. Maybe, too, he had forgotten to turn it in to the conductor of the train, or the ticket agent at Kansas City.

Not much, perhaps—but that ticket was another queer thing, to go along with the others. It gave me an idea, and I acted on it.

I acted on it—and by the time I got around to the main office of the express company, about two o'clock in the afternoon, I had either solved one of the most amazing cases it had ever been my province to handle—else I was in the way of making an unmitigated fool of myself. Just that, and nothing else.

McFee greeted me.

"We weighed up that express matter," he said, "and there are two items which do not tally out. One is a carboy of chemicals; must have been billed wrong, since the weight is stamped on the crate by the manufacturer; the bill over-weights it. The other is a parcel—but here it is," he broke off, pointing to a package about ten inches long and seven or eight wide, perhaps eight inches thick. It was wrapped in heavy manila paper, and was stoutly tied. "It is under-weight. That is, our weight is less than the stamped weight, by eight ounces."

I picked the package up, copied the name and address into my book, and handed it to McFee.

"Lock it up," I told him. "It's valuable. It contains two magazines—one on top and the other on the bottom. Between them there is one hundred thousand dollars in bills. The express loot, in short. You can look inside—"

He was already doing that, but I didn't wait for his comments. I had other work to do.

At the door I paused and called back to him standing there with both hands full of bank notes:

"By the way, you can turn Ducret loose now."

Then I started out to locate Jim Warren.

Three-quarters of an hour later, Jim and I got out of my car on a side street far out in South Kansas City, and one of my assistants drove it off. Then we made our way into Fifty-Eighth Street, several blocks from our stopping point, and rang the bell of No. 282, a brick house which stood back from the street about fifty feet. The door opened presently, and we stepped unceremoniously inside.

5

——

"WE ARE OFFICERS," Jim told the frightened woman who answered our ring. "No harm will be done you if you don't make a fuss. Answer our questions, and do as we say, and you won't regret our visit."

We displayed our badges, and the woman grew calmer.

What do you wish to know?" she quavered.

"You have a roomer named Carter Bancroft?"

"Yes."

"Describe him."

"He's a nice looking young man," the woman began, "very quiet and well behav—"

"I mean his looks," Jim cut in.

"He's tall, stoops a bit, wears horn-rimmed spectacles, and always dresses in a blue suit."

"What color is his hair and eyes?"

"He has blue eyes and light hair. He travels for—I think it is for a Bible publishing house, and is very quiet and well behav—"

"Yes, we understand that. Is he in at present?

"No. I'm expecting him, though. He should have returned last night."

"Oh! He isn't here every night, then?" Jim said.

"No. Only about once a week. Usually Friday."

"All right, Mrs.—"

"Jeems, sir—Sarah Jeems," the woman supplied.

"Well, Mrs. Jeems, you will precede us to Mr. Bancroft's room," Jim ordered.

She led the way upstairs, unlocked a door at the front and ushered us into a small, well furnished bedroom.

"This it?" Jim queried suspiciously.

"Oh, yes, sir!" Mrs. Jeems declared. "This is Mr. Bancroft's room."

"Have you one room vacant, on this floor?" I asked at this point.

"My own bedroom is on this floor."

"Well, Mrs. Jeems," I told her, "I'm sorry, but you must go into your room, and allow us to lock you in. You must remain quite still, and we will release you soon. Believe me, it is for your own protection."

Dazed and wondering, Mrs. Jeems retired to her room, and Jim turned the key on her, after first ascertaining that Bancroft was the only roomer she had, and there was no other person in the house. Then the two of us sat down in Bancroft's room, and waited.

It was shortly after dark, and we were sitting there quietly with the light out, that we heard a key turn in the downstairs door, and later a heavy foot upon the stairs.

Jim slipped his gun out, and I closed my right hand over the butt of my own in its shoulder holster.

The footsteps came on to the door behind which we sat, a key was inserted, and a tall, stoop-shouldered young man, wearing horn-rimmed glasses, stepped part way inside, and pressed the light button. He stopped abruptly at sight of us, his face going suddenly white.

"Walk right in, Ducret," I invited. "Of course you don't hope to fool us with that thin disguise."

He came in. There was nothing else he could do—unless he wanted to die there on the threshold.

"I—I—well, what—"

He stammered, choked, fell silent.

"The jig's up. Don't try any funny business," Jim said, searching him and removing an automatic pistol. "Sit down, and we'll try and make matters clear to you."

Ducret sank down on the side of the bed, eyes staring—not at Jim, but at me. I took things in hand then.

"You are under arrest for killing Stanley Jefferson—a dirty, dastardly crime! You, a working mate—but we'll let that pass," I said, trying to smother the ire within me. "When you first conceived the idea of robbing the express company, you probably had no thought of killing anybody. Later, when it became apparent that your kind of plot wouldn't work out unless you bumped your pardner off, you cold-bloodedly went on with it.

"As a first step in your plans, you rented this room and bought a trunk—the one you thought to fool the police with. It was necessary for that trunk to have a certain weight—about what a medium sized man would scale. You probably considered sand, maybe stone—in the end you bought three fifty-pound bags of rock salt. It was cheap, and easily come by. You placed the three bags inside the trunk, after you had transformed it into the padded, knock-down affair it now is: then you were confronted by the necessity of getting it to Memphis.

"You were clever, there, I'll have to say. You had a dray-man cart it to the station, purchase a ticket to Memphis and check the thing through. A clever dodge—but you slipped up. The drayman reported to you, and gave you the trunk check and the ticket. You placed the ticket in your pocket, and forgot it. I found it.

"Arriving in Memphis on the same train that carried the trunk, you sent for it, had it taken to a storage house, probably; where, makes no difference. On the day that trunk was needed, you had it carted to the express company and shipped to Kansas City. Just after the train pulled out of Fort Scott, the final division before reaching the Kansas City terminus you shot your pardner through the head, killing him."

A gasp came from the man on the bed. "You—you lie!" he shouted. "It all happened like I described! It did, as God—"

"Never mind the profanity!" Jim blazed, drawing his blackjack. "Any more interruptions, and I'll use this!" he threatened.

"The trunk was not the only express matter you sent to Kansas City by that train," I resumed. "You sent a package of magazines to yourself, under your assumed name, at this address. That was another shrewd bit—but you slipped up there also.

"Jefferson dead, you rifled the safe. After that you dug out the package of magazines, removed all but two, placed the packages of bank notes between them and rewrapped it. You could do that easily, using the same paper. It was necessary, however, to break the wax seal put upon the package where the selvedge of the paper crossed. Plenty of the same kind of sealing wax the Memphis office used, in the car, of course. You counterfeited the seal, restoring the package, apparently untampered with.

"As I said, that was a fine idea—but you slipped in two places there. You carelessly laid the stick of sealing wax on top of the stove, which was at your elbow. That is one slip. The other is, you destroyed one too many magazines. The light weight of the package betrayed you.

"The package fixed and restored to the pile, where it would finally, you figured, reach you at this address and be signed for by your landlady, you then proceeded to put that clever trunk idea into execution. You opened it, removed the three bags of salt, and punched the holes through the paper. Even the wrench, supposedly used by the bandit in liberating himself, was left lying on the bottom.

"Would the investigators, putting themselves in the bandit's place, come to the conclusion that no sane person would take a chance on finding themselves trapped by having something heavy on the lid? You had cleverly antic-ipated that, by making it apparent that the trunk could be taken to pieces, if necessary. You even got inside with your shoes on, and left a bit of earth there. That was good—it fooled me completely.

"The rock salt. You dragged the sacks to the left-hand door of the car and, after pulling out of Paola, proceeded to throw the salt out. There was the fatal slip. Some of those particles of salt were carried back to the smoker—one of them nearly blinding Warren. Had you really used chat, or had the salt—but what's the use? The rock salt was the most enlightening clue of all the numberless ones you, keen though you were, left behind.

"The salt disposed of, remained the sacks. You could have

thrown them out the car door, but they might be dug up by somebody and, in some way, appear again. You decided to burn them, along with the magazines.

"You did burn the whole business—making several slips there. As a matter of fact, you pulled more boners than I can count, including the original one—the conception of the job in the first place.

"The heat from those burning sacks and magazines melted the stick of sealing wax on top of the stove—and that melted wax was my first clue. Some of the particles of salt, which adhered to the insides of the sacks, sifted down through the grate into the ash tray. Salt won't burn, you know.

"Once I decided that there had been no bandit in that trunk, the case was clear—and the discovery of the rock salt determined that point. The only thing left to do then was to figure out what had become of the money. I had you safe—"

I stopped abruptly. Ducret had been crouching on the side of his bed, and across the bed was an open, unscreened window. It was a desperate chance, but he took it.

With a powerful spring, he hurled himself toward the opening—and then is when I clamped my hand on the substance of that which I mentioned at the start. When Jim dug us out of the wreck of the bed, Ducret was quite peaceful—and would be for some time to come.

He woke up just as we reached headquarters—in time to sign a confession before the chief of police went home.

THE RIVERTON TANGLE

*The Once Splendid Hotel in Which Father and
Son Met Unknown Death Stood Deserted Until
One Man's Ambition Betrayed Another's Crime*

1

THE HOTEL OF DOOM

WHEN THE REV. Amos T. Hemming came into the office that morning and asked the boy for an interview with the head of the Kaw Valley Detective Bureau, I was very willing for him to have it. With half a dozen high-salaried operatives cooling their heels in the office at my expense, I had a keen ear for inquiries of that sort.

I met him at the door, and invited him into my private shop.

"Mr. Tug Norton?"

The caller was a spare man, in the middle sixties, I judged, and had all the earmarks of a clergyman—white collar and tie, black frock-coat, steel-rimmed spectacles, and all. For further evidence of his calling, the purple bookmark of a testament protruded from a pocket of his coat.

He had mild gray eyes, and a placid expression. That is to say, placidity was the normal expression of his face, but it now showed some signs of worry, and a certain twitching of his thin, clean-shaven lips told me that he was none too sure of himself in the matter then engaging him.

I nodded in reply to his question, and asked him to be seated.

"First," he informed me, "I must have your promise not to divulge what I am about to say."

"Certainly, sir," I assured him. "You may safely confide in me. Our firm makes a specialty of keeping inviolate the confidences of its clients."

After a moment's hesitation he nodded gravely, and sat down.

"My name is Amos T. Hemming," he imparted, "and I am one of the owners of the Riverton Hotel. Perhaps you are familiar with the history of the former resort?"

I nodded, and my mental ears pricked. The Riverton Hotel, a once popular resort in the hills west of the city, had quite an interesting history, and some of it was very recent. I said nothing, and let him talk.

"The building, one of the largest and most ornate of the day in this section, has stood uninhabited, save for a caretaker, for the past few months," he resumed. "It is in a state of bad repair, but is, nevertheless, a valuable property. Situated upon a three hundred-acre tract of fertile land,

*"Take care of her, Bob," I called, and turned to face a
vision in a nightdress and cascade of yellow hair*

possessing many fine springs, some of recognized medici-
nal value, accessible from Kansas City by interurban, motor
car and the Missouri, it should bring a high price in the
real estate market."

He paused, seemed to think ahead for a moment, and
went on speaking in his monotonous, slightly complain-
ing voice:

"Wilbur Cowden, former president of the hotel
company, died there one night a year ago, and under conditions which never have been cleared up satisfactorily. He
was found dead in his bedroom in the hotel, with a bullet
in his brain, a revolver on the floor. After what purported
to be a thorough investigation, the public was informed
that he had taken his own life.

"Now, it developed directly afterward that Cowden had
realized upon such private property as he possessed—
stocks, bonds, and some valuable real estate in the East,

and should have been in possession of something like one hundred thousand dollars at the time of his demise.

"The administrators, aided by friends, have never been able to find a trace of the money. His one-third interest in the hotel constituted his sole visible asset. A daughter and son, the latter since dead, inherited the father's share, and the young woman still holds it."

He ceased speaking, and gave me a queer glance from eyes that were half closed, then spoke with what I deemed considerable reluctance:

"You may have heard some talk about the despoiling of the interior of the hotel building, shortly after it was closed, by persons evidently seeking hidden valuables, it being narrated about that Wilbur Cowden had concealed his money on the premises. We did all we could to stop the vandalism, and succeeded pretty well, but every now and then fresh evidence of the work of treasure hunters is found. Some still believe the tale.

"Six months after the death of Wilbur Cowden, Samuel, his son, came from the East and took up residence in the hotel with his sister. A month later he was discovered dead on the floor of his room at the top of the building. He, too, had been shot, and the pistol was on the floor at his side.

"Suicide, this time, without a doubt—such was the verdict. The motive for the act was never forthcoming, although the young man's record in the East was investigated for a possible clew. The matter made a great deal of talk. Father and son—hereditary suicidal tendency on the part of the young man, was the prevalent belief. After a month or so the public in general forgot the occurrence.

"But hotel patrons, actual and prospective, did not forget.

To make a long story short, the two mysterious deaths occurring in the hotel so close together simply ruined the place for its purpose. People shiver over such things. Four months ago we closed the building, and have not been warranted in opening it since."

"You think then," I remarked during the pause that followed, "that the two suicides—"

"They were anything but that!"

The interruption was voiced vehemently, and Mr. Hemming's face grew red with annoyance.

"Ah! Now we are going to get down to cases," I thought. "He'll come through in a minute."

"What is it you require of me?" I asked.

"I told Grayle and Miss Cowden, and I now say to you: Those supposed suicides were murders, pure and simple! To regard them as anything else is absurd!"

I let that pass for a moment. "The persons just named are your co-owners?" I queried.

"Yes. Dr. Herbert Grayle, who conducts a sanatorium near Riverton station, and Mary Cowden, who occupies property close by. Each owns equal shares with me in the place. We met last night to consult about the possibility of selling the property, or taking action looking toward dissipating the pall which hangs over it. I suggested that you be brought into the case, but the proposal was vetoed. Of no use, my partners said."

"Now, Mr. Hemmings, just why are you skeptical regarding the assumption that those two deaths were suicides?" I asked.

"I knew Wilbur Cowden well, and there never was a saner man," Hemming declared. "I got rather well acquainted with the son, and his mentality was far above the average. He was calm, self-possessed, and normal in conduct at all times. He declared to me, as well as to others, that his father had not died by his own hand. It was his conviction that he had been killed for his money."

"Did not the disappearance of so large a sum of money strike the police as odd?"

"They took no stock in the existence of it!" was the indignant response. "Claimed that if he really had such a sum he had speculated and lost it. Even gave that as a good reason for his killing himself!"

"Did the son have knowledge of the existence of the money?"

"He knew only that his father had sold considerable property in the East. What disposition he made of the proceeds of such sales was unknown, both to Samuel and Miss Cowden."

"Do you know that he had it?"

Hemming's face paled, and he gave me a disturbed look. After a moment of palpable debate, he answered:

"At the risk of directing suspicion to myself," he said, "I am going to answer that question. I do know that he had it. It came to him from his brokers, by express, and was in currency. Mr. Cowden and I were close friends; he trusted me.

"Two days before his death he called me into the hotel office, told me about the money, and said that he had made an offer to purchase certain real estate in the county. The money was for that purpose, should his offer be accepted. He did not say with whom he was bargaining."

"Now, get back to your purpose in coming to me," I

requested. "You say your partners objected to calling me in?"

"They did. But I, acting alone, wish to engage you to uncover the truth about those deaths. Once the facts are known—that they were murders—and the guilty brought to justice, the pall which now hangs over the place will be no more. I want to restore a valuable property—as well as punish the murderer of my old associate—and it must be done!"

"A good deal of time has passed," I reminded him. "I might as well start hunting for the proverbial needle— unless a bit of luck breaks for me. Still, hunting is my business. If you are prepared to pay, I'm prepared to cast off on the trail."

He drew a check-book from his pocket and sat down at my desk. "What do you require as a retainer?" he queried.

I mentioned the sum—and made it large. To take up a trail after all the regular sleuths in the country have been nosing along it, is worth money—provided you take it with the intention of giving value received. I did intend to. My business is based upon just such service.

He never even batted an eye, but wrote the check and placed it in my hand.

2

THREE AGAINST EACH OTHER

"NOW," HE REMINDED, "neither of my partners are to know that I have called you in. That I insist upon."

"They won't," I assured him. "One question: Where are the quarters of the caretaker located, and what is his name?"

"Thomas Burdick, the caretaker, lives in two rooms in the southeast corner of the basement," he informed me. "He has been with the hotel company since it was established five years ago, and Mr. Cowden had employed him prior to that. I consider him a reliable person. I have no other information to give you, that I can now think of.

"This may seem a far-fetched procedure, but, if followed back to that night a year ago when Wilbur Cowden died, and the real facts uncovered, I firmly believe it will be established that his death, and the subsequent death of the son, was not suicide. Then the cloud will be cleared away from the property, and it will once more be valuable."

He rose to go.

"I shall begin at once," I told him. "Where may I find you, when I wish to communicate with you?"

He gave the address of a well known hotel in the city, saying he had resided there since closing the Riverton.

"Remember," he said in parting, "that money is no object, so long as I get results!"

Statements like that sound good in my ears.

The First State Bank cashed the check without even looking up Hemming's balance—which augured well—and I returned to my shop to study the case over. A hard one, if I was a capable judge.

"Dr. Grayle to see you, sir!"

I confess it kind of took my breath, that announcement. Grayle, too! Another owner wanting a private detective!

"Show him in," I directed.

A muscular man of about forty years entered immediately. His dress was that of a business man who knows the value of good clothes, and his clean-shaven face was gravely professional. It was only when he sat down near me that a faint odor of drugs became noticeable, marking him for what he was.

"I've heard of you and your organization, Mr. Norton," he opened, voice deep and pleasant, large gray eyes level with mine. "Never thought I'd be needing your professional services, but I am. Don't know just what I want done, either. The truth of the matter is, I'm a victim, in a business way, of circumstances which have, I believe, a remedy. I want you to get some facts for me—facts, understand?"

"It is our business, doctor, to find out facts," I reminded him. "And we will undertake to nail yours for you. Just what is the nature of the trouble?"

Could he be wanting me for something entirely unconnected with Hemming's job? Had I been wrong in leaping to the conclusion that he had reconsidered his objection of the night before, and now wanted me to take a hand in the Riverton case? Grayle cleared his throat, presaging a somewhat lengthy statement.

"I am one of three owners of the Riverton Hotel property," he began, and followed with a lot of history concerning the hotel—the second time I had heard it that day.

"Now," he summed up, "here's where I stand: If those two deaths were suicides, then that fact should be established so thoroughly by way of the newspaper columns that all doubt in the minds of the people will be wiped out, and the matter dismissed and forgotten. If they were murders, as has been hinted, then that should be established and the murderer brought to justice.

"Once he is captured and executed, in case he really exists, the stigma attached to the neighborhood—a horror in the minds of all who know about it—will fade out. In either case, my sanatorium will be saved while, as matters stand, patients, nervous to begin with, shudder at the nearness of my place to the grounds. It is the mystery that gets them. It matters not to me what your findings are, so that the truth is laid bare."

"I see. Your business will benefit either way."

"Exactly. And my interest in the hotel property will be restored to its former value. I must insist, though, that neither of my associates know that I have seen you. I may count on your silence?"

"Absolutely," I replied, and waited.

"The fee?"

I named a retainer—another generous one. He paid it in cash, without a murmur. Taking fees from two persons for work to be done on the same case may seem a little queer. Each had, however, hired me for his own private ends—

and those ends were different. I quieted my conscience and pocketed the retainer.

"I shall begin investigations at once," I assured him, as he rose, "and will keep you informed. Good day."

"Why do they want to keep their activities hidden from each other?" was the question which popped into my mind when Grayle had gone. "Why didn't they get together, and hire me to find out the truth? One wants it proven that two accepted suicides were really murders, and the other wants me to hew to the line and let the chips fall where they will—the latter being the course I would pursue in any case.

"Well, Tug," I assured myself in all sincerity, "here's a sure enough tangle—and the time to start work on it is now!"

"A lady to see you, sir!"

I turned, just as a slender, elegantly dressed woman, her features dim under a veil, entered the room. I could—and did—guess at her identity. The third owner of the Riverton property.

"Be seated," I invited, allowing none of the excitement I was beginning to feel to show in my manner.

"Mr. Norton," she said, addressing me in about the sweetest tones I ever heard come from a woman's throat, "it is customary, I believe, for persons to employ private investigators to solve mysteries. Am I not right?"

"In most cases," I replied, "detectives have such ends to serve."

Maybe I had guessed wrong about this young woman. I could tell by the way she began that hers was not the usual proposition.

"What may I do for you?" I queried.

"I want you not to—I mean, I wish to employ you not to undertake to solve the mystery shrouding the deaths at Riverton!" she exclaimed, as though, having nerved herself to it, she wished to get her mission over with as quickly as possible. "Should you be asked to undertake such a case, I will pay you any fee you may name if only you will refuse to do it! Shall I consider you to be in my employ?"

Right then I began to believe there might be something underhanded in those deaths. The daughter wanting to hire me not to investigate them! Prior to her coming I had kept an open mind in the matter, leaning, if it could be called such, to the theory entertained by the police after their investigation. Now, however, I began to consider the case from a more serious angle.

"That is rather an odd request," I said to the young woman. "In case I should accept, I must know the name of my employer."

She looked frightened, her face paling under the veil.

"No!" she exclaimed. "That is not necessary!" After a visible effort she composed herself, opened her hand bag and took out a roll of bills. "See, I came prepared. Would a thousand dollars be sufficient for the present? I can and will pay more, if other and larger fees are offered you!"

"How shall I communicate with you, in the latter eventuality?" I queried.

"I will communicate with you, at frequent intervals," she evaded. "You will accept my offer, then?"

I shook my head. "No." I answered. "I have never taken a fee of that character, and I don't believe I'll begin now. Sorry, but there is nothing doing!"

She gasped, getting hastily to her feet. "You—you have already been engaged!" she cried accusingly. "You have already been set on the trail! Don't deny it! Oh, will nothing dissuade you?"

"Nothing," I told her sternly.

"Then," she exclaimed, drawing herself up, "let me warn you! If you value your life, drop your activities now! Stay away from the Riverton property! Heed my words, for I shall not warn again! Stay away from the hotel and its grounds!"

She turned quickly and dashed out of the room—her exit in keeping with her melodramatic utterance.

I promptly signaled one of my idle, high-priced assistants to pick up her trail.

Two of the owners wanting my services as an investigator, and the third—for I would have bet the young woman was Mary Cowden—wanting to hire me to keep my nose out!

3

AN UNEARTHLY SCREAM

I DID NOT waste any time speculating about my unnamed caller, or whether her warning was worth serious consideration. Steele, my operative, would take care of her. Ten minutes after her exit I was on my way to the river front, all set for action.

There are three easy routes to the Riverton property. One is by way of the Leavenworth Interurban, which runs cars at half hour intervals between Kansas City and Fort Leavenworth. The hotel building lies fifteen miles northwest of the limits of Kansas City, Kansas, and half a mile north of Riverton Station, which is on the electric railway.

There was a time when Riverton Station gave promise of becoming a substantial suburban village, but with the discontinuance of the resort its prospects faded. Riverton became a name on a pine board attached to a small shelter house on the right of way, and nothing else. A few minutes' walk, over a good road, takes one to the hotel grounds.

The second route lies over the State highway, which traverses the section, east and west, two miles south of the station. A hard surface road, excellent but lonely, reaches out like a long, white arm and connects the highway with Riverton.

The third, and seldom used, route is provided by the Missouri River.

I chose the latter route, and started upstream in a small motor boat alone, after night had fallen. I had no intention of allowing any one to know of my arrival, and I particularly did not want my woman caller to learn of it. I had not forgotten her, by a long shot, even though her warning had impressed me as being a bit of melodramatic nonsense. Steele would dig her out, of course, and find out whether or not she had teeth.

After passing the Quindaro Pumping Station, Kansas City's source of water supply, I entered sparsely settled country, wooded and hilly. My boat was an open one, equipped with a powerful engine, and I made good time up to the hotel property, passing it in the direction of Lansing and Leavenworth and anchoring in the weeds and brush at the foot of an island known to me.

Back in the woods, hidden from the river, was a log shack used by duck hunters in season. It was equipped with a stove, bunks, and, in short, everything necessary for my needs, should I find it advisable to use it.

About nine o'clock, using a skiff I had towed alongside the motor boat, I dropped downstream and tied up about midway of the lonely stretch of river front constituting part of the hotel grounds, and about two hundred yards above the deserted wharf and boathouse.

The building stood a quarter of a mile back, concealed from view from the river by a big grove of timber. The character of the land was hilly, and it would be possible to approach the house without being seen, even in the daytime, by taking advantage of the hills and shallow hollows. After night it was no trick at all.

Skirting a deep draw which ended in a weedy depression, choked with stunted willows and river grass which grew almost to the water's edge, I followed along it until I came to higher ground, a knoll from which the vague bulk of the building could be made out.

There I stopped for five minutes, searching the pile for a light—something to show the presence of human beings. The caretaker, I knew, lived on the lower floor, in a sort of half basement. Not a glimmer showed, however, and I glanced at the luminous dial of my watch. It was ten o'clock.

Moving carefully, so as to avoid striking my feet against the rocks and small bowlders with which the ground was strewn, I approached the main wing of the building, coming up to it at the point nearest the river. Standing there, the lights of the two houses were visible.

The lights to the south, about a quarter mile distant in the direction of the interurban station, were numerous, and I identified the place as Grayle's sanatorium. A like distance to the north, on top of a hill, two lights appeared. One at the front and the other at the back of a house. Those lights, I surmised, were shining in the home of Mary Cowden.

Having gotten the lay of the land, with reference to the location of the sanatorium and the probable position of Miss Cowden's place, I next turned my attention to the big, stone building in the shadow of which I stood—whose mysteries I had set myself to solve.

A basement window gave ready access to the lower floor,

and presently I was inside, my flash light playing down a dusty, cobwebby corridor which led off southward and extended the full length of the front. There were doors opening upon it on either hand. A worn rug covered the floor.

At the south end of that corridor the quarters of the caretaker were located, and his quarters were my immediate objective. Fixing the direction in my mind, I shut off my flash and proceeded slowly southward in the darkness, feeling along the east wall with my hands. It took perhaps ten minutes to negotiate the corridor, and when I at length came to the end I played my flash for a moment on the door of the last room, then tapped gently upon it.

I got no answer. After waiting a minute, I tapped again, louder. The soft blows of my knuckles awoke responsive echoes in the passage, but that was all. I tried the door and found that it was locked. Then I knocked on the one next above it, getting no response.

That did not put me out any. If the caretaker happened to be in I meant to have a talk with him. If absent, I had planned to have a look at the inside of his rooms. My bunch of keys soon solved the mechanism of the lock on the first door—arguing, I thought, that the occupant was not at home—and I stepped inside.

My flash revealed the character of the place. It was a combination kitchen and dining room, furnished with odds and ends of what had once been good stuff, musty with the smell of food, and masked from outside observance by two closely drawn shades. A closed door indicated the way into the bedroom on the north. I pushed it open, stepped inside—then stood tense, listening.

Had some one moved in the corridor outside? A foot, carelessly allowed to drag—

A rat squeaked, and ran through the door I had just opened. I grinned and set the button on my flash, flooding the room with light.

At that instant, as though the flash of light had set it off, the stillness of the place was shattered by a shrill, unearthly scream. It rose to a pitch which, to my ears, seemed impossible of attainment by a human voice—and came to an abrupt end at the highest reach, as though some one had choked off the sound.

Immediately thereafter a heavy thud, seemingly on the floor above, shook the building, there came the sound of some one running across a carpeted floor—then silence.

I backed out of the room I was on the point of entering, shut off my light and stood motionless, my mind working. Should I investigate the rooms above, seeking the source of that disturbance?

I do not play hunches. Nevertheless, I have a sort of instinct for which I have the greatest respect—an intuitive feeling which warns me, at times, that danger is near. Such a feeling stirred within me now.

The next instant I had opened the west window of the room, crawled through, and was running toward Riverton Station as fast as my feet would take me.

4

MISS MARY COWDEN, INVALID

I HAD NOT covered half the distance to the station when it flashed into my mind why I was running; the reason, retarded a bit, crystallized.

That terrible scream was too well timed. It was almost coincidental with my arrival inside the building. My woman caller had warned me not to set foot on the premises—that, subconsciously, was why I did not tarry.

Nature endowed me with a man's portion of courage, but when the urge to run first and investigate afterward comes suddenly and strongly upon me I obey it. I recall several times when my life has been saved by doing just that.

Whether or not it had been so saved this time remained to be seen.

What I most desired at the moment was to get in touch with my operative, Steele, whom I had put on the trail of the woman. After that we would together consider the advisability of exploring the rooms of the hotel. Frankly, I did not like the thought of doing so at night. Too many chances to shoot from an intersecting corridor, or some shadowed nook or cranny.

Besides, that same intuitive prohibition was still strong within me. That cry had sounded phony—and if it was phony it had been employed for the purpose of decoying me up those dark stairs to my death.

I knew just where I should find Steele. He had been instructed to call the office as soon as he ran his quarry to earth, and, in case I was not there, to plant himself where he could watch the Riverton Interurban Station, himself unseen. He was to wait there for further orders. Unless the woman had led him a longer chase than I had reason to suspect she would, Steele would certainly be on hand.

I passed the sanatorium, skirting the foot of a long lawn on the right of the road, circled due south and reached the station without meeting any one. The place was dark, the incandescent lamp which once adorned the little shanty having long since disappeared. Taking out my flash I allowed its rays to play upon the weather-beaten wall on the south, shut it off, then played it again.

Two minutes thereafter Steele was beside me.

"Well," I asked in an undertone, "where did she lead you? To a little cottage north and east of the hotel building?"

"No," Steele replied. "She went directly to Grayle's Sanatorium, entered by the main door, and is there yet. At least, she had not left when I came here an hour ago."

That was a facer.

I thought swiftly, and a possible explanation came. Miss Cowden and Dr. Grayle were both opposed to an investigation, according to Hemming. Grayle reconsidered his position and called me in on his own hook. Miss Cowden, suspecting that I had been engaged by Hemming, had hastened to acquaint Grayle with the fact.

But why the haste? Why all the agitation over a mere

investigation of the mystery? Should not Miss Cowden be deeply interested in knowing just how her father and brother met death? If a normal daughter and sister, she should welcome the opportunity to set at rest the doubts concerning the manner of their taking off.

Also, why, in the event she had hastened to tell Grayle, had she lingered so long at the sanatorium? Who was occupying her cottage that night? I distinctly saw its lighted windows, and knew some one was inside. Possibly a maid, cook or companion.

At any rate, I had to dig Miss Cowden out and get her full measure before taking another step in the case. I could not afford to delay another hour. She had information which I must, by one means or another, make my own.

"We are going to pay a visit in the vicinity, Steele," I informed my operative. "It is a bit late for it, but we are going to make the call regardless. Come."

We struck off in a roundabout way for the cottage of Mary Cowden, and as we walked I related to Steele all that had happened since Hemming entered my office that day.

We had reached the hilltop on which the Cowden cottage stood—lonely and forlorn—when I finished recounting my experience in the hotel building. Steele, lacking the opportunity, made no comment.

The cottage was a small, one-story affair, sadly in need of paint. We approached the front door, through the glass of which a dim light shone. I rapped on the panel.

Footsteps inside, then the door was opened widely, as though some person was expected, and a tall, angular woman filled the aperture. A smile, half formed on rather grim lips, gave place to a tightening of the lines of her mouth, and she closed the door almost shut.

"What do you want?" came the demand.

"It is very important that I see Miss Cowden," I informed her in my politest tone. "Tell her that I have recon—"

"I'll tell her nothing!" snapped the guardian of the door. "Miss Cowden is ill in bed, and can see no one!"

"Ill?" I repeated questionably. "How long has she been so?"

"That isn't any of your business," was the reply. "But if it will do you any good to know, she has been a semi-invalid since her father's death a year ago. Lately she has been confined to her bed. Now get out, and leave us be!"

And that was that! Ill in bed—had been almost a year!

Was the old woman lying?

I acted suddenly. Displaying my badge with one hand, I swept her aside with the other and entered.

"Take care of her, Bob!" I called.

"Help!" cried the woman. "Thieves! Help!"

Just who she hoped to raise with that shout was a question in my mind. She made no more noise, however.

"Another cheep out of you," I heard Steele saying sternly, "and we'll run you in!"

What else he said I do not know. My entire attention was centered elsewhere.

An inner door opened wide, and in the aperture stood a vision in white nightdress, a great mass of yellow hair fluffed about her head and cascading down her back. One look assured me that the young woman was ill, and that, in all probability, she had been so for some time.

"What do you wish, gentlemen?" she asked in a soft, weak voice.

"Are—are you Miss Mary Cowden?" I asked, inclined to stammer.

"I am," was the calm reply, while her blue eyes, unnaturally large, looked me in the face without the least trace of fear in them.

"Then," I said, "we are not gentlemen! We're just a pair of roughnecks who beg your pardon and ask your permission to retire!"

I had forced my way into that house without the least compunction, believing that I was about to enter the presence of the flashing eyed, healthy cheeked brunette who had called on me that afternoon. I had been willing to do so because I firmly believed she held the key to some, if not all, of the mysteries in which I was professionally concerned. And I had found only a sick, helpless girl!

Miss Cowden smiled, a slim white hand supporting her in the doorway.

"I believe a mistake has been made—an honest one," she said. "Perhaps it will be better to explain."

"You are very good to say so," I declared. "And you are right as to the mistake. I cannot, however, make the matter clearer than to say that I am a reputable detective officer, engaged upon an investigation in this vicinity. Our mistake here was due to a case of—er, mixed identities. We shall not trouble you again."

I was in the act of backing out.

"I knew the two of you for policemen, the minute I saw your ugly mugs!" snarled the ex-guardian of the door.

"Gentlemen! Huh! Get right back to bed, Miss Mary," she ordered, hurrying to her charge.

"Never mind Cora," Miss Cowden apologized. "She is good clear through, even though at times a bit abrupt. Tell me one thing, and then you may go."

I nodded acquiescence.

"Is your presence here concerned with the misfortunes of my family—the death of my father and brother?"

Darn it! I couldn't add a lie to my other offence against her.

"Yes, Miss Cowden," I replied.

"Then I shall tell you that you are engaged uselessly," the young woman declared. "My father killed himself because of two things: One, he lost heavily in speculation. Secondly, insanity runs in the Cowden family, and he was insane when he committed the act.

"My brother, Samuel, inherited the suicidal tendency, and killed himself after nearly a month during which he suffered from insomnia. What I say is true. Why keep such things alive? I am content to let my dead rest in peace. What right has any outsider to interfere?"

During that speech I regained my normal wits—no longer felt put out over our intrusion. Here was something worth hearing.

"How do you know Mr. Cowden lost in speculation?" I asked.

"I know he did speculate—had always done so—and died poor."

"How did you learn that he had an insane streak?"

"I have the word of one of the most skillful of physicians on that point," came the surprising answer. "One who specializes in nervous disorders—disorders of the brain."

"Who?" I demanded.

"Dr. Herbert Grayle," she replied.

"Did he tell you about your brother, too?"

"Yes."

"About the insomnia?"

"No. Brother himself told me that—not more than three or four days before he died."

I had blundered onto a gold mine of information—yet I dared not dig deeper. I could see that Miss Cowden was growing fatigued. There was only one thing to do under the circumstances.

"We shall retire now, Miss Cowden," I told her. "But I should like your promise to see me for a few minutes some time later—say within a few days. Will you?"

She nodded. "I shall—and perhaps I can convince you that I know the right of things."

"Perhaps," I assented. "Good night."

5

FROM AMBUSH—A SILENCER

OUTSIDE I PAUSED and spoke out what was on my mind.

"Grayle!" I exclaimed. "He told me he knew nothing about the deaths, other than reports of the police and vague rumors that Cowden and his son had been murdered. Now it appears that he has told this girl positively that both were insane, and committed suicide because of the malady. What do you make of that?"

"Well," replied Steele, after a moment's consideration, "it might be a bit of propaganda he's planting in the girl's mind."

Propaganda!

But why? Could it be possible that Grayle—well known as a specialist in mental diseases, of high standing in his profession, apparently wealthy and prosperous, had had a hand in killing Wilbur Cowden and his son?

On top of that came another question demanding an answer:

Since the mysterious woman who wanted me to keep out of the case was not Mary Cowden, who the devil was she?

"Steele," I said, "there is a lot of hard thinking necessary right at this point. I've got to make something jibe with something else, so to speak, and do it now. We'll row up the river to Cobb's Island, cook a bite to eat—I've provisions in the motor boat—and see if we can find a loose end.

"Darby has instructions to meet me here before daylight, unless otherwise instructed, and he'll have the dope on the past history of this Cowden affair. Maybe that will give us a lead. Anyhow, I'm hungry, so the island it is."

We struck off in silence toward where I had left my skiff. The way wound about among hills and hollows—the hills and hollows and the springs which had made Riverton Hotel such an asset as a resort—and angled above the building, missing it by about half a quarter.

"What do you make of that maid, back yonder?" Steele asked after a bit.

"Nothing important," I replied. "Loyal to her mistress, I think."

"And the mistress?"

"Straight as a fiddle-string," I asserted without hesitation. "She's square. Believes what she told us to be true."

"And Grayle. You say he gave you no hint that he attributed the Cowden deaths to suicidal insanity?"

"He failed to touch upon his belief, if he held it," I replied. "Quite the contrary. He led me to believe he had an absolutely open mind as to the motives behind the deaths. Might have been suicide, might have been murder. Either way, he wanted the truth made known."

"Humph!" was Steele's sole comment.

We fell silent—and lucky for us we did.

We were just ascending from a shallow hollow and rounding a knoll which was topped by a number of large bowlders, when I heard the click of boot-soles against rocks—just a faint noise, but enough.

I dropped flat to earth on the instant, dragging Steele down with me.

A flash of flame seared the darkness a hundred feet away from us—and, instead of the loud explosion I expected, there came a subdued report. A sound which, if noted at all, would not have attracted much attention, unless, as in our case, the spurt of flame had been seen.

Some one was shooting at us with a gun equipped with a silencer!

I rolled behind a bowlder, Steele with me, and we whipped out our guns.

"Listen!" I breathed.

Again came that muffled report, and my eyes caught a faint, brief illumination at a point farther west of our position than I had expected the marksman to be. My ears gave me the answer.

"He's running—hear him? Running away from us!"

There were no more reports—else, if any, they were too distant for our straining ears to hear them.

"Well, Steele," I remarked, "was he, or wasn't he?"

"Was he or wasn't he what?" Steele growled.

"Shooting at us?"

"I didn't hear the sound of a bullet whining around us," replied the operative thoughtfully. "And he ran from instead of toward us. That might be explained by the circumstance that we, behind the bowlder, had him at the same disadvantage he had us at first, only for that second shot. I pass."

"Well, he's gone, and we may as well proceed. We'll go over this ground in the morning."

We resumed our way toward the river, passing the spot where the marksman must have been, Steele moodily in the lead.

There was a faint moon, and as we came opposite a large bowlder on our right—the one, I surmised, which afforded the ambush—something lying on the ground against the white of the rock, caught my eye. Steele passed on, and I stepped aside and picked the object up.

For a moment I stared incredulously at the thing I held in my hand—then, stuffing it in my pocket, I followed Steele.

6

A PURPLE BOOK-MARK

A SHORT WHILE later we sat at a table in the hunters' cabin on Cobb's Island, fed and comfortable.

"I'm going to do a little thinking aloud, Steele," I remarked. "You can check me up if I get too far off. Now:

"The Riverton Hotel is not of ultramodern construction—that is to say, its rooms are not soundproof. After Wilbur Cowden's death, no one could be found who heard the report of the pistol which killed him.

"I recall that the police explained that by pointing out the fact that the bullet taken from Cowden's brain had undoubtedly been fired from the pistol beside him. If no one heard it, that did not have a vital bearing on the matter, they said. The hotel was in a very prosperous state at the time, most rooms filled, and Cowden's apartment was not an isolated one. Yet nobody heard the shot.

"Consider further: Samuel Cowden was shot to death in the same wing and on the same floor of the building, six or seven months later—and no one heard the report. Yet he, too, was killed by a bullet fired from the revolver found beside him. Revolvers, in both instances, by the way, which the police have been unable to trace."

"What does that prove—no one hearing the shots?"
Steele queried.

"It doesn't prove anything," I told him, "but it does
establish a mighty strong argument in favor of the murder
theory. It argues, to my mind, that silencers were used on
those revolvers. None was on either when found—and a
corpse couldn't remove one."

Steele nodded agreement, and I went on thinking aloud:

"Cowden, by his own statement, was in possession of
a large sum of money which he had got together under
conditions savoring of a desire for secrecy. He, according
to Hemming, admitted having the money two days before
his death. No money was found in the apartment, nor has
any clew to its whereabouts since been turned up.

"A wall safe in his room stood open—opened by some
one who knew the combination, since it was uninjured. No
finger marks on the safe or in the room of an incriminating
character. The police investigation so divulged.

"Why the secrecy about the money, on Cowden's part?
Did he actually have it?"

"It would seem that he did have it, and that he was killed
for the purpose of robbery. Furthermore, the assassin did
not get what he came for."

"How do you make that out?" Steele demanded, sitting
up.

"The fact that directly after the police withdrew from
the case, and before Samuel Cowden came to take up residence at the hotel, some one who had the run of the place
began searching Wilbur's apartment for something. What?
Money, of course.

"That search might have been instituted by the daughter, or, perhaps, a servant who believed in the existence of the money. But I am assuming for the present that it was conducted by the murderer. Other circumstances strengthen that theory. Here they are:

"Samuel Cowden arrives. He states publicly that he believes his father to have been murdered, and says that Cowden had sold considerable property in the East and should have possessed a large sum of money.

"Now, the sister told us to-night that Samuel had been a victim of insomnia for a long while. Hemming stated to me that Samuel was calm, self-possessed, normal—in short, eminently sane. Ever observe the demeanor of persons afflicted with the disease of sleeplessness?

"You have, of course. And they are not sane—at least, they are highly abnormal mentally.

"Here is what I think was the matter with Samuel Cowden: He believed in the existence of the money, and he spent many nights searching for it. Sister probably caught him up late at night and he explained his prowling by attributing it to sleeplessness. He, too, thought the murderer had failed to find what he sought.

"Now, if I have it right, Samuel's 'sleeplessness' supplied the motive for his murder. The man who killed Cowden feared the son would find the hidden money. You see, the killer knew the money was in the building the night he shot Cowden. The search still goes on.

"Now, in view of the circumstances I have mentioned, I feel warranted in believing that both the Cowdens were murdered, and in searching for the murderer. He, or an accomplice, is still in the vicinity. The continued prowling in the building establishes that.

"Now we come to one whom I consider a very important person: The woman whom I erroneously believed to be Mary Cowden. She must be found. I believe she has knowledge, guilty or otherwise, that will give us just the light we need. She should not be hard to locate.

"Another thing: I am convinced that the scream I heard in the building was meant to decoy me upstairs. Hence it follows that some one was expecting me. Who? There are only three persons who could have expected me:

"Hemming, Grayle, and the woman.

"Count Miss Cowden out of it. Also Cora, the maid. She's a hard customer, but honest. Where does that bring us? To Hemming, Grayle, the mysterious woman—and one other. I haven't mentioned him yet.

"Thomas Burdick, the caretaker. He wasn't in last night—at least he was not visible. Gone, you may say, but not forgotten nor overlooked. We will investigate him to-morrow. Also give the hotel a thorough going over. Try to account for the disturbance I heard."

"I follow you," said Steele during the pause, "and your reasoning sounds plausible enough. It seems to me, though, you have overlooked one significant point."

"Namely?"

"That attack made on us to-night in the hotel grounds," he explained, eyeing me speculatively. "Seems to me that needs some looking into, too."

"It does," I replied, rising. "But that thing to-night is about the hardest nut of all—else it makes everything as clear as spring water. Look this over."

I tossed the object, which I had picked up at the scene of the shooting, upon the table.

"A book-mark!" Steele exclaimed, examining it closely. "Purple. Has a Scriptural line done in silver letters on it!"

"Yeah," I corroborated. Then added: "Hemming had it, or one like it, in his pocket when he was in my office. Now," I told him, "think that over, if you wish, but I'm going to sleep."

When I turned in, Steele was still staring at the book-mark.

7

ON THE TRAIL OF THE NIGHT PROWLER

JIM DARBY, ANOTHER operative connected with The Kaw Valley Bureau, arrived by motor boat, reaching the cabin before daylight and rousing us out for an early breakfast.

Jim brought all the dope available concerning the matter in hand. Most of it had been gleaned from our own files during the night. It was of little value, except that it tagged the individuals with whom the case dealt.

The Rev. Amos T. Hemming, the report disclosed, had once been a minister affiliated with a well-known orthodox religious sect. He had held pastorates in Kansas City, St. Joseph, and other large towns in the State. His record was absolutely spotless.

After his retirement, seven years previous to the current date, he had invested part of a legacy left him by a bachelor brother in the Riverton property and, acting with Wilbur Cowden, developed and promoted the hotel venture.

Grayle, who had established a sanatorium a year previously, came into the company later. Hemming's whereabouts on the night of the first death in the building was indicated. According to his own statement, borne out by employees and guests, he had been present at the Riverton.

Wilbur Cowden, an Englishman, had come to America ten years before. He had resided in New York City for three years. Moving to Kansas City, he directly became acquainted with Hemming, and joined him in the project he was promoting. There was nothing against him, so far as could be learned.

No enemies, so far as could be determined. Information from New York City gave out the fact that he had sold approximately one hundred thousand dollars' worth of holdings there, a month before his death, and that the money had been sent to him by express. No reason for having it sent on in cash could be assigned.

A widespread appeal to the banks of the country failed to divulge the whereabouts of the money. None had an account with Cowden; none had safe deposit boxes against his name. There the record ceased.

Herbert Grayle was a graduate of an Eastern university; had practiced his profession in Boston for a number of years succeeding his graduation, then removed to Kansas City. For five years thereafter he practiced in the city. Then he set up his sanatorium at Riverton.

His record had nothing against it. He had married in Boston, and was living with his wife, seemingly in harmony. Rated as fairly wealthy, and prospering in his present venture. Nothing more about him, except that he had been at the Riverton the night of the tragedy. He was, however, not only a stock-holder, but house physician for the hotel.

Samuel Cowden was given a clean bill, both in the East

and during his short residence at the hotel. Apparently a sane, well-behaved young man.

Thomas Burdick, head porter while the hotel was in operation, was an Englishman who had always been "in service." Wilbur Cowden had employed him as a butler in New York. When Cowden removed to Kansas City, Burdick came along. There was not a black mark against Burdick.

References from former employers in England, proven to be authentic, gave him an excellent character extending over many years. There was nothing about his actions before or since the closing of the hotel to arouse suspicion. Drank sparingly, and attended to business. Had been at the hotel the night of the tragedy.

All the above named were, according to the report, present at the hotel the night of the second killing.

There was nothing in the reports of the physicians who examined the bodies of Cowden and his son to contradict the theory of suicide.

The doors to the apartment, in both instances, had been found locked and the keys in the locks. On the other hand, in each instance windows opening on fire escapes had been found lowered from the top—hence not latched.

That was all of value.

"All right, Jim," I said, after I had digested the report, "here's a job for you. Go to the office and tell Davis and Blount to report at the Riverton Hotel at once. Then go to the Hotel Allerton, in the city, and locate Parson Hemming.

"If he is not there, find out where he is—and don't stop until you do. After you find him, give him this, and observe his actions. Tell him I sent it. If you are alone with him—well, it might be as well to be watchful, with your hand on your gun."

I handed Darby the book-mark.

"Won't that give him an opportunity to make a quick get-away?" Steele remonstrated. "Unless, of course, you are going to tell Jim to pinch him. You haven't a thing on the parson, you know."

"I'm not going to make a pinch, nor will he attempt to get away," I replied. "That book-mark will, I figure, force his hand. The parson has not been entirely above board with me. He will come through now, or I miss my guess."

Steele said no more, and Darby departed downriver.

"Why did you warn Jim to have a hand on his gun?" Steele wanted to know as we landed at the wharf and started toward the point where the book-mark had been found.

"I may be mistaken in my idea of Hemming," I replied soberly. "If I'm correct, he won't think of doing any shooting. If I'm wrong, most anything might happen."

While not exactly plainly marked, the trail of the gunman was not hard to pick up. It led away to the west, betraying its course by reason of scuffed earth and pebbles. Evidently he had been running swiftly. Following a straight course west for two hundred yards, the trail veered to the north, then turned east down a draw and became much plainer in the soft earth around a spring.

Tracks were not the only marks there. Blood stains, fresh and profuse, reddened the ground.

"Wasn't shooting at us, after all!" Steele exclaimed. "The man that bird cracked down on got hit!"

"Evidently. Probably stopped at the spring to bathe the wound and stop the bleeding. He knew his way to the spring, and it follows he is familiar with the grounds. See anything else?"

Steele answered in a negative. The blood and the tracks were all. The floor of the valley was of a character rendering trailing an impossibility. We lost our quarry there.

"May not have to hunt far to find him," Steele remarked, significantly. "Don't you think it's about time to interview Mr. Thomas Burdick?"

I nodded. "That's exactly what is in my mind."

A few minutes later we were battering at a basement door at the south end of the building.

8

LEADING A DUAL LIFE?

IT TOOK A deal of pounding to get results. Just when I had begun to think that the caretaker's absence had been prolonged through the night, the basement door opened and a sleepy-looking man appeared.

He was an Englishman, no mistaking that. A typical stage serving man from Old England, though he did not mix his H's and I's.

"You wished something?" he queried, drawing a faded dressing-gown closely about him and cocking a half opened eye at me.

"Certainly, my man," I replied. "Else why would I be knocking you up so soon after daylight?"

"And what is it?" he wanted to know.

"Are you Thomas Burdick?"

"I am, sir."

"Then lead the way inside, Thomas," I ordered. "Get some clothes on and show us about the place. Also, get the stiffness out of your tongue, because there'll be questions."

"And who may you be, sir?" he inquired respectfully, retiring and permitting us to enter.

I displayed my shield, watching him closely when I did so. He merely blinked.

"I'll be getting dressed, sir, then will be at your service," he hastened to assure me.

A few minutes later, under the guidance of Burdick, we made a hasty tour of the rooms on the floor directly above, peering into closets, under beds, and back of draperies. In view of the commotion of the night before on that floor, I might have found a corpse. As it turned out, I found nothing.

Dust lay heavy upon the fine rugs of the rooms, in the corridor and on the floor of the big office. In that dust were footprints—lots of them. So many, in fact, they were of no value to me whatever.

"Now, Burdick," I said, motioning him to a chair before the desk in the office, "where were you last night? Here?"

"I was not, sir," he answered. "That is, I was not here during the early part. I get lonesome, having nothing much to do, you might say, and go in to a cinema occasionally. As it happens, I was at one last evening."

"Do you ever hear any one moving about in the building on those nights when you are here?" I asked.

"Can't say that I do, sir. Sometimes I have heard noises, but there are birds—pigeons and bats—at night. Some of the windows are broken."

Half an hour's questioning yielded absolutely nothing of any importance. Burdick was either as innocent as a child in arms, else too slick for me. I inclined to the former belief. The man certainly showed nothing of the crook in his face. I'd take him, ordinarily, to be a good, honest servant, such as can seldom be found outside of England—except when they are imported to this country.

"Now, Burdick," I instructed, "you will accompany my

friend here to the top floor. You will show him the apartment in which Mr. Cowden met his death, and the one in which young Mr. Cowden died. You will remain with Mr. Steele until he has made such investigations as he desires. That clear?"

"Perfectly, sir." He arose, standing respectfully at attention.

Steele signified his readiness, and the caretaker led the way up the wide staircase.

Five minutes later I was inside Burdick's rooms, shaking them down with speed and thoroughness.

I may as well say, right here, that I did not expect to find anything of an incriminating nature in the caretaker's room. I had no reason to suspect him in the murders; on the contrary, I was persuaded that he would be utterly incapable of shedding human blood. Still, those rooms could not be overlooked; to search them was necessary, if only to satisfy myself that I was right in my estimate of the man.

The rooms were in perfect order—neat and clean. I searched carefully, poking into every drawer and box, every nook and cranny, but could find nothing suspicious.

In one corner of the bedroom was a built-in clothes closet, and hanging neatly upon hooks on its back wall was the caretaker's wardrobe. The pockets of the clothing yielded nothing. I closed the door, and sized up the outer measurements of the cupboard, mentally comparing them with the interior.

Then I laughed. Removing the clothing from the hooks, I easily found a loose nail which released a false back, and swung it open on its hinges. The thing was so clumsily arranged it could not escape my eye even when I was only half looking for it.

I played my flash inside the hidden nook—and found nothing. At least, nothing in the way of stolen money. But my search did not go unrewarded.

On a hook inside the crypt hung a gentleman's full-dress suit. It was of late pattern and of the finest material. An opera hat hung upon another hook. A fine linen shirt was also there—and, yes, an Inverness cape, further search revealed. Patent pumps were on the floor.

In a hidden cupboard in the room of a servant! All the regalia needed to make up the outward semblance of a gentleman of wealth and leisure!

I searched the pockets, and these articles were brought out:

A handsome gold watch, English pattern, and running; a fancy gold penknife; pearl shirt-studs; gold cigarette case; a checkbook; the stubs of two theater tickets; two hundred dollars in notes—and a card case.

According to one of the cards in the case, I was at the moment handling the property of one George Fitzgeorge Barrowdale, address: The St. Vrain Apartments, Kansas City, Missouri.

After restoring the articles, I replaced the false back, hung the clothing up as each garment had been before, and then sat down for a moment to think.

Five minutes later I gave it up. Was Burdick, the care-taker, Mr. George Fitzgeorge Barrowdale, the gentleman? Was the worthy Thomas leading a double life?

It looked so—and would not, of course, be difficult to determine. The finding of that hidden cupboard placed the caretaker in an entirely different light. He was guilty—but of what? The hiding of the clothes showed him to be under cover with something. It remained to determine as speedily as possible just what that something was.

I returned to the upper floor, and sat down to await the return of Steele and Burdick. Thinking over the strange denouement the cupboard had yielded, I was in a brown study when a heavy knocking on the main door drew my attention.

Looking through the glass of the panel, I perceived Dr. Grayle standing outside. A hand was cupped over his eyes, and he was peering into the dark interior—evidently in search of some one.

9

LYING AS A METHOD

I RELEASED THE catch and swung the door open.

"Good morning, doctor," I greeted, holding out my hand. "You are an early bird like myself, it seems."

Grayle gave my hand a firm grip. "I saw your arrival from my dressing room window—at least, I thought I recognized you," he told me, smiling genially. "Hurried into my clothes and ran up to get a word with you while I have time. My day starts early, and ends late. I have patients in the city, you know, as well as in the sanatorium."

I nodded, and we sat down. "Anything special on your mind, doctor?" I inquired, proffering my cigarette case.

"No—both to the question and the smoke," he laughed, waving the case away. "No tobacco before breakfast for me. As for my running up here, I did so out of curiosity alone. Had a notion you might have run onto something. Quite anxious about this unfortunate business, you know. The sooner it is brought to an end, one way or another, the sooner I'll have my hospital on its customary basis.

"Would you believe it, I see patients in town every day at their homes who should be at my place, but refuse to come here because of my nearness to this building. Normal persons would not have that antipathy—but, of course, Mr. Norton, my patients are anything but mentally normal."

I nodded my comprehension of his delicate position. "Too bad. But I think the matter will be straightened out before many hours pass. In fact, between you and me—and I mean just that, between you and me, and no other—I struck a lead this morning which almost clears up everything. By late evening, I should say, the mystery enshrouding this old place will be a mystery no longer."

Grayle looked at me in well bred astonishment. "So soon?" he exclaimed. "Why, you have only been on the grounds since about seven this morning. It is now barely nine! I must say, Mr. Norton, that you work rapidly!"

There was skepticism in Grayle's tones which he was not able to wholly conceal. I did not blame him for that.

"A great deal can be done in a short while, doctor," I reminded him. "Especially when one digs in intelligently and works hard."

"Very true. And am I to be taken further into your confidence?"

"A bit later, perhaps. Not now. You see, I might be mistaken—and we detectives—at least some of us—are peculiarly susceptible to ridicule. I confess myself to be."

"Not unlike physicians, in that respect," Grayle commented with a grin.

"I had intended to look you up, doctor, some time to-day," I said, changing the conversation to another channel. "There are a few minor details which are not yet quite clear—among them, the reason for Cowden's secrecy about that money."

"I can make that clear," Grayle said. "Cowden had the

money—at least he told me so. I think the only other person in his confidence concerning it was Mr. Hemming. As to the secrecy, Cowden wished to purchase certain lands in this and an adjoining county; he got the notion that they held oil in large quantities.

"Near-by discoveries of oil may have influenced his belief. Be that as it may, he had bargained for a large tract, all farm lands, for which he was to pay in the neighborhood of sixty thousand dollars. That tract was, however, only part of the acreage he desired to control.

"He wished to buy the first body secretly, holding the deeds from record until he secured options on the balance. It was to be a cash transaction, and on the quiet. Such deals are not uncommon."

"I do not find that you gave that out when the police made their examination," I stated. "Why, doctor?"

"I was not asked, for one thing. Another, I talked with Miss Cowden, and she informed me that she and her brother might carry out her father's plans in regard to the lands, should the missing money be found. She, at the time, thought her father had placed it in a bank somewhere, and that it would be recovered. Pending Samuel Cowden's arrival, I held my tongue and told no one."

"Quite a sufficient reason, sir, seeing that the knowledge as to Cowden's intended use of the money could be of no service in the investigation," I commented. "Divulged, your information might have ruined the deal, in case the son and daughter desired to carry it through. Ever hear of a chap named George Fitzgeorge Barrowdale?"

Grayle's face grew thoughtful. Clearly he was trying to recall the name. Finally he shook his head. "Never before," he answered positively. And I was equally positive that he never had.

"You have been skeptical, doctor, about Cowden's money having been on the premises the night of his death. Let me tell you now that it was here. I know not the amount, but, large or small, it was here. I am very positive that I can lay my hand on the sum within, say, two hours."

Grayle came bolt upright, amazement in every line of his face.

"Oh, now, my dear chap—" he began expostulating.

"Fact."

"But—but however have you been able to learn so much in so short a time?"

"Ever hear of Dupin, that crack dick of Poe's?" I asked.

"Surely," he replied puzzled.

"Well, by eliminating the places a given object could not be, he narrowed his field of search to the places it might be—then laid his hand on the place it had to be. I followed this Dupin's tactics in regard to the money. The treasure hunters, who have nearly wrecked the top floor of the wing where Cowden died, did much to help. They narrowed my field by proving conclusively that the cache was not there. They helped a lot."

"Are—why, man, you are not joking, surely!" Grayle exclaimed. "You really mean that in so short a time—"

"I mean that I can lay my hand on the Cowden money," I stated slowly. "There is one chance in a thousand that I may be mistaken—and I'm betting against that chance."

"Well, by George, I'd like to be there when you do it!" he declared. "I'd like to see with my own eyes the sort of hiding place which has been able to defy the persons who have devoted much time and attention to finding it! I would indeed!"

I laughed. "I'll tell you about it, at least. That much I'll promise," I told him.

At that moment Steele and Burdick came downstairs, and I got up with relief. My conversation with the doctor had begun to pall, and I panted for action.

Had I been lying to Grayle? In some things, yes. In others, no.

I anticipated certain near events, that was all. Burdick, I was certain, knew where Cowden's money was—and what Burdick knew soon would be shared with me.

10

AWAY TO THE CITY, WILLY-NILLY

I INTRODUCED STEELE and Grayle.

"Ah, Burdick," greeted the doctor affably, after shaking hands with the operative, "I haven't seen much of you lately. Health good?"

"Thank you, sir; it is very good," Burdick replied bowing. "May I inquire concerning Mistress Grayle, sir?"

"Quite well, Burdick, thank you," Grayle replied.

He turned to the door, and, hand upon knob, addressed me:

"Don't forget to let me in on that business you spoke of, if possible," he said. "I'd like to see with my own eyes!"

With a laugh and a friendly farewell he was gone.

"What did you find, Steele?"

"Things on the floor where Cowden had his apartments are in a condition suggesting the passage of a cyclone," he replied. "Woodwork torn away, holes dug in the plaster, floorboards pried up and all the furniture literally pulled to pieces."

"And you failed to hear the noise, Burdick?" I queried, turning on the caretaker.

He was quite self-possessed. "I am aware that some one is hunting the place for Mr. Cowden's money," he stated calmly. "More than one person, probably. But, sir, I am not supposed to hear or see what goes on in that respect."

"Why not?" I demanded.

"There be those who have the right to do what they wish with the property," he answered simply.

It was enough. I dismissed him.

"Hurry to town," I ordered Steele. "Go to the St. Vrain, and dig out George Fitzgeorge Barrowdale. Get his description. Then search his apartment. He is not, I think, there. After that, interview the president of the Gateway National and find out how much Barrowdale carries there. You may find deposit books on other banks in his apartment. Get the amount. Also," I added, as he was about to depart, "tell the cashier at the office to send me out half a dozen one hundred-dollar bills, and a lot of ones, twos and the like. That's all, and step on it!"

Steele hesitated a moment, opened his lips to speak, thought better of it—then decamped.

As soon as he was gone I looked up Burdick again.

"Dr. Grayle's wife a pretty woman?" I queried.

"Beautiful, sir!" he exclaimed fervently. "A most excellent lady, sir."

"Hum. Describe her."

"Medium size lady, sir. Dark hair and brown eyes. Very wonderful complexion. Lovely, sir, Mistress Grayle is!"

"Ever notice her hands?"

"Er—oh, yes, sir! Her hands, they are small and white and—"

I broke into his rhapsody.

"First joint of the little finger of her left hand missing?"

"I was about to mention that, sir," said Burdick. "Automobile crash, two years ago. Left hand mangled, but cured and restored, sir, except for the joint you mention. That had to be amputated. Very sad, sir; very sad indeed!"

"Yes—sad, very sad!"

I had located the woman of mystery—now that I did not particularly need her.

Grayle's wife. Her motive in coming to me was clear enough, now. Many things were clear—yet not everything. Those lacking in lucidity, however, would soon crystallize into a complete transparency.

I had one person to interview, one report to receive—then the finale!

I returned upstairs, just in time to open the front door to another caller:

The Rev. Amos T. Hemming, pale, apologetic, eager, hurried into the room. He was followed by Darby.

"I—I fear that I have not been entirely frank with you, Mr. Norton," Hemming began, sitting down as though somewhat exhausted.

"I'm certain you have not," I retorted. "First, though, how badly were you wounded last night, and where?"

He gasped. "A—a flesh wound, only, and in the left arm," he stammered. "How did you guess—"

"I didn't guess. The way in which you carry your arm told me enough. Now—explain."

I waited.

"There is not a great deal to explain. Samuel Cowden convinced me that Wilbur's money had not been found by his murderer—else why had a search of the apartment been made by an unknown person, or persons, so soon after his death? I helped Samuel hunt—"

"Did any one else know that hunt was going on?"

"Grayle did—and laughed at us. Burdick knew also."

"Go ahead."

"After Samuel was killed I continued to look for the money, more convinced than ever that it was in the building. I give my word of honor, however, that my sole purpose was to find the money and give it to the owner—Miss Mary Cowden. The child is almost penniless, and needs it."

"Why did you keep that from me?"

"I felt that I would present a very ridiculous figure should I admit being engaged in such a thing," he blurted out. "At my age, and considering my calling. That, sir, is why."

"You came last night to have a final look for the money?"

"Yes. I did not expect you would get on the case so quickly. I wanted one more trial before you came."

"Now—about the shooting?"

"I was on the point of entering through a basement window, when I saw a man stealing away toward Mary Cowden's cottage. I followed—clumsily, it seems. When I came to a place where some large rocks are the man shot at me. He missed and I ran. The second shot struck me in the arm. I eluded him, bathed the wound and wrapped it up, then returned to the city. That, sir, is all—and the solemn truth!"

"Anything further on your mind—anything else you've overlooked?"

"Nothing. I have told all."

I arose. "I shall have to ask you not to leave the room to which I am going to ask you to retire, until I give permission. Have I your promise?"

Hemming turned a frightened face to me. "Am I under ar— Oh, surely, Mr. Norton, I am not a prisoner?"

"No—not yet," I assured him. "Perhaps not ever—on this case. But I want you here until I have cleared up certain points. You have nothing to fear, if you obey orders. What say?"

"I am in your hands," he replied. "Every order from you shall be respected."

I sent him into the manager's room back of the office, and my two men, Davis and Blount, arriving at the moment, I assigned them to him for company.

"Darby," I ordered, "go below stairs and keep Burdick company. Don't pinch him, understand—just keep him company."

Jim departed, and for the next three hours I sat in one of the deep chairs with which the office was furnished, and thought hard.

I had Hemming under guard, Burdick watched, and knew where I could get hold of Grayle when I wanted him.

The question was: Which one do I want?

I knew, or at least thought I knew, the answer—but things were in a state now where a false step would prove fatal. I had to be right—had to.

At the end of three hours Steele came back. His face wore a frown which was half a grin. Sitting down beside me he broke his news.

"The Honorable George Fitzgeorge Barrowdale, from the description given me by the clerk of the St. Vrain, smells suspiciously like our friend Burdick," he said, and waited.

"I was almost certain of that—wanted it established. Go on."

"He has been living at the St. Vrain for nine months— off and on. That means that he has kept a swell suite of rooms there, but uses them only occasionally—maybe a couple of nights a week. In the rooms I found two deposit books—First State and Mechanics. Brother Barrowdale appears to be wealthy—his total deposits in all three banks being exactly eighty-three thousand, two hundred and ten dollars."

"I hoped so. Been living a gay and fast life, eh?"

"Keeps a car. Sober enough, but loves the bright lights. Highly respected by the hotel management—all clean, it seems. Enough to pinch him, eh?"

"Sure. Tell Darby to bring him up."

A few minutes later Jim and Steele arrived with a very disturbed Burdick in tow.

I arose and looked him in the eyes.

"Well, Honorable George, you have come a cropper it seems," I remarked casually. "You might have known you would. Too bad, my boy, too bad!"

"Upon my honor, sir—"

"Shut up! You haven't got any honor! Take him into the room with Hemming," I ordered. "I'll join you directly."

With drooping shoulders and bowed head Burdick walked into the room back of the office, accompanied by Steele and Darby.

Five minutes later I followed.

A two-hour conference in that room had the following sequel:

Hemming and Burdick, closely guarded by Steele, Davis,

Darby and Blount, departed for the city in an automobile. I stood on the porch and watched them as the car rolled past the sanatorium on its way to the State Road and out of sight.

11

"YOU PLAYED INTO MY HANDS!"

RETURNING FROM AN hour's stroll about the hotel grounds, during which I had called at the cottage of Miss Cowden, found her considerably improved in condition and chatted for a few minutes with her, I sauntered up the drive way of Grayle's place and rang the doorbell.

Grayle himself answered the call.

"I have caught my crook," I told him, speaking in a low voice, as we walked together to the front of the veranda. "Sent him in this afternoon, along with one who may or may not be an accomplice—"

"So!" the doctor exclaimed. "That was the meaning of the procession which passed my door a couple of hours ago! Burdick—you think him guilty?"

"Positive of it."

"But Hemming—he was in the car too! Surely he is not involved?"

"Hum. A few hours will determine that," I grunted. "Anyhow, I've made my pinch, and there remains but one thing more to do—the final act in the drama. You said you wanted to see where the money had been hidden, and I'm going to grant your request. It is now six o'clock, and I have supper to get. Suppose you come to the hotel at eight. We'll unearth the treasure together."

"Fine!" Grayle exclaimed. "I will be free at that hour, and delighted to attend! By the by," he said as an afterthought, "take your dinner with me—unless, of course, you have arranged for one of your men to return with some?"

"I sent the boys in with the prisoners," I replied. "I can attend to the rest of the matter alone. As for dinner, I shall gladly accept your invitation."

Grayle laughed. "Still fearful of ridicule, in case the cache isn't productive after all?" he chided. "Well, there will be just the two of us—and I'll keep my mouth closed. We dine at seven."

"At seven then," I agreed.

Seven o'clock found me at the doctor's table. We two dined alone, and I wondered if I should be permitted a sight of the brunette lady—Mrs. Grayle. The meal, at which we idled, passed and she failed to appear.

"Mrs. Grayle is confined to her room with a slight cold," the doctor volunteered near the end of dinner. "She regrets not being able to—"

"Oh, that's all right," I interrupted. "Some other time, perhaps. Shall we get along?"

"I'll slip on a light overcoat, the night air is somewhat chill, then join you," Grayle replied.

We walked over to the hotel, discussing the future of the place, now that the pall was about to be dissipated, and various other things. Arrived, I opened the main door and we entered.

"You are going to be greatly surprised, doctor," I told him, as I pressed the button on an electric lantern which stood on the desk. "If I have figured things correctly, the hiding place is going to give you a jolt—so unexpected, and all that. Come, we will go to the quarters of the caretaker."

"Burdick! Has he had that money hidden in his rooms all this time? When did you find it?"

Grayle's tones were eager—the eagerness of a boy engaged upon an exciting adventure.

"All in good time," I said, opening the door of Burdick's bedroom. "Now," I went on when inside and the door closed, "you hold the light and I'll do the searching."

"Oh—you've got to search for it! I thought M. Dupin was going to lay his hand right on it!" The doctor laughed heartily.

"I will before I'm through," I gritted. "My process of elimination assures me that the loot is in this room. Burdick can be made to tell, of course, but it may take time. I've been too busy to search thoroughly here, besides I wanted to oblige you by letting you help. If you still desire to do so, all right; if not, I'll go ahead alone."

"By all means, old chap, I want to help!" declared Grayle. "Go right ahead, and I'll hold the light!"

He did so, offering suggestions now and then, while I proceeded to nearly wreck that room. Just as Grayle had begun to cast suggestive glances toward the partly open door into the kitchen I shouted:

"I have it! Here, doc, hold the light this way!"

He wheeled toward me. I was prowling inside the cupboard which I had seemingly thoroughly searched before.

"This thing seems to have a false back—dimensions

are not quite right. A little closer with the light. There—I have it!"

I released the nail which secured the false back, and swung it open.

An exclamation of surprise came from Grayle. I turned, with the comment:

"Clumsy? I'll say so. But nobody ever thought of investigating here, so it passed unnoticed."

"Go ahead!" urged the doctor breathlessly. "Heavens, man, I'm all on edge!"

"Well," I agreed, drawing a deep breath, "here goes!"

I bent over, felt about on the floor of the crypt, then straightened up and turned to Grayle. In my hand I held a bundle—seemingly a tightly rolled shirt. My fingers trembled as I unrolled it—and exposed a flat package of bank notes.

"By God!" I breathed with excitement and relief in my tones. "I was right, after all!"

Grayle's eyes were fixed in fascination upon the loot, his face expressing amazement, incredulity—then, in a flash, ferocity.

With a swift movement of his right hand he snatched a revolver from the side pocket of his overcoat—a revolver equipped with a silencer.

"You poor, damned fool!" he almost shouted. "You played right into my hands! What a nut! What a numskull!"

I stood silent, as though unable to believe him serious. Then I spoke:

"Put the gun up, doc!" I ordered. "This is no time for funny stuff!"

"Funny!" he laughed suddenly—a nasty, wolfish growl. "It is funny—to me! Old Cowden's money is mine at last!"

"Say!" I bellowed. "You can't get away with anything like that! Suppose I'd let you walk off with the stuff? Where are your senses?"

"You," he snarled, "won't offer any objections—because you're going to die."

He swung the gun up—there was a flash and a heavy report.

No silencer was on Steele's gun, which he fired through a crack in the kitchen door. His marksmanship, upon which I had risked so much, was accurate as ever, and Grayle's pistol dropped to the floor, while its owner grasped a shattered wrist in agony.

The next moment he was overborne, manacled, and in the light of a couple of torches he saw Steele, Darby and Davis gathered round.

"They went only a short distance toward the city, doc," I taunted sardonically, "then came back by way of the river. They, too, wanted to witness the last act of the play. Had to have witnesses, in fact, because, while I believed you to be guilty as hell itself, I had nothing positive on you. I have now—plenty. So, my dear doctor, it is you who are a numskull—you who have played into my hands!"

Fortunately, looks do not kill, for the shafts of rage which Grayle shot toward me were murderous indeed.

12

THE KEY TO THE SITUATION

QUITE A GATHERING assembled in the office of the Riverton Hotel a short while later.

Grayle, wrist bandaged, sat in a chair against the wall, flanked by Steele and Darby. He had not opened his lips since the scene in the basement.

Hemming and Burdick were present, and a few minutes later a motor car brought Miss Cowden, looking actually beautiful with the color of excitement on her cheeks, her maid, and Davis.

Miss Cowden was made comfortable, and assured me that she felt equal to the ordeal she was about to undergo, and which my visit that afternoon had prepared her for.

"We are all assembled," I remarked to them, glancing at my watch, "except—ah, I hear footsteps, and, if I mistake not, the missing ones are about to join us."

All eyes were directed toward the main door, which opened to admit Blount—and my woman of mystery, Mrs. Grayle.

The doctor spoke then:

"My wife!" he ejaculated, attempting to rise. His guards drew him back into the chair.

Mrs. Grayle, her color gone, cast one frightened glance around the circle, then fixed her eyes upon me.

"I—I tried to prevent this," she wailed. "But you wouldn't stay out! Oh, Herbert, my husband, what shall we do now?"

"Shut up!" blazed the doctor. "Don't talk!"

"Oh, let her talk, doc, let her talk," I reproved. "She tried to save you, and couldn't. She can't hurt you now. Be seated, please, Mrs. Grayle."

Assisted by Blount, she staggered to a chair and cowered in it.

"There are a few loose ends to tie together, folks," I told them. "We are going to tie them now. First I will say that the moment I became convinced that Wilbur Cowden was killed for his money, which was clear enough to me, owing to the fact that Samuel was killed later and under precisely the same conditions as his father, I knew I could pick the murderer from among three persons:

"Hemming, Burdick, and Grayle.

"They had the opportunity, still had access to the property after the deaths, which enabled them to search the place at will. Hemming and Grayle both knew Cowden had the money, and I strongly suspected that Burdick, the trusted servant, knew it also.

"Hemming did not fit in with my ideas of a killer. He came to me in good faith, and hired me to take the case. Miss Cowden, prompted by Grayle who had also persuaded her that there was nothing in the murder theory since both her father and brother were insane, objected to reopening the matter. So did Grayle—for different reasons.

"Grayle first aroused my suspicions when he arrived so close on the heels of Hemming—with an entire change of front. He wanted me, too. I suspected he had been watching Hemming, and when sure that the latter had called upon me, he came right over and hired me also—a bit too quickly. Wanted me to be his man—give him my confidence later, in case he failed to kill me when I got on the job.

"He did fail, although he tried last night. Mrs. Grayle fell a bit too hard, however, after she finished that scream. So hard, I knew it was not a human being, but a heavy piece of furniture, such as would jar the wing I was in.

"Now I am going to let Burdick tell his own story. He really was the key to the whole thing. Come, Burdick!"

Burdick, who had aged visibly during the past few hours, nevertheless spoke clearly when he began his tale.

"Two weeks before he died, Mr. Cowden came to me in my rooms in the basement," his story ran. "He had employed me for a period covering almost ten years. He trusted me—and I was trustworthy. There was nothing in which I could have been traitor to him. He knew it.

" 'Burdick,' said my master, 'I have here a large sum of money which I do not wish to bank. Neither do I feel safe in keeping it about me or in the office or my apartment. Do you hide it down here in your rooms and have an eye to it. Nobody would ever think of searching for anything valuable there.'

"I accepted the trust—very proudly. And, as God is my witness, had Mr. Cowden been alive on the day I was to deliver it back to him, I should have done so—intact.

"But he was killed. I had not the same feeling of loyalty to Miss Mary and Mr. Samuel Cowden. I knew little of the young gentleman, and had had but infrequent contacts with the young mistress. When the news reached me that the master was dead—I was tempted.

"For many years I had longed to live as the gentleman whom I had served did. I wanted to be a gentleman along with them. Mr. Cowden was dead, and no one dreamed I had the money. Why not keep it and become what I longed with all my heart to be?

"I hid the package outside the building, kept my mouth closed and, later began living the double life which was the occasion of my detection. Last night I—well, frankly, I imbibed a bit too freely, and returned here dressed in clothing I dared not expose. I had done so a time or two previously, so had constructed a secret compartment in which to conceal the clothing used in my other station.

"I hid the dress-clothes, and Mr. Norton found them. The watch had not run down, so he knew the clothes had been there only a short while, and that I must have knowledge of them. The English name I had assumed caused him to suspect that Barrowdale and Burdick were one and the same.

"That is all, only this: I had no knowledge, either before or after, of the murder of Mr. Cowden and Mr. Samuel, only what everybody else knew. Furthermore, I have spent only a small portion of the money, and have already agreed to turn the balance back to Miss Mary. I did not run away, because I feared I would attract attention.

"As God is present, I regret the part I have played."

He ceased speaking, voice breaking and lips trembling. I cast a glance at Mary Cowden and saw nothing in her face save pity and forgiveness. I knew then that Burdick had no need to fear.

"When I discovered Burdick's part in the thing," I resumed, "that narrowed my field to two possible suspects in so far as the killing of Mr. Cowden and his son was concerned. I knew that the servant had not killed the master, because he had the money. Had the murderer found what he was looking for, there would have been no second killing.

"Samuel Cowden let it be known that he was searching for his father's hidden wealth, and from the manner in which he was going about it, there was every likelihood that he would eventually turn it up. That is why he was killed.

"The murderer feared to lose the money, which he hoped to find, and killed him. He used the fire escape, just as he did in the former killing.

"Hemming and Grayle. There was my choice. Hemming did not seem to fit—yet he might.

"Last night Dr. Grayle was to have taken some medicine to Miss Cowden's cottage, but, fearing that I might come to the hotel that night, he watched inside the building, his deadly revolver with its silencer in hand. Mrs. Grayle, whether willing or unwilling, was with him. I did not bite—refused to decoy.

"After I had left the hotel, he remembered the medicine, and later started with it to the cottage. Mr. Hemming saw him and followed, only to be discovered and wounded by the doctor.

"The murderer with the deadly silencer was abroad again. Hemming was the victim. That seemed to narrow the field to Grayle.

"But—I had to be sure. So I framed him. He came to

the hotel to see me recover the loot, thinking me alone. If I found the money, what more simple than to slay me, who would be entirely unsuspicious of him, and finally gain the money for which he had wantonly and callously killed two men?

"He tried to kill me, when I produced that bogus package, and failed, but in doing so gave evidence against himself which I think will send him to the chair."

It did. Under terrific pressure, he broke down in time, and owned his acts. Mrs. Grayle disappeared shortly thereafter, and I hope she found peace some time, somewhere. I do not believe she was at heart a bad woman.

The Riverton Hotel is now in a flourishing condition, run by Miss Cowden and Dr. Hemming—and, in consequence of its restoration, the Kaw Valley Bureau is flourishing, too.

BENEFICIAL FIRES

Suddenly Blazing Crimson Against the
Black Sky Was the First Warning, and While
Men Cursed the Incendiary Slunk Away

1

THE KAW VALLEY DETECTIVE BUREAU, of which I, Tug
Norton, am founder, owner, manager, and chief operative,
was, early in its third year of existence, going through one
of those periods of inactivity which always cause me to
feel as if I'm slipping into the hands of receivers. Even the
husbands and wives of Kansas City were walking in paths
straight and narrow, else they were all remarkably adept
at covering up.

At any rate, nobody seemed to want anybody watched;
all the old mysteries had been solved, else gone into the
limbo of the unsolvable, and the crooks seemed to have
declared a benevolent protectorate for the benefit of K.C.

I sat at the desk in my private workshop, studying things
over, and wondering which three or four of my half dozen
high-priced assistants I should drop, or, indeed, whether I
hadn't better drop them all off the pay roll and myself out
the window—when, without the customary warning of a
card, Jared B. Hatton walked in.

"Nobby," the boy who generally hangs around in the
outer office, was burying a relative—for the tenth time
that season—out at Muelebach Field, the Blues and the
Colonels officiating at the sad rites, and that accounts for
Jared walking in unannounced.

My feelings were not hurt; I exhibited no least symptom

The fat man with the star on his vest took Halsey's arm—
while he turned to order Lafe Crump off the scene

of indignation over the invasion of my privacy; I did not, because I didn't feel that way. In fact, I felt jubilant. For, if I knew the earmarks, Jared B. Hatton was a blood brother to Ready Money.

After the introduction:

"I am a resident of Bonner Springs, Kansas," Mr. Hatton stated, "and as the case—or rather the cases—I want investigated will take you to that place or its vicinity, I want to say in the beginning that I and my associates, are prepared to find your fee a reasonably large one. Expenses to be paid by us, too, of course."

I bowed. "When the Kaw Valley accepts a case outside of the city," I assured him, "the fee must of necessity be large. Expenses are never padded, certainly, but they must be paid, no matter what they total. Our record for honesty is your guarantee."

Mr. Hatton bowed also. "I accept your terms. Now it is for you to decide whether you will accept the commission."

That was already decided!

"Proceed, Mr. Hatton."

"The farmers in the Bonner Springs section have, for the past six months, suffered greatly from fires—all of them of unknown, or, perhaps I should say, unaccountable origin. In some cases residences have been destroyed, but in the majority of instances barns have been lost.

"Now, Mr. Norton, the loss of a barn may mean very little or it may mean a great deal. That is according to the size and contents of the building itself. Now, in each and every case of the destruction of a barn, in our district, the loss has been great. Many fine cattle and horses have burned, and much grain, hay, and equipment also. It appears that only the most prosperous of the farmers have suffered. That is what seems to me unaccountable."

"Horses and cattle, huh?"

I pondered that—and my gorge began to rise. Ever hear a horse voice his terror and agony when the flames—

But enough of that. I have, and my hard and fast belief is this: a man who will destroy an animal that way, would take keen pleasure in murdering women and babies.

"Yes, horses and cattle, and many of them," Hatton broke

in on my thoughts to affirm. "That's what runs the total of the losses up so high. Fine stock, Mr. Norton, in each case."

"Insurance?" I queried.

"Oh, yes. That, of course. But insurance upon farm buildings and stock is never very high. Inadequate fire protection in the rural districts accounts for that. No loss, in the fires I speak of, was more than half covered by insurance."

"That lets the owners out—even if common sense didn't," I commented.

"Meaning?"

"One or two farmers in a community might burn their own stuff for the sake of the insurance premium, but to think that a dozen or so would do so is all bosh. Poor reasoning. Now," I went on, "you doubtless have a theory as to the origin of those fires?"

Mr. Halton nodded thoughtfully for a full moment— and I studied him in the interim.

He was a massive man, all bone and muscle, and appeared to be about fifty years old. His eyes were gray, large, and overshadowed by bushy, iron-gray brows. Hair that color, too—iron-gray. He was clean-shaven, and the color of his skin testified that whatever else he might be, he was a farmer along with it. One of the prosperous ones, at that.

"I have two theories," he said after a bit. "One is that an insane person—insane with the incendiary form of insanity—is responsible for the fires."

He paused, eying me, and evidently expecting a comment.

"That theory has its drawbacks," I told him. "Such persons set off fires merely for love of watching them burn.

They do not discriminate. Your 'bug' does discriminate.
Hence he is not insane, over fires, at least."

"Exactly!" exclaimed Hatton, pleased at what was
patently an agreement with his own ideas. "I did not hold
to that theory very tenaciously. At first it seemed likely,
but later I was forced to seek another. The fires are being
set by some person who vindictively hates either the entire
community, or, has it in for those particular men who have
suffered."

"Now you are coming close to the mark," I approved.
"Still, a man would need a large capacity for hating, to fill
the bill. Know any such person?"

He shook his head negatively. "He certainly is outside
of my knowledge."

"Any other theories?"

"None whatever."

"What about your own officers—county and others?
What have they done?"

"They've done everything they seem able to think of.
Used bloodhounds, kept watch over barns in the vicinity,
followed everything which remotely resembled a clue—
and have given up."

"Humph! Don't blame 'em! Looks like one of those
'give-it-up' cases."

Mr. Hatton's face fell.

"But I'll take it!" I assured him hastily. "It's in my line.
When others fall down, the private agency comes into its
own. That is always the way. Now, as to the retainer?"

"Name it."

I did—and got it, then and there.

"You mentioned associates. Just whom, besides yourself,

am I working for, Mr. Hatton?" I asked, as an afterthought when he was preparing to leave.

"I forgot to mention that I am president of the farmers' grange organization in our district," Hatton explained. "At a meeting, two days ago, it was unanimously voted to employ a private agency to go to the bottom of things. You are the employee of the organization, Mr. Norton, but if you wish my guarantee—"

"Oh, no!" I exclaimed, waving away the thought. "The grange association of your county is plenty guarantee for me. Merely wished to know just what backing I had. That's all."

"Very well." Mr. Hatton was on his feet again.

"You may not hear from me for several days, Mr. Hatton," I informed him when he was in the act of departing. "But I will be on the job. When necessary, or advisable, I will communicate with you in Bonner Springs. Good day, sir."

When he had gone I sat down to think things over. The more I thought, the hotter I got. It seemed like one of those horse-destroying fires was burning right in my office.

Presently that fire seemed to get right under my chair—and I got up and went into action.

2

BONNER SPRINGS LIES in the hills of Kansas, twenty-four speedometer miles from the Missouri line. It is a small town and perches on a hillside above the Kaw River. There is much wealth, however, in Bonner and its trade section, the country being peculiarly well adapted to fruit growing and to stock raising.

In a motor boat, accompanied by Jim Steele, my right-hand man, I set out up the Kaw on the morning following Hatton's visit. We did not linger in Bonner, but, in our character of fishermen, bought some supplies and later made camp a mile above the place, on the river bank. Then we proceeded to fish.

In the meantime, Joe Benson, another operative, had registered at the hotel in the Springs. Joe arrived wearing a derby hat, square-toed shoes, blue serge suit, and a suspicious look. He sported a black, stubby mustache under which a black cigar reposed.

Joe is, in fine, my stock detective. Whenever I want a dick to show up on a job and do it so the whole country will see and know in spite of clumsy efforts at secrecy, Joe does his stuff.

In the present instance his job was to pose, and ask questions. He was to query everybody in the town, make a great show of activity—while Steele and I did the work.

If he learned anything of value, which was improbable, we had means of intercommunication.

"What's to do, chief, besides loaf around camp?" Steele asked, after we had got located and had our hooks wet.

"Jim," I answered, "there is no way to get at this thing that I can see, except to wait until another fire occurs. That's bad, since it means the sacrifice of more horses and cattle, to say nothing of barns and other things. But we've got to have a starting point, and a fresh fire is the only thing I figure can give it. We've got to watch the skies at night, and be off at the first hint of red. That's all."

We divided the night between us, one watching while the other slept, and continued to divide them for two more nights—then the heavens suddenly were aflame. It happened about two o'clock in the morning.

Jim shook me awake.

"Fire to the west!" he exclaimed. "Looks to be a mile off! Maybe more! Hustle!"

I did. A moment after I was wide awake we were off in the direction of the blaze, which became greater in volume as each moment passed. It looked like the whole world in that direction was going up in smoke—or, perhaps, like a volcano in full eruption. There is something terrifying about a fire in the country at night.

We ran on across fields, passing farmhouses in which lights were showing and men and women hurrying about. There had been no alarm. Just the great blaze against the sky—and deathly silence. But men in the country have a way of knowing when fires break out—a sort of sensitiveness which warns them. Many joined us on our way.

When we reached the scene—Sam Hammond's place,

and a large one—the big barn was a mere red skeleton against a background of darkness. In one side a great mass of slowly burning hay glowed; in a corner grain was burning.

Other things were burning, too. In the cow section, where the milkers were kept overnight to avoid seeking them in the pastures before day, and in the horse stalls on the south. Smoldering heaps. Lifeless, thank God, before we arrived.

"Damned murdering devil!"

Steele was speaking.

"You are right! And it's been going on for six months—just like this!"

I looked up and found the speaker to be a squarely built young man, whose red hair made his pale face seem ghastly in the light of fire. His blue eyes had a hunted, harassed look, and there were lines of worry in his face.

"I'm Halsey," he volunteered, walking closer. "Adjuster for the insurance company. If this sort of thing keeps up—well, look at me! I'll be in my grave with worry! Twelve times during the last six months I've been called on to view such as this—to say nothing of having to go into the details later. It's awful!"

"If you don't like your job, why don't you quit?" demanded a jeering voice, and I looked another stranger over.

A tall, long-haired, ill-kept specimen of the human race he was. A hoocher, I could tell at a glance. He was half drunk at the moment, and his red-rimmed eyes sparkled with vindictiveness while he waited for Halsey to get back.

"On your way, Crump!" snapped the adjuster, turning from him. "The time has passed when I'd be willing to have anybody see me in your company. Go and mix with your kind, and let decent people alone!"

"Decent!" blazed the derelict. "You call it decent to take a man's bread and butter out of his mouth? Huh? You call that decent?"

He moved closer, and I noticed his hard, dirty fists closing and unclosing.

The insurance adjuster was somewhat smaller than Crump, though both were about the same age—thirty, or thereabout. He was a game one, I was to learn.

Before I could make a move to interfere, if I had had a mind to, he was at Crump like a tiger. One cleanly-delivered blow, and the derelict sprawled on the ground.

"Get up, you carrion!" Halsey said vehemently. "I've got more where that one came from!"

A fat man with a star on his vest interposed at that juncture.

"Stop that scrapping!" he ordered authoritatively, taking Halsey by an arm.

"You know better than this, George! As for you, Lafe Crump, if you don't take yourself off, right now, I'll clap you in the calaboose! Git!"

"Calaboose! Ha! Ha! Ha! That's Lafe's home, anyhow! Why don't you use some other kind of threat, Joe—one with teeth in it?"

Another citizen was introducing himself. This one was long past middle age—nearly sixty, I'd judge—and if ever I have seen spite, anarchy, deviltry, sarcasm, and impudence bottled up in one human being, he had it. His whiskered face was one big wrinkle of repulsiveness.

"They ain't no call for you to butt in, Tucker!" Joe Hart,

the deputy sheriff, cracked back. "Shut up, or I'll lodge you down there, too!"

"Me? Ha, ha, ha, ha! Oh, no, Joe! Not me, Henry Tucker! I've got too much money! I'm rich! The calaboose is for such as Crump—he's pore, since they done took his job away from him!"

"Kicked me out!" cried Crump, getting up, but withdrawing, nevertheless. "Kicked me out, so's to put George Halsey in! But I'll git even! See if I don't!"

"Git!" The deputy started toward the speaker, who took to his heels and disappeared across the road into the darkness.

During all this I had not opened my mouth—but my ears had been wide. My interest was, to put it mildly, enlisted. The fire, as a fire, no longer drew me.

The blaze was dying down, leaving a glowing mass of wreckage, and Steele touched me on the arm.

"Hadn't we better take a look around?" he asked.

"I think I've struck a lead, Jim," I replied. "That ruin can't tell us much—but I think I know somebody who can."

I walked across to Halsey, and drew him aside.

"Does your company keep a man on the ground all the time?" I asked. "Are things that bad?"

"On the ground? Oh, I see, you are a stranger, and don't understand. By the way," he asked, suddenly suspicious, "who are you?"

"I'm Oscar Toombs," I replied. "Me and my friend Askew, yonder, are out for a little fishing. Camped above Bonner. Saw the blaze and ran over."

"Oh!" he said evidently relieved. "That's all right. Strangers naturally arouse my interest, in view of what's been going on. It's like this, Mr. Toombs:

"A couple of years ago the farmers in this section got tired of paying extortionate fire insurance rates, so they got together and organized the Farmers' Mutual Insurance Society. All local farmers. Headquarters, quite naturally, at Bonner Springs. I'm adjuster for the company, and live in town."

"So. Well, who is the gink you clouted."

"Crump? Oh, he's a nobody, now. Used to have the job I've got now. Boozed so much they had to throw him out. He hates the company, and me too, of course."

I pondered that. Then: "And the whiskered bundle of hate and ridicule—who is he?"

Halsey laughed. "You mean old Henry Tucker. He's the worst old drawback this county ever saw. Independently wealthy, he never has joined the farmers in anything. Never a member of the grange, or the insurance company— anything, in fine, looking to the betterment of the section. Hates everybody and everything. Lives to himself—no family—and is the miser he looks to be. Always comes around in time to knock whatever happens to be afoot. That's Henry."

"Humph! Every community has one, maybe more, but I'll say this section is doubly cursed in that respect. Old Henry has deviltry enough for a dozen!"

"You've gauged him accurately."

"By the by, what company used to operate here, before the Farmers' Mutual?" I asked.

Halsey gave me a quick, searching look. "You betray a lot of interest in our affairs, Mr. Toombs," he said, rather coldly.

I laughed. "I may as well confess it, Mr. Halsey," I said, "I'm a writer—a sort of fiction hound. Things like this help me a lot. I always pry into matters of this kind, and with no other motive than to gather material for future use. Pardon me, if I seem to be too nosey."

Halsey's face relaxed. He smiled.

"I was a bit abrupt," he apologized. "Put it down to anxiety and the eternal harassment of my position. The Kansas Midland used to have the business in this section, as well as over a considerable portion of the balance of the State," he explained. "But, as I said, they were almighty high in the matter of rates, and they lost out here."

"Thanks," I replied. "Guess I'll be off and get some sleep. There's a few hours left before dawn. See you again, Mr. Halsey."

3

STEELE AND I returned slowly to camp, each of us thinking and keeping his thoughts to himself. Sitting beside our
camp fire, newly built up, afterward, Steele suddenly asked:

"Well, which is the bug—Crump or the old devil,
Tucker?"

I took my eyes off the coals, where I had been concentrating, and asked:

"Why pick on those two?"

"Looks plain enough to me," Jim asserted. "One hates
the company, and wants revenge. The other hates the whole
darn community—"

"Jim," I broke in, "either of those chaps may be the firebug. I'm not saying they're not. Either would probably be
capable of it. But—and mark this—those fires are not 'hate'
fires, or 'revenge' fires. Put that down."

"What kind, then?" Jim asked quizzically.

"They are what you might call 'beneficial' fires," I
returned.

"Just how?"

"Nobody is going around burning all those barns just
to satisfy his feelings, be they hate or whatnot. Those fires
are benefiting somebody. I mean in a very material way.
No doubt about it."

Jim was thoughtful for a long moment. Then he looked up quickly, his face incredulous.

"Tug," he said sharply, "you are not intimating that the Kansas Midland would—"

"Hell, no!" I told him peevishly. "Certainly the Kansas Midland Insurance Company would not stoop to such tactics to get this business back! I'm not turning idiot in my old age, Jim!"

"Well," Jim argued aggrievedly, "here's a situation. All the losers by these fires are, according to the adjuster, Halsey, insured in the Farmers' Mutual. The Mutual has routed the Kansas Midland from the field, causing them a large loss in business. You say the fires are due to cupidity—that they benefit somebody. All right—who?"

I made no answer. The question was an insult.

"Of course, Tug, I don't expect an answer right off the reel," Jim hastened to say, "but that's the question in my mind. Who? And, so far as I'm concerned, it's answered. I'm damned certain either Crump or the old devil, Tucker, is the actual bug—no matter who gets the profit. The Kansas outfit would benefit, and it could hire the dirty work done, couldn't it?"

"Yeah. It could. But it didn't. As for Crump and Tucker, I grant they are worthy suspects—but as tools only. We'll watch 'em both."

"Hoping they—or one of them—will lead us to the gink higher up—the employer?"

"Nope. To prevent more fires."

"Damn it!" exclaimed Jim. "Can't you tell a fellow something?"

"Yeah," I answered. "Get in the boat and take a letter

to Jerry Bidwill, the public accountant, you know. That's something. I'll write the letter. You wait for his answer—if it's a week."

I went inside the tent, leaving my subordinate glowering from his log. I had an idea—and I didn't want Jim to see it explode later under my feet, if it should happen to be that kind of idea.

It was after daybreak when Steele departed for Kansas City on the job assigned him, and, two hours later, I was sitting on the front veranda of Jared Hatton's house. It was a fine place, on a hilltop just outside of the village and overlooking the Kaw.

"It's like this, Mr. Hatton," I said, after his cordial greeting was over, "there are two persons hereabouts whom you might have mentioned when I asked you if you knew any one who had hate enough inside him to fit the character of firebug. One is Crump, the other an old devil with whiskers and a grouch. Name of Tucker, I believe."

Hatton gave me a glance of surprise. "Surely," he said, "you don't suspect either of them? Why, man. Crump is so far gone in liquor he spends half his time sleeping off drunks. On the occasion of at least two fires he was, to my knowledge, in the town jail.

"And Tucker—well, he's mean enough, unquestionably. But the man is more given to words than acts. He's been here ever since I can remember, and nothing criminal has ever been attributed to him. Frankly. I think you are wrong."

"Maybe so. But Crump has a, to him, very real reason for wanting to injure the Farmers' Mutual, and there is no telling what might hatch in his liquored brain. Do you happen to know the exact whereabouts of old Tucker, on the nights of those two fires you spoke of, while Crump was in jail?"

"Why, no. I can't say where he was. At home, probably."

"Humph. Might not Tucker and Crump be working together, each for the gratification of his own personal grievances?"

"They might, of course. Though I'll confess I never considered them for a minute."

"Do you know of anybody, other than Crump, who might have a grudge against the Farmers' Mutual?" I asked.

Hatton shook his head. "Not a soul."

"How is the stock in that concern held? Apportioned, I mean?"

"Each of twenty-four original subscribers hold equal shares—one share to a man. When a fire occurs, we all chip in and pay our *pro rata* of the loss. When a new member enters, he takes a share of stock, then meets his *pro rata*, when loss occurs, as do the rest. It is not, Mr. Norton, a money making organization. Merely an association of farmers, formed for mutual protection against the high rates of the old insurance companies."

"I see. You are, of course, a member?"

"One of the original ones, yes."

"How, may I ask, is the Mutual bearing up under its losses?"

Hatton shook his head ominously. "A few more fires," he said, "and there will be no Mutual. We are, frankly, fighting with our backs to the wall."

"Are any of you involved further than your stock?"

"No. But we could easily be, should we continue to operate."

"Now, Mr. Hatton, who of your acquaintance would benefit by the wrecking of the Mutual?" I asked sharply. "Think. Those fires are benefiting some one in a financial sense. Who? That question has got to be answered."

Hatton looked at me for a long moment, as though he did not quite understand my drift. Then he saw, or thought he saw, the point, and his face was transformed by a frown.

"Surely, Mr. Norton, you are not thinking that the Kansas Midland, or any of the old companies, are at the bottom of this thing?"

There was distress in his voice.

"I don't think any such thing!" I declared. "I'm not fool enough to think that the Midland would employ such tactics. The point I'm making is this. Some individual, or group of individuals, may be attempting to force the Mutual out of the field, to make room for himself. That is one theory. Another:

"If a group of real estate operators—unprincipled, it goes without saying—had their eyes on some land down this way, wanted to get it cheaply, and believed they could force a lot of you fellows into the market by bankrupting your insurance company and destroying your property— do you get the idea?"

Mr. Hatton got it. He came slowly to his feet, his big hands clenched at his sides.

"By the eternal, Mr. Norton!" he cried, a rasp in his voice. I believe you have put your finger on the spot! Real estate sharks! Why man, they'd do anything! That would account for it all—the theory you have just outlined! It would never have occurred to me!"

I smirked. "My trade, Mr. Hatton, is to figure out things

like that. Now, do this: run over in your mind all the real estate sharks you know of—not local, necessarily—who might be of the stripe to concoct such a scheme, make a list, and let me have it—say to-morrow. I will call here for it, or send. Will you attend to that?"

"I certainly will, Mr. Norton," he agreed, walking with me to the front gate. "You shall have the list to-morrow. In the meantime, what are you doing to prevent further depredations?"

"I have a plan which I intend to put into execution at once—to-morrow night, most likely," I replied. "I may need your assistance in that also. If so, I'll look you up."

With that I departed, having given Mr. Hatton the surprise of his existence.

Down in Main Street I ran across Joe Benson—rather, he ran across me. Joe buttonholed me, a stranger in town, and, in the hearing of a score of natives, pumped me dry—and, incidentally, reported that he had learned nothing whatever of the least importance.

"Watch Lafe Crump, town drunkard," I imparted, then made my escape.

Shortly after dawn the following morning Steele came up river. He handed me a letter from Jerry Bidwill, public accountant, a friend of mine—and, incidentally, in the know of practically all the big financial transactions going on in Kansas City. What he did not already have knowledge of he had ways of finding out about.

I went inside the tent and read the report. For a long time thereafter I sat thinking, and thinking hard. Then I called Steele in.

4

—

AN HOUR LATER I looked up Halsey, the adjuster, in the village.

"How many farmers, belonging to the Mutual, have not yet been burned out?" I asked.

"Twelve—an even dozen," he replied without hesitation.

"Give me a list of their names."

He looked at me with a grin. "For one of your fiction tales?" he asked.

Because I want it," I replied tersely. "You know, by now, or ought to know, who I am. If you don't, then ask Jared Hatton. But, mind you, young man, keep it under your hat."

He became serious at once. "I do know who you are, of course," he told me. "That list shall be yours within ten minutes."

He was as good as his word.

While I talked with Halsey, Steele was in a telephone booth, getting in touch with our office in Kansas City. He was calling for reinforcements.

With the list given me by Halsey in my pocket I climbed the hill to Hatton's place. Finding him about, I went straight into business.

"Here is a list of six farmers," I explained, "all of whom are members of Mutual. I have six men at my disposal, including myself—all thoroughly reliable. Now, it is impossible, or impractical, to watch the barns and houses of all the insured, but I am going to watch these six until, sooner or later, the firebug visits one of them. When he does, his finish has come."

Hatton nodded approvingly.

"Now, your part is to get word secretly to the six farmers on the list. Tell each that a man will be in his barn to-night, and for several nights to come, probably. Caution them all to keep quiet. That is all. Will you get it done at once?"

"Immediately," he replied, and indicated his motor car, which stood under a shed. "I'll do it in person. In the meantime," he fished a folded slip of paper out of his pocket, "here is the list of real estate sharks you asked for."

"Thanks. I'll look it over."

I took the paper and departed.

After dark three more fishermen joined Steele and me in camp. Later Joe Benson came along.

"Steele has spent the day learning the locations you are each to occupy to-night, boys," I told them. "He'll give each of you directions. Now, as to what you are to do, I have only this to say: lay low, keep watch, and if the firebug shows up—get him."

After the last of my men had departed I struck off for the farm farthest out of all. Reaching the barnyard, I slipped into a shed under which old machinery parts were kept, and took up my vigil.

Just who would receive a visit from the firebug was problematical, but I was willing to bet that he would show up.

Fate willed that I should be the one. It was nearing two o'clock in the morning when I saw a shadow creep from a sheep pen near the barn and flit toward the big structure. Silently I slipped out of hiding and took up his trail. I wanted to catch him in the act.

Among the many pens and sheds in the lot, there were a dozen, I lost him. Cursing myself, I turned back and started a circle of the barn—only to gasp, then start running for the southeast corner, where a blaze suddenly shot up. I could smell oil burning.

Footsteps running rapidly away from the scene, and in the direction of the very shed under which I had hidden, gave me the location, and I sprinted for it.

In the darkness beyond the shed a long tongue of flame suddenly speared a horizontal course toward me, there was the spiteful crack of a pistol, and a bullet whizzed by my head.

The next shot was mine—and I didn't miss. Just the vaguest outline of a man where that flame had been, but I got him.

Running rapidly, calling aloud to those in the farmhouse, I flashed a light into the face of a panting, struggling figure on the ground.

Then I got a shock.

The man I had shot was George Halsey!

Halsey, adjuster for the Mutual! Halsey was the firebug—caught in the act!

Excited shouts back of me told me that the farmer was on the job, and I saw at a glance that the fire was being successfully combatted. I bent over Halsey, who was yet alive.

"Can you hear, Halsey?" I asked.

He ceased writhing, after a moment, raised his stricken eyes to me, and asked:

"Am—I hit—bad?"

"You are going out—yes," I answered, for I had seen men die before. "Better come through!"

"Get—pencil—paper—witnesses!" he panted. "Hurry! Man, hurry!"

There, in the light of a lantern held by Roscoe Bell, the farmer, and in the presence of his wife and son, the deposition of George Halsey was taken down.

5

WHEN I CLIMBED the hill to Jared Hatton's house, next morning about seven o'clock, I was accompanied by the president of the Farmers' Mutual, a member of the grange, and Steele. Mr. Hatton came out and made us welcome.

Outside of a very few persons, my companions included, nothing of the past night's happenings had become known. There were certain steps to take which required secrecy for a short while longer.

"Mr. Hatton," I began, after we were seated, "I have some news for you. The firebug has been caught."

Hatton's face went blank. He stared at me, then in turn at the faces of the others present. After a moment he voiced his astonishment.

"Why, this is indeed news!" he declared. "I had not heard that the community had been visited by another fire!" He turned to me.

"I called up each of the men you had me visit yesterday to warn them that their places would be under guard for some time to come—or, at least, until the firebug was taken. Each informed me that the night had passed without incident."

I nodded. "The fire occurred at the home of a farmer not on that list I gave you," I explained. "You see, Mr. Hatton, I hit upon a scheme for protecting the remaining farmers in the Mutual. Those men who were warned were safe. I knew that. Therefore I devoted my attention, and the attention of my men, to the remaining six—who had not been notified that they would be guarded. In doing so I protected all twelve. Do you get the idea?"

"I'll confess that I don't," Jared acknowledged. "But that is not, perhaps, essential. What I should like to know is the identity of the scoundrel who has been setting the fires. Who is he?"

I shook my head negatively. "All in good time," I told him. "Please keep looking until you vision my little plan in all its phases. It is not, I assure you, very abstruse. Think a moment."

Hatton's face grew red. He looked at me with a cold eye.

"I must ask you to explain, Mr. Norton," he said. "I'll confess I'm not good at riddles."

"This is not a riddle," I told him sharply.

"Here is the whole thing in a nutshell:

"I knew that the homes of the men who had been notified that they were to be guarded would not be visited by the firebug. I knew it because I knew the bug would have a list of those places before nightfall—as a warning to keep away from them. Also he would know where he might act in perfect safety among the remaining six insured. With me and my men safely stowed away he might carry his torch about with assured immunity. That's why the list was made out—and given to you."

Hatton's face went paler, and his hands clenched tightly. Again his eyes sought the faces of those gathered on the porch. But he could read nothing there. Finally he turned once more to me.

"You—you figured that in some manner your plans would leak out?" he queried, his voice shaky. "That the firebug would get word of them?"

I nodded. "Yeah," I answered. "I figured you would warn your tool, Halsey, that all was safe in one quarter—and damned unsafe in another. You did just that, Hatton—and Halsey, misled, paid for your mistake with his life."

There was an awful silence on the porch at that announcement—and accusation. Steele, sitting on a balustrade, tensed his long frame, and his eyes were glued to the face of the big man near the door.

All the others watched Hatton closely.

Finally the latter spoke, and his voice rattled like dry leaves.

"Halsey—died?" he asked. "Who—who shot him?"

"I did," I answered.

"Did he talk?"

"More than that. He made a deposition."

"A confession, you mean? He owned up in writing? Before witnesses?"

"Yes, before several of them," I informed him. "The game is up, Hatton. Why keep up the stall?"

I've met a lot of crooks in my time, but none who beat Jared B. Hatton for pure nerve. As I watched a change came over him. The developments so far had shaken him, but when he saw how the wind was blowing he staged as complete a recovery as it has ever been my privilege to witness. He simply froze—became the iciest iceberg on record.

"Perhaps you will explain your meaning, Mr. Norton?" he requested, looking me squarely in the eyes and never batting his. "Your accusation is clear enough, although, in your poor way, you have sought to make it very subtle. You are trying to connect me up, in some way, with Halsey. That is clear. Go on, please."

"I will!" I snapped. Then I read Halsey's deposition.

It set forth that Jared Hatton had employed him, by paying him a large lump sum and promising to make him independent when the Mutual should go out of business, to set fire to the barns of those insured in the latter company. It told a lot more, but that was the gist of the thing.

Hatton laughed coolly. "And do you think that thing would convince a jury?"

"Shut up!" I barked. "I've had all I want out of you, you dirty horse-burning thief! Another word, until I've finished my case against you, and I'll let Steele, there, sap you—like he's itching to do right now. You shut up, and listen, damn you!"

I was mad. Madder, I think, than I have ever been before at a man I had trapped. He'd burned horses, damn him, and done it to add more dollars to the dirty pile he'd amassed! Yeah, I was mad!

Hatton's face went a bit pale, and he appealed to his fellow citizens on the porch to see he got fair play.

"We are going to see to that, Hatton," Lee Narrows, president of the Mutual, assured him. "Just that!"

Jared sat down, and I went on.

"When Hatton came to my office and hired me he did so because the vote of his grange had driven him to do it. He tried to stuff me with the idea that all this burning was the result of hatred on the part of some person. He saw I wouldn't fall for the theory that an insane person was doing it. But he did think I might believe that some person was causing the destruction to satisfy an insatiable hatred.

"Well, I had more respect for Hatton's intelligence. I knew he didn't believe any such rot. I knew that he must know, as I did, that those were beneficial fires—fires that added profits, either actual or potential, to somebody's bank roll.

"I looked Jared up, after he left, learned that he was very wealthy, and that he was regarded as a remarkably good business man. That clinched it.

"Well, I found out what was afoot, after I came here. Somebody was seeking to put the Mutual out of business—and succeeding. Who?

"Not the Kansas Midland. That company would never resort to such tactics. No other insurance company would. Yet that was the aim of those fires—the destruction of the Mutual. Who would benefit?

"Then it struck me right between the eyes. The Kansas Midland would not stoop to such—but how about a big stockholder in the Midland?

"Don't you see, men? He would not be fighting just this little organization. He would be fighting the idea—an idea which, if successful, would undoubtedly spread over the entire State. What, then, would become of his stock in the Midland?

"Gentlemen, I found that stockholder. My information—and I can verify it—is that the Kaw Valley Trust Company, of Kansas City, holds forty-five per cent, of Kansas Midland stock, nearly a million dollars' worth—as an agent for Jared B. Hatton!"

I ceased, and all eyes were fixed upon the big figure of Jared. He sat quite still.

"That is a damnable lie!" he said coolly.

"A denial of it, if it is proved true, is equivalent to an acknowledgment of guilt in this other matter, Hatton," I reminded him. "And you know it's true."

His face went white at that. He had overlooked a bet.

"I came up here, scared Jared by telling him I thought it might be the work of the Midland—or let him think such was in my mind. Then I gave him a pleasant surprise by cooking up an impossible yarn about a group of real estate sharks being at the bottom of it. He balked at the insinuation that an insurance company might be at the bottom, but cottoned to the other idea instantly.

"Now, gentlemen," I went on, "with the damning evidence of that secretly held stock, and the deposition of Halsey which names Jared B. Hatton as his principal, all back of me, I arrest Jared—"

Hatton leaped from his chair, his arm came up, and a gun flashed in the morning sunlight.

"Damn you—"

Then Steele landed.

Hatton went down the hill to the lockup, his unconscious form borne between the four of us.

THE QUEEN'S PATTERAN

*Daybreak Found Me Looking Out Over
the City's Housetops, Joplin, I Thought, Was
Destined to Become a Second Pompeii*

1

FOUR STRANGE CLIENTS

THIS BIT OF intimate history concerns itself largely with the activities of a smart crook who played for astoundingly high stakes, intending to retire on his winnings and run straight thereafter. Unfortunately for him he delayed a trifle too long, and was carried off on a stretcher.

Lots of them do that. Nothing unique in the fact that he postponed his reformation, and, in consequence thereof, found himself in the center of a zone of danger with all avenues of escape cut off. Certainly nothing original in that.

Richard the Third pulled just such a boner. So did Napoleon. So have other high-grade crooks, beginning back in the age when man first began to covet the mules, and maidservants, and other assets of his neighbors, and extending right down to the immediate present.

But I'll say, here and now, that no case of record in the archives of the Kaw Valley Detective Bureau, of which I, Tug Norton, am founder, owner and chief operative, even approaches what I am about to relate, insofar as bizarre and unique features are concerned.

Neither has it a counterpart, within the range of my

knowledge, in downright black deviltry, and deep-laid skullduggery.

Listen! I'm going to prove it!

In the month of June of last year, Orlando the Second's young and exquisitely charming queen, being then in the very heart of America's boasted civilization—geographically, at least—disappeared during the dark hours intervening between the setting and the rising of the sun, leaving behind her in a welter of blood, the dead body of her aged consort—the jeweled hilt of her own dainty but deadly dagger protruding from his breast, its needlelike point in his heart.

In America? Yes, right here in the United States.

Orlando's queen, Zelena, disappeared on the fifteenth day of June, and the body of the aged monarch was discovered upon the trampled grass of a cleared spot in the midst of a dump of hazel-brush on the east bank of Shoal River, early on the following morning. The handsomely appointed motor van in which the royal pair were known to have traveled had also vanished.

I say vanished because, while the marks of its tires were

"Go right ahead!" I told him—as he held the match for his mother

easy to trace from the highway into the timber where the dead king lay, a recent rain having rendered the earth soft and spongy, no returning traces were visible.

There were no wheel marks leading from the spot in any direction, for the simple reason that there was no other direction in which the van could have gone.

Shoal River, shallow but wide at that point, barred progress on the north and west, and great mountains of crushed stone—called chat—intervened on the east.

The river was not deep enough to conceal the van, had it been driven into it, and, while it is true that an expert driver, with a powerful car, might have forded the stream, there could be no possible object in doing so.

For, on the opposite bank of the watercourse, arose huge, tumbled cones of chat, waste from the lead and zinc mills which long ago operated there. They were insurmountable obstacles in the way of passage.

Those chat piles were banked one above another for a distance of three miles to the north, and approximately an equal distance westward, in some instances attaining a height of two hundred feet above ground. To drive a motor car across that barren and treacherous waste was simply impossible.

There was, then, only one point of egress from the place where the van had stood in the brush, and that was back the way it had come. That it had not returned that way was established beyond doubt. The ground, still soft, would have retained the wheel impressions. None were there. The van, however, was gone.

So was Queen Zelena—and one hundred thousand dollars in currency which Orlando carried on his ill-fated wedding journey.

All that I read in the newspapers, which gave a great deal of space to the matter when it occurred, then dropped it in typical newspaper fashion. The accounts entertained me and, I confess, I was persuaded that the whole thing was cooked up by highly imaginative reporters.

That the dead body of a Spanish gypsy had been found on the banks of Shoal River, five miles from the city of Joplin, in Missouri, was, of course, a matter of police record in that place. But, I thought likely, the rest of the yarn was just a fine bit of embroidery from the expert needles of the gentlemen of the press.

I was to learn better.

On the morning of June 21, just a week after the murdered man had been found, the door of my office in Kansas City was opened by the boy who does such jobs for me, and the strangest quartet of persons I have ever met crossed the threshold.

The persons themselves were of a strange culture; they

were strange in physical make-up and in manner. The story they told outstranged anything I had ever heard—and, make no mistake about it, I've seen and heard a lot of unusual things in my time, at that.

2

"WE ARE ROMS"

ONE WOMAN AND three men entered the room. One of
the men escorted the woman to a chair, the most comfortable one there, and seated her with a grave and respectful
bow.

The woman was worth a good, long look. Her delicately
modeled face had the hue of ancient ivory, and possessed
also an unblemished smoothness. Her large and brilliant
eyes were a deep violet, and long, silken lashes fringed
them.

From beneath hair as white as the breast of a swan, the
lobes of shell-like ears appeared. Pendent from her ears
were enormous circles of gold, set with sparkling gems.

A turban-like headdress of fine silk, colorful, and harmo-
nizing with the rest of her costume, concealed her head
from a line low on her forehead, and fell in graceful folds
upon her shoulders. The gown she wore was also of silk,
of a pattern with the turban, and most unusual in design.

Imagine my astonishment when this seemingly delicate
and highbred lady fumbled in a beaded bag secured to a
girdle of richly colored beads, produced a French brier pipe
with a long amber stem, filled it with tobacco, which she
packed into the bowl daintily with the index finger of a

small, bejeweled hand, and lit from a match which the man beside her applied. She undoubtedly enjoyed the delicate whiffs of smoke she drew through the long stem.

"Your pardon, sir," said the young man who had applied the match. His English was good, though possessing an accent pronouncedly Latin. "The smoke is soothing to madam's, my mother's, nerves—and she has great need of composure."

"Go right ahead!" I told him. "All of you light up, if you want to. I'm a tobacco hound myself. Nothing like a pipe of good tobacco to cheer a man up and make him at peace with himself and all the neighbors."

I ran a swift glance over the speaker, wondering all the while what had brought so singular a group to me. He was slight—about five feet and eight inches tall, I judged. Weight not over a hundred and forty. I had often heard of graceful men, but had not, I'm frank to say, met many such.

This chap had it—oceans of it. He might have been one of those old parlor-trained cavaliers, from the way he carried himself.

A sack suit of dark cloth—velvet-corduroy, I took it to be—sat well upon him, and, from the top of his sleek black head to the toes of his highly polished black shoes, he was spic and span.

The other two men were very like him in dress. They were younger, much the same in size, and possessed also the same grace of movement and the same calm self-possession.

They also had this in common: skin as dark and rich in color as the shell of a ripe chestnut; black eyes fringed with long lashes; full, red lips, and hair that would have made a raven seem merely dun-colored in comparison.

Foreigners? Sure. But what nationality were they? I had never seen their like before, that was certain.

"You are, I presume, Mr. Tug Norton?"

The query came from the elder of the young men, who seated himself gracefully and opened up.

"At your service," I assured him.

"We, my brothers and my mother, are Roms," he explained. "Romanies, we are sometimes called. Gypsies, too, is a designation with which we are not unfamiliar. But Roms, Romanies or gypsies, we are in deep distress, and have come to you with our burden."

I bowed. Somehow, when that chap spoke those words, I suddenly felt my sympathy go out to him—Rom, Romany or gypsy; black, white or yellow. He had no need to tell me that he and his whole outfit were in trouble. They showed it in their faces.

"I shall be happy to aid you in any way I can, Mr.—" I paused.

"Pardon me. I am Bardo Lorel. My brothers are Danjefo, and Ricco. My mother," he ended with a smile, "is Madam Lorel."

"All right," I replied. "Now we know each other, suppose we proceed to business. In the first place, who sent you to me?"

"A gentleman in the City of Joplin, in Missouri," Bardo Lorel answered. "The chief of police, in fine."

Bang! My memory-gun fired right then and there! Attentive already, I became doubly so.

"You wish to engage me for an investigation of some

kind?" I asked, seeing that he expected me to say something.

"Very certainly!" he exclaimed. "The police gentleman spoke very good of you, and for that we came."

The old lady, pipe-stem held daintily between her jeweled fingers, was leaning forward in an intent attitude. It was as though she had some difficulty in following what was being said. Bardo gave her a smile and a nod, then uttered a few words in a lingo which was beyond me. She smiled in return, and gave me a friendly glance from her brilliant eyes.

"Madam, my mother, understands very little English," Bardo explained. "You will pardon if I translate occasionally?"

"Absolutely!" I assented. "Go right ahead with your story, and translate whenever you want to."

"Thank you. Our sister, Zelena, lately the bride of Orlando Seton, king of all Spanish-American Roms in this country, has been foully dealt with, and we have come to beg your aid in discovering her, whether she is living or dead.

"It is the opinion of the police of Joplin that my sister, a queen in Romany, assassinated her husband, and fled with his money. Fled," he paused, and a dark flush dyed his face, "with a lover—an apostate Rom.

"It is unspeakable, that! Unbelievable! So obnoxious to us, her people, as well as to every Rom in America, that we freely will pay such a sum as would cover the floor of this room with a carpet of pure gold, to disprove it! It is for that we came to you!"

My breath halted suddenly, somewhere between my

lungs and my Adam's apple. It was a large room in which we sat—a very large room. The Kaw Valley Bureau could use a carpet of that size and texture! No doubt about it!

But I did not betray my state of almost suspended animation. I got my breath to working again and replied gravely:

"I have no doubt, if I take your case, we shall have no difficulty in arranging the terms. Suppose, now, you give me the details? Your sister disappeared a week ago. I read about it in the papers. Much time has been lost, and the trail has grown cold. In such matters it is highly desirable to act with dispatch. Why—pardon the question—are you so certain of your sister's innocence?"

The answer was given in simple dignity, for all that it burned with suppressed heat.

"She is a maiden of Romany. Mere desertion of her husband, the King Orlando, to give herself into the arms of a lover, would bring about instant expulsion from her family and her race. Complete ostracism for life would follow. Her name would be despised and hated by every man and woman in whom the blood of Romany flows, and the Curse of Curses would be placed upon her.

"Sir," he asked quietly, "is it possible to believe that a young woman, educated in the best of American and European colleges, tenderly and carefully reared, elevated as few maidens of our race can be elevated, would flee from her chosen husband, after driving a dagger into his heart while he slept, to become the slave-woman of an apostate gypsy?"

I shook my head negatively. "It doesn't seem plausible that she would," I answered. "Now, let's have the facts in the case."

3

DANJEFO'S STORY

BARDO BOWED A graceful assent. "I shall request that you hear Danjefo, my brother," he said, turning to the young man. "He it was who first arrived beside the place of *lalo pani*, after word came to us at our *tan* near St. Louis, that Orlando, the *baro manu* was *mullo*—"

Madam Lord's fingers relaxed and the French brier thudded softly upon the rug at her feet. Covering her face with her hands, she shook with a passion of grief, and her rich, musical voice interrupted wailingly.

"Orlando! Orlando! *Puru manu! Baro manu! Mullo! Mullo!*"

"Listen!" I exclaimed dazedly. "I savvy only one language, and am not any too strong in it! If I'm to get the gist of this thing, it'll have to be laid down in pure and simple American! What is this *lulu panee*, and *maynew moolew* stuff?"

"Your pardon!" Bardo begged contritely. "It is that I very often find no English words when excitement is within me. *Lalo pani* means red water. It was beside this place of red water, Shoal River it is named, that Orlando, the *baro manu*—the great man—was killed—"

Again that liquid voice in interruption.

"Orlando! *Puru manu! Baro manu! Mullo! Mullo!*"

"Please, mother!" Bardo reproved in gentle tones, then turned to me in explanation. "Mother grieves greatly because Orlando, *puru manu*—old man, old friend—is *mullo*—is dead. We Lorels are blood kin to the Setons, being the same family. Orlando and madam, my mother, were small together, and attached friends through life. Now, *rye*—sir, I mean—we shall get on. *Tucue,* Danjefo, *chipe.*"

I passed that *tookew chippy* in silence. I suppose Bardo was ordering his brother to spill it. At any rate, Danjefo began speaking immediately.

"Mr. Norton, *rye,* you must know in the beginning that there are strata of culture in Romany, just as there are in America—in all countries and all races. Not to burden you with tiresomeness, I shall only say that we, the Lorel family, are not of the *dukkering* type of Rom—that is to say, we do not breed fortune-tellers—dukkers. We, the Lorels," he informed me in accents of deep pride, "are *kalo-ratt.* And, while we *rokker* in all the various departures from the *kalo jib,* we are not to be confused—"

"But I am!" I broke in. "Confused is my middle initial, at the moment! Make him cut out the *rats* and *ducks,* Bardo, old chap, and get down to brass tacks!"

Bardo gave me a faint smile of amusement, then spoke softly to Danjefo. "*Tucue,* Danjefo, *rokker gorgio chipe!*"

Evidently Danjefo had received a good calling down in words he could savvy, for he flushed slightly, and he was duly apologetic when he again spoke to me.

"Your pardon, *rye,*" he begged. "We Lorels are of the pure blood, or Black Gypsy—*kalo-ratt.* Our tongue is naturally the original Sanskrida—or Black Language. The *kalo jib*. All that may seem to you to be beside the matter at issue. It is not, however.

"To understand what I must make you comprehend, it is needful for you to know how widely we Black Gypsies differ from the lower cultures, as, for instance, the *dukker-ing*, or fortune-telling type."

"All right, Dan," I assured him. "I understand that you are the real, Simon-pure article. Knew it, of course, when you came in—although I couldn't dope out just what tribe you belonged to. Now cultures, strata, and all such being settled, let's have the facts."

"My sister, who was Zelena Lorel," Danjefo's story ran, "was promised to Orlando II, King of Romany, when she was twelve years old. Such is quite common among we Roms. She was educated most carefully in order that she might not demean herself later in accordance with her high station.

"Romany maidens do not, as a usual thing, select the man they marry. That is best done by their elders and parents. Zelena understood that, and prepared her mind and heart for it.

"Orlando Seton was sixty years old when he died. He was married to my sister two weeks ago, she being just turned eighteen. Sheva, the former queen, had proven to be barren, and Orlando possessed no child. Should he die without male issue, his title, which is hereditary, would pass to a nephew—Tannello Seton.

"It happens that, in addition to youth and great mental and physical strength, Tannello Seton possesses great charm of person—is, in fine, what you *gorgios* call classy.

Was there a deep attachment between my sister, Zelena, and this Tannello? It would appear that there was, at least, much love in his heart for her.

"It was of no hope—that love. This Tannello knew it. For, at the time of the *sonacai can*—pardon, once again, *rye!* I here allude to the time of the golden moon, when we of Romany hold great *festas*, and the good things of the fields are brought in.

"At that time, two years ago, the troth of our sister and Orlando was pledged. Once publicly pledged, it may not, in Romany, be broken.

"Tannello, covering his face with the silken cloth from his head, turned his back upon his family—and upon all Romany! An apostate gypsy! That is what Tannello became thenceforward!

"He became a *gorgio!* Non-gypsy!

"Very rich, this Tannello is. So, for that matter, are all the *kalo-ratt*. Very educated, also, is Tannello. In the great school of the Missouri State, of Columbia, he became a learned engineer for mining.

"Having repudiated all connection with Romany, because of this great love which he must keep inside of his heart and never again give it *chipe*, he removed his *tan* to Joplin *Foros*—but I forget once more. This Tannello removed his house to Joplin City. There he now engages in engineering for the zinc and lead, with much good fortune.

"Two weeks ago Orlando and my sister, his queen, set out from St. Louis on a wedding journey. They went alone, for such is the custom in Romany. In Orlando's magnificent motor van, especially for the occasion, they traveled. Toward this Joplin City they went.

"Why? Because Orlando wished to view some vast properties which he holds, as King of Romany, near that place. Many years ago he invested much money in a tract of two hundred acres, in the vicinity of Shoal River, and, far-sighted *manu* that he was, the property was rapidly fruitful. I do not understand in just what manner it was so fruitful, but that it was soon to be I have Orlando's word on it.

"There is another something important for you to know. As king of the gypsies, Orlando was master of fabulous money—the tribal treasury. The beginning of this treasury was in the time of Ramo Cooper—understand, *rye*, in Romany it is the custom to assume surnames such as those borne by the native sons of our adopted country.

"Ramo Cooper was the first king of the Black, or pure blood Spanish Roms. The treasury has been handed down and down, from one king to another, accumulating vastly all the while. No one, save Orlando and those who know its resting place, can say how great the sum now is—but it is enormous—"

"Hold on!" I broke in. "Don't you folks do any banking?"

"We have not great confidence in the banks of the *gorgios*," was the dignified answer. "You have heard of the wandering Jews? Yes? Ah, *rye*, we of Romany—old, even, as those Jews—are wanderers too!

"Since the records of our tribes run, and they are far, far back, any wood has been our home! We have lived in many nations, and known many peoples, but never have we mingled with them! Persecution has dogged our *patteran*, the whole world over! Can you ask, then, why we of Romany do not trust the *gorgio* banks?"

I could get the Rom's slant there, right enough.

"They do have a habit of going busted right frequently," I acknowledged. "Have you got any idea of the whereabouts of that bunch of kale?"

"Pardon?" Danjefo raised his delicate eyebrows inquiringly.

"No. I beg yours. I'm speaking in a sort of *rat* language myself! What I mean is this: Have you got any idea where the tribe's treasure is cached?"

"Cached—ah, I know! Hidden. That is how you mean! No. Only the king, the four oldest men of the tribe, or family, and the king's consort, may know the whereabouts of its keeping. They, alone, have the key, and are able to read the *patteran*."

I marked that *patteran* thing in my mind for future reference.

"Your sister, then, knew—or, let us hope—knows where the jack is holed up?"

"I—I am not sure, *rye*—"

"Where the treasure is planted," I explained.

"Oh, yes! Zelena was informed of that on her wedding day."

I thought I began to see a light. I did not, however, mention it, since it was only a feeble flicker at best. Just a flicker.

"Orlando, it is reported carried a hundred thousand dollars with him on that journey. Know anything about that?" I asked.

"I know not the amount, only that it was large," Danjefo replied. "Hidden within a secret compartment of the *wardo*—the van, I mean—was a large sum which belonged to the general fund. I have no doubt that Orlando carried it for the sole purpose of adding it to the principal."

"Who, besides Orlando and his queen, might have known about the secret compartment?"

"None save Orlando, Zelena, and the workman who constructed it could have known the secret of the compartment," Danjefo said. "That something of the sort existed was known only to us, the immediate members of the family."

"Could this Tannello chap have savvied it?"

"Impossible!"

Maybe so, I thought. But Zelena could darn well have tipped him off about it. I didn't mention that, either.

"What else?" I asked.

"There is but little. Orlando made camp in the brush near Renne's Mill, which stands on a shoal-like shelf of rock under the east bank of Shoal River—whose water is deeply red.

"When morning came, a fisherman found him lying beside the dead ashes of his fire, a dagger belonging to my sister driven into his heart. Zelena was gone, leaving no *patteran*. Nor was there *patteran* to indicate whence the *wardo* had departed. That *rye*, is all!"

"All right. Now, give me the low-down on that *patteran* stuff."

Danjefo looked at his brother Bardo in a dilemma of helplessness, and the latter spoke.

"It is hard to define to you the exact meaning of *patteran*," he said, dark brows drawn in an effort for clarity of speech. "It means differently, in our *chipe*. That is, it expresses much.

In the sense, however, employed by Danjefo, it means what the *gorgios* would call a trail."

"Well," I exclaimed, "why in the name of Julius K. Caesar didn't you say so and be done with it? In a nutshell, you want me to pick up the queen's trail, and follow it out to its end. I'm glad you were able to find an Americanese equivalent for it—because I wouldn't have recognized a *patteran* if it'd been wrapped round my neck! Find the little gypsy queen—that right?"

"Yes! Yes!" exclaimed the men of the party in unison, while madam, the mother, sensing what the emotion was over, rapped loudly, and applaudingly on the arm of her chair with the bowl of the brier pipe.

"Good!" I declared. "I'm your man. Now," I went on, eying Bardo Lorel, who seemed to be the head of the group, "having in mind that carpet you mentioned at the beginning of this interesting conversation, suppose you present it in installments—a rug at a time. And, in view of the fact that running about the country on out-of-town cases is expensive, let me have the first rug now."

Did he? Yes—and from a roll of material that would have staggered the colossus of Rhodes himself!

For an employer of his high type, I would undertake to find the *patteran* of the lost tribes of Israel, to say nothing of a runaway queen, who doubtless would not be hard to recover—once I learned where the Tannello chap was keeping her!

4

I LOOK UPON THE KING

"JIM," I REMARKED to my chief assistant, shortly before the K.C.S. passenger train pulled into Joplin next morning, "I've got this thing well doped out."

Jim stretched and yawned. "Yeah?" he said disinterestedly. "A cup of hot coffee would entertain me a lot better right now than listening to your theories could possibly do! Is this a place called Joplin, and, if so, when?"

It was five o'clock in the morning, and Jim Steele was not in the best of humor. I had decided, at the last minute, to take Steele with me. Mixing around with the Roms might prove somewhat dangerous, and Jim is a mighty handy man in a scrimmage. Besides, I could easily afford the extravagance of Steele's companionship, thanks to the strip of carpet Bardo had slipped me.

"We will raise Joplin in about fifteen minutes," I said, glancing at my watch. "In the meantime, I'm going to talk. Whether or not you listen is a matter of indifference to me. Here goes.

"It is patent that Zelena, despite her foreign extraction, has become acclimated—in fine, thoroughly Americanized. She bumped off the old king, her lord and master, without the slightest compunction, grabbed his roll, and beat it with the man she loves.

"Sadie Simpkins, of Post Oak, Oklahoma, couldn't have done a better job of it. I consider, then, the Americanization of Zelena Lorel established—written in gore with the point of her own dagger.

"It is necessary to get such a slant at Zelena, in order to make my theory stand up. Danjefo said that no Romany maiden would do such a thing. All right. But all that traveling and educating and mingling Zelena did, altered her completely.

"Higher education wiped her mind clean of any fear of such bugaboos as the curse of curses—whatever it is. She ceased, long ago, to be a Rom, and became, instead, an out and out American.

"She emphatically did not love the old boy, King Orlando II. Dan and his outfit know that perfectly well. She married him because, being in Romany, she had to do as the Roms ordered her to do.

"But you can bet your next month's salary—which, thanks to Bardo, you stand a good chance of getting—that she and Tannello framed this deal before he hid his face and backed off from his family.

"Think of it! Zelena, being queen of the gypsies, would share her consort's knowledge of the whereabouts of the big money. And, you can also wager, the queen steered the old man toward Joplin—where Tan is putting up. Between them they staged the killing.

"You may argue that the four oldest men of the tribe would, immediately upon learning of the fate of their king, remove the treasure to some other spot. Against that I will say: Suppose the money is mostly in gold, which it quite likely is, and is therefore not so easy to move.

"Suppose, too, that they, like all the rest of the Roms, believe Zelena to be entirely innocent; that she was kidnaped or slain. There would, then, be no need for rehiding the treasure. Don't you see, it is only in case they think Zelena has turned traitor, murderess and apostate, that they would transfer the tribal hoard to another place.

"They emphatically do not believe their queen is guilty. Therefore, I maintain that the treasure is where it was before Orlando died—and that it will stay there, so far as the Roms are concerned.

"What then? Zelena and Tannello will, one of these fine dark nights, dig up the treasure, and take an extended trip to other parts. That, Jim, is my view of the case."

Nine hundred and ninety-nine out of one thousand present day American men would have doped the case out precisely as I had done for Jim. It was the only plausible explanation—the natural one. Sadie Simpkins would have done it, under like conditions, and Zelena and Sadie are sisters, just under the skin.

Jim Steele slept through my pronouncement, hearing none of it—a circumstance for which I was afterward devoutly thankful.

Joplin at last. We stepped from the train into the Van Noy Restaurant, going thence to the police station. There we procured cards which enabled us to view the body of the dead gypsy.

It had been kept in storage at the morgue, pending final disposition at the bands of the subjects of the little kingdom—little, but none the less real and vital in the minds and lives of those belonging to it.

The Lorels had not traveled to Joplin with us. That would not have been permitted, had they wished to do so. In a high-powered car, they sped on ahead of us, leaving shortly after our interview the afternoon before.

So, attracting no attention, since the city was as yet hardly awake, we entered the morgue and looked upon the remains of Orlando II, a king in Romany.

I shall never forget the fine features, crowned by long hair, the hue of new silver, of Orlando Seton. There was something there which defies description. Real nobility of expression. That is as near as I can come to it. The dark face was clean-shaven, showing the wide mouth and the thin, fine lips perfectly. I could imagine that he was a just and worthy ruler—peace to his ashes.

That look at Orlando sobered me. Prior to it, I had been inclined to treat the whole matter rather lightly. Not that I was not duly regretful of the tragic side of it. I was. But, for the life of me, I had been unable to take a serious view of the little gypsy kingdom, its monarch, its treasure, and its comic air of dignity as portrayed by Bardo and the other Lorels.

The tragedy was, to my mind, just another of those all too frequent human triangles. Just another pitiful attempt on the part of a man and a woman to rearrange the social order to suit themselves—and do it with a dagger.

The police of Joplin held a like opinion. They had ticketed the little queen as a faithless wife, widowed by her own hand, and gone to the arms of a former lover.

Tannello Seton, well-known in the city, was absent—

had been since the day previous to the murder. That was, in itself, strongly substantiative of their theory. They had investigated, learned nothing to oppose the conclusion they felt was the right one, and had dropped the case, insofar as any great activity was concerned.

"Them gyps are a close-mouthed lot," the night sergeant commented, as he filled out our cards. "They won't tell anything—just like the wops. No doubt they will, in time, get their queen back, along with her lover, and mete out justice in their own way. We won't ever know how the case ends. Gyps are that way."

I viewed the dagger—a slender, flexible strip of finest steel, with a guard of old silver and a handle of jade set with rubies, emeralds and sapphires. Truly a lovely bit of work, worthy of Cellini.

Later in the morning, after the chief came down, I was permitted to take possession of the dagger, upon my promise to guard it well and hold it available should it be wanted. That, because the chief was an old friend—a former buddy on the force in Kansas City.

"Jim," I asked, when we were seated in a small roadster, guided by Officer Lakely, *en route* to Renne's Mill, five miles east of Joplin, "did—er—did you hear me when I was outlining my ideas in this matter, just before we unloaded at Joplin?"

"Naw, Tug," he answered. "I was asleep. Say," he went on, "did it strike you that the old fellow back yonder in the morgue was a real somebody in his time?"

That was it. Somebody. You bet Orlando Seton had been somebody. That was what I had sensed when I looked upon his dead face. A real man had been struck down in a cowardly manner. That thought was a solemn one, and changed my entire attitude toward the dead sovereign and his kingdom in the land of the free.

5

AGAINST A WALL OF ROCK

A CONCRETE ROAD, leaving Joplin on the east, runs in almost a straight line for a distance of four miles, then turns sharply north and, at the end of a mile, turns east again and crosses a narrow bridge over Shoal River. Two hundred yards north of the east end of the bridge is Renne's Mill. There my quest for the queen's *patteran* began.

Shoal River, at that point, is not above two hundred yards wide when at normal stage, as it was the morning I first looked upon it. From bank to bank, however, the distance is perhaps an additional hundred yards.

The west shore is low, almost on a level with the plain through which the river runs, but the east bank is high and almost wholly formed of rock which rises in narrow ledges from the bed. Both shores are wooded densely, and below the bridge on the south side the river is divided by a narrow island which is also completely covered with trees and underbrush.

Just beyond the east end of the bridge a narrow, rutted trail, lined with water-willows and sword-grass, leaves the highway, drops steeply down into the bed of the stream and follows over a rocky bar which, at low water time, is high and dry. Fifty feet from the point of divergence from the highway, the trail loses itself from view in the woods and undergrowth.

The mill—an old-time water-power grist mill, long since deserted and turned over to the sole occupancy of pigeons, bats and owls—stands on a base of rock masonry down in the bed of the stream, raised above danger from flooding, save perhaps in times of extremely high water.

The stream, even when at a normal stage, washes the foundation of the structure. Above the site the river tumbles down a series of rock shelves or ledges, forming a natural stairway over which the water ripples musically.

Attached to the lower shelf is a wing-dam of man-made masonry, which diverts part of the flow to the east shore and conducts it beneath the mill, through a causeway and over the wheel on the south side of the building. The water-wheel was no longer there, save in fragments strewn about the scene of its former location.

The mill building is fifty feet square, constructed of wood, and stands four stories above its foundation. No paint had touched its walls for many years, and the windows were boarded up where the glass panes had fallen out.

The doors, too, were barricaded, though the timbers used for that purpose were so insecure from decay that they no longer presented a very formidable bar to ingress, should any one desire to enter.

The trail from the highway passes the mill on the east, and ends in the brush under the high bank of the river, a hundred feet north of the site and almost on the edge of the stream which circles in from a northeasterly direction.

It was along this trail over the bar, which was composed of gravel and sandy earth in which the wheel marks had been distinctly visible a week before, that the gypsies' motor van had traveled.

Where the trail ended in the brush, it had stood, concealed from the highway, and visible only from a point directly across the river. For reasons which shall be made clear almost directly, there was little chance of observation from the territory over the river.

In a small clearing the King of the Roms had built his supper-fire, and the heap of ashes still remained. Lakely, our policeman guide, pointed out the spot where the body had been found. It had lain on the bare earth, face upward, five feet south of the heap of ashes.

There was not so much as a pocket knife on his person; no money, and no letters or papers of any kind. Identification had, however, been easy, since Orlando Seton was not unknown in the district.

"The dagger," Lakely informed us, "was driven clear to the guard in the old man's left breast. Doubtless he died instantly. Probably stabbed in his sleep."

"About the missing van," I queried, "how do you know that it stood here? How did you determine the spot on which it is said to have rested?"

"Just here, north of the fire, its hood pointed eastward, the van undoubtedly stood," Lakely stated. "The wheel marks were slightly deeper here than anywhere else, and there was another means of determining its location.

"There was a leak in the differential-housing which permitted the oil to drip and form a small pool on the ground. The van, without doubt, stood for some time just where I have indicated."

"I merely wanted to satisfy myself that you fellows were

not just dreaming there had been a van here," I offered. "You see, it is hard to believe that a vehicle of any kind could cross the bar into the brush, just after a rain, and get out again without leaving unmistakable traces of the return trip.

"Certain, are you, that the thing wasn't backed out, its tires following the first impressions?"

Lakely grinned. "I'll give you my flivver, spare tire, motor-meter and all extras included, if you'll back it or any other car out of this place in the manner you suggest," he bantered.

"It couldn't be done, of course. However, an expert driver might have backed the car out, following the old tracks so closely as to deceive any but the most careful inspection. You made such an inspection, doubtless?"

"We didn't use a magnifying glass," Lakely returned sarcastically, "but we did use our eyes aplenty. No car returned from this clump of brush to the highway that night, unless it flew or was picked up and carried over. That's flat!"

"Thanks. I'll take your word for it, Lakely," I laughed. "It is, you will grant, impossible for the car to have climbed the bank on the east. The river barred it on the north and west.

"It is true that a daring driver might have forded the stream—it is shallow enough—but I would hate to tackle the job. Besides, where would he have gone, after the crossing? He would have found himself up against a solid wall of rock, unable to move ten feet from the river."

I pointed to the white hills of chat which covered the landscape in that direction for miles around. In the foreground the chat began to pile up beyond the river bank, rising in a slope to a broad peak perhaps seventy feet high. Beyond that first peak a second loomed, higher by fifty feet than the one in front.

Just northeast of the first mountain, with a sloping valley of loose chat between, a second heap of waste arose. It was higher even than the others, and was, in turn, overshadowed by other and higher cones beyond.

It was as though a thousand enormous tents had been pitched on a wide, elevated base, the sloping walls of each overlapping its neighbors, and those in the background towering higher and higher until they were lost in the mist of distance.

Waste from ancient mills, it was. Crushed rock which once imprisoned particles of ore, and, after the crusher had abstracted its value, was carried out by conveyors and piled mountain-high upon the ground.

"What lies over there in the valleys between those high cones?" I asked Lakely.

"Loose chat, and lakes of water. Some of them are as much as fifty feet in depth. Just what conditions are over there, though, may not be positively stated, for it would be as much as a man's life is worth to venture there.

"If nothing else got him, sliding chat would. Except on the long easy slopes, such as appears yonder on the first pile and which has been hardened in its place, having lain so long, the chat mountains are always changing.

"The noise of the avalanches are plainly to be heard at times. I wouldn't climb up the side of one of those ghostly heaps for all the money there is in Joplin! And we've got a mighty rich town here, at that!"

"All right" I agreed, "I won't ask you to—nor will I do

so myself. There could be no reason for it, since it is manifestly impossible for the motor van to have climbed those walls. What I want to know is this:

"Since the van did not return whence it came, and could not leave this spot in another direction—what then, in the name of Christopher Columbus, became of it?"

Lakely shrugged. "There's lots of people would pay handsomely for the correct answer to that question," he replied. "I'd give a month's wages to know the explanation myself!"

"You don't believe in ghosts, do you?" I demanded. "You don't believe in witches, fairies, goblins, and the like? Of course you don't. Well then, that car got out of here in a perfectly plausible manner. It wasn't wafted away by unseen and unseeable powers of witchcraft, nor was it a hybrid, partaking of the characters of motor car and airplane.

"It could not have flown. Yet it is gone. Any place big enough and free enough from obstructions to permit the passage of a motor van is big enough and plain enough for a man to follow—and that's what I intend to do.

"Discovery of the whereabouts of that car not only will answer the mystery of its disappearance, but it will, I have not the slightest doubt, clear up this case entirely. That motor van must be found!"

6

WHAT I FOUND

"YEAH," LAKELY AGREED. "I'd say the van is the key to the riddle. I'll add, Norton, that you've laid out a nice little job for yourself, when you go prowling for it. Every man the force could spare for the hunt has looked high and low for the thing—and all we drew was a blank. Maybe you'll have better luck. Who knows?"

I was only half hearing what the Joplin cop was saying, my eyes and my attention being fixed upon a number of stakes, or square timbers, which dotted the sides and the tops of the chat mountains at intervals, the upright ends barely visible above ground.

"What are those timbers?" I inquired, pointing them out.

"At various times each has served as a support for the 'out' end of a chat-carrier," Lakely explained. "Let us say that a mill stands where we now are. The ore rock is crushed into chat inside the mill, the mineral extracted.

"The refuse—the crushed rock—falls into the buckets of a carrier, the far end of which is secured to a stake over on yonder dump—only there is no dump of any appreciable size there at the moment, let us say. Gradually the chat builds itself into a mountain, another timber is set up, the

241

dump end of the carrier switched to its new location, and
the process of mountain-building repeated, over and over.
Do you get it now?"

I nodded. It was quite clear. The abandoned stakes were
not salvaged, since they were strongly seated in the earth
far below, spliced out in sections as needed, and firmly
imbedded in chat. Curiosity satisfied, I forgot the stakes.

The character of the soil lying between the spot where
the van had been and the river next interested me. I found
that it was not really soil, but rock, with just enough earth-
filled fissures and depressions to invite and sustain the
vegetation which clothed the place.

"About this Tannello Seton," I next put to Lakely. "How
does he stand in the community?"

"Good citizen, for all we know to the contrary. Expert
in his line—mine engineering. Been here a couple of years.
Lives well. Has an apartment at the Seymour, the swell-
est in town. Fine looking chap, and athletic along with it.
Baseball star, I understand, while at M.U. Rotten, his going
bad like he has, I say."

"Yeah. Get any trace of him, since he is supposed to have
left the city, the day previous to the murder?"

"None. He left the Seymour at nine o'clock on the morning before Orlando was found dead, carrying a suit case.
Never said where he was going, but told the clerk he would
be gone for some time—possibly two or three weeks. He
did not leave by train, we made certain, and his car is in
the garage where he usually kept it. That's all we know."

"Looks like it's about all you need to know," I
commented. "It only remains to dig him up, and put the
rope round his neck. Leaving his car behind looks bad,

taken in conjunction with the fact that he did not leave town by train. Looks like he had no intention of going away. Still hunting him?"

"Well, no," was the answer. "We'll pick him up, of course, if he shows here. But we are not wearing ourselves out chasing round after him. No need to. We couldn't convict him if we brought him to trial most likely. The gyps are a slick lot. Close-mouthed.

"But you can bet all you are worth, or ever hope to have, that Tannello Seton will answer for his crime. He'll answer before a court of his own people, in some secret and secluded spot, and be dealt with according to their notions of what constitutes retribution.

"The world ain't big enough for him to hide in, once the gyps take up his—now what the devil do they call it?"

"Patteran," I supplied wisely. "Yeah the gyps are great *patteraners,* you can lay to that! In the meantime, let's see what we have here."

I walked a few steps into the brush, stooped over and retrieved a soiled envelope which I had been eying for some time without giving it much thought until the moment. There was an inclosure, and I withdrew it. A single sheet of paper, typed on the business letterhead of a real estate dealer in Joplin, Vincent Shipp, by name.

"Here's something you sleuths overlooked," I remarked, watching Lakely's face struggling to dissemble a rueful expression. "This letter was evidently brought to the spot by Orlando Seton, since it is addressed to him at St. Louis. It is dated ten days prior to the king's arrival and subsequent death. I'll read it."

The letter was as follows:

Joplin, Mo., June 5, 1926.

Orlando, Seton, Esq.,

Box 840, Station X. St. Louis, Mo.:

My dear Sir—Your recent favor to hand, and I note with satisfaction that you have at last concluded to discuss the possible sale of your Renne's Mill property. In that you are wise, for I honestly believe the tract is now at the very peak of its value.

As I have already informed you on more than one occasion a development syndicate of this city has signified a strong desire to talk terms, looking to the immediate purchase of the entire acreage. The ground is ideal for its purpose—a suburban addition to Joplin which will provide attractive home sites and, at the same time, offer unusual recreational features. The time to sell, therefore, is *now!*

The date of your expected arrival, as given in your letter, is fortunately timed. You will arrive on the fourteenth, and on the evening of the fifteenth will occur the monthly meeting of the syndicate referred to herein. I shall, therefore, meet you at your camp beside the mill on the morning of the fifteenth. We will thresh this thing out, and, I hope, be prepared to submit a proposition to the interested parties without delay.

Trusting that nothing shall intervene to prevent your safe arrival on the 14th inst., I beg to remain,

Cordially yours,

VINCENT SHIPP

"Well," Lakely demanded, his face all smiles again, "what if we did overlook that thing? Let me tell you, every realtor in this city and the adjoining territory has been angling to get old Orlando's signature on a deed for the Renne's Mill property.

"It is badly wanted, not only by the syndicate mentioned in the letter, but by a lot of other capitalists. It's right in line with the city's growth, and is also convenient for cabin sites to catch the streams of summer tourists. Yeah, we overlooked it—but it don't mean a damned thing! Roll a corn shuck round that and smoke it, Norton, old-timer!"

"I'll chew on it instead," I retorted, placing the letter in my pocket. "Who is this Vincent Shipp?"

"A Joplin realtor, as the letterhead states. Offices in the National Bank Building—also set forth in the heading," Lakely answered, grinning. "Want to call on him?"

"Maybe. Been here long?"

"Oh, ten years or such matter. Handles only the biggest kind of deals. Rich. Finest chap you ever met. Scion of the Southern aristocracy, said aristocracy having had its habitat in the dear, dead days, in and around the Crescent City, down in Louisiana.

"Mixture of French and Spanish— Creole, I believe they term it—and proud as Lucifer, and all the little Lucifers. That's about all I can tell you."

Lakely was becoming facetious, but that troubled me not. Instinct informed me that my nose was at least sniffing at the beginning of the little queen's *patteran*.

Important or not, the letter gave me something to work on—and that was precisely what I wanted.

"Has the blue blood figured in your inquiries up to date?" I asked.

"Nope."

"Kind of strange, don't you think, that he should fail to

come forward with his bit, seeing that he expected to meet the old chap at his camp the morning his body was found?"

"Say, Norton, what are you trying to get at?" Lakely demanded. "Why, man, if all the realtors who wrote letters from this place to Orlando had reported at headquarters and made their little spiels, virtually half the able-bodied males in that business would have been represented!

"Since the boom they are thick as fleas—almost as hard to enumerate as it would be to check up on Old Man Carter to determine how many oats he had! You are sleuthing in the wrong direction, if you go after that Vincent bird! Take it from me!"

"I have one more question to ask you, Lakely," I said.

"Shoot it, old-timer!" Lakely commanded, suppressing his hilarity to a minimum of effervescence.

"Can you find your way back to the city—alone?"

7

I EXPLORE THE MILL

LAKELY, REALLY NOT a bad chap, bowed with mock deference and retired to the runabout, where he sat eating peanuts which he left us long enough to purchase at a quaint little roadside store on the east bank of the river, a square-built house of native stone, where wares calculated to catch the eyes of tourists were displayed.

I could get Lakely's view of things with ease. Should I, a private detective from out of town, succeed where the Joplin men had failed—oh, what a plucking of feathers there would be! I knew my old buddy, the chief, well enough to picture the scene at headquarters in such an eventuality. Yes, I could see Lakely's side of it—without the aid of glasses.

Ever try to work with somebody standing by, good-humoredly ridiculing your best efforts? It isn't conducive to effective labor, brain or hand, and I was glad enough to be rid of the Joplin cop.

Steele, who had been nosing about the vicinity of the mill, much like a bird-dog in a sago field, was sitting on a ledge of rock beside the river when I joined him.

"I know, now, why the gyps call it the place of red water—in their outlandish lingo," he said, pointing down.

"Contaminated from washing soil impregnated with zinc. That's what colors the water, and makes it look like it might have its source in some gigantic slaughterhouse."

"Interesting, Jim," I remarked sarcastically. "But—has it taken you all this time to dope that?"

"Not exactly," Jim replied, no whit disturbed. "There's a tunnel through the masonry on which the mill stands—a big one. A waterway, I judge, through which the stream was conducted over the wheel. The bed of the river, however, has shifted during recent years, and the tunnel is above the flow, except, possibly when the flood season is on. I poked into it, found only a lot of waste left there when last the stream flowed through, then came out."

"Well, what of it?"

"Nothing—only, since the tunnel is large enough for you to walk through without requiring any tiresome effort, you might give it the once over. We are hunting for a vanished van, remember—and a tunnel so close to the spot where said van was last known to be is rather suggestive."

"I follow you," was my answer. There might be something in what Jim hinted at.

On Steele's heels, I made my way to the entrance of the tunnel—a burrow formed by arching the stone of the mill's foundation so as to leave a passage nearly six feet high by three feet wide clear through the groundwork from north to south. At the south end, remains of the crib and wheel could be seen.

We spent an hour inside, going over every inch of that tunnel, sounding the walls and hunting for loose stones, and finding nothing of the sort. Of course, no motor van could have been driven into such narrow confines, but, as Steele had said, one tunnel suggested another.

The car was not inside the mill—where it could have been driven, seeing that the elevated runway up to the wide, double doors on the east was substantial enough to have supported it.

Might it not be beneath the mill? Concealed within a space in one or the other halves of the foundation—granting that the stonework was not solid, as it had every appearance of being, and that a secret room of such character existed.

Far-fetched? Surely. But then, bear in mind, a motor van had vanished utterly. It was somewhere, and, it stood to reason, not far away. We had to consider every possibility—since there was an utter lack of probabilities—no matter how silly they appeared to be.

In respect to our exploration beneath the mill, I grant that it was time lost. We found nothing enlightening there.

"Any use going through the old buzzard-roost?" Jim queried, when we had withdrawn to the bank again.

"It won't do any harm," I opined. "It has been combed from foundation to rooftop, I know. But we haven't had a look yet. Come on."

We entered by way of a door from which the barricading timbers had been removed, and found ourselves on the first floor of the mill. It was covered with a thick film of dust, and the hewn timbers of its framework, as well as the walls, were draped in thick sheaths of cobwebs.

Bits of old belting, broken machinery and other debris, littered the place. Footprints were everywhere, which was to be expected, since the Joplin police force had been over the place.

Each floor resembled the other, with scarcely any variations. Rickety stairways enabled us to climb, and finally we stood beneath the roof.

"You didn't expect to find anything here, did you?" Jim queried.

"No," I replied. "But," I went on, crossing the moldy floor to a window which looked out to the north, "the view from here is worth the exertion."

Beneath me, across the river and unfolding as far as my eyes could see, lay the most desolate tract of country it had ever been my lot to view. Chat. An ocean of chat. Imagine several thousand large, grayish tarpaulins, sewed together and spread over a grove of trees of varying heights, covering a plot of ground three miles square, the gigantic blanket sagging in the spaces between the trees, and many of those low spots transformed into lakes by the summer rains. Not a spear of grass, a shrub—anything, save a sea of chat!

Nothing, that is, except those interminable rows of black, weather-stained timbers already noted, thrusting gauntly up in strong relief against a ghostly background.

The place gave me the shivers—yet it fascinated me.

"Nothing could live over there," I found myself thinking. "Not even birds and animals. To venture the dangers of the spot would be the height of madness—suicide, in fact. Damn such a place, anyhow!"

Deeply, unreasonably irritated, I was in the act of turning away, when I caught sight of something fluttering in the wind which, I had been told, seemed ever to harrow the waste. It gave me a start, seeing something with movement suggesting life in that awful stretch of barrenness.

In another moment I was moving from the window in deep disgust. What I had seen was only a length of cable, or rope, dangling from one of the distant timbers, shaken to and fro in the wind. Further inspection disclosed other bits of rope on other timbers. Parts of the rigging-ropes which had long ago held the chat-carriers in place, I knew.

"Let's leave this dismal roost for bats and owls!" Jim exclaimed, dodging frantically to avoid the swoop of a horned-owl which, disturbed by our presence, appeared most resentful. "Damn the view!"

"Yeah!" I echoed. "Damn the view! If ever absolute desolation lay under mortal eyes, it does from yonder window. B-b-b-r-r-r-r!"

The warm sunlight was most welcome when we stood outside again.

8

BLACK ICE

IN THE AFTERNOON, while Jim took in the sights of the city, an elevator deposited me on the fifth floor of the Joplin National Bank Building, whence it was no trick at all to find the handsome suite occupied by Vincent Shipp, realtor.

Finding Mr. Shipp, however, was not so easy.

"Mr. Shipp is in," I was informed by a businesslike young woman in the reception room, "but he is in conference, and can see no one—unless," she hesitated, then went on, "you have most urgent business."

"I have," I told her. "Tell him I came to confer with him about the Renne's Mill property."

Mr. Shipp was deeply in conference with himself, as I learned two minutes later. At least there was no one else in the room when the young woman ushered me in.

He was, in some ways, a strikingly handsome man. Just under six feet in height, he was admirably proportioned—very slightly inclined toward thinness. His hands and feet were small—betraying, according to the Hoyle of the blue-bloods, patrician breeding.

His head might have been considered a trifle larger than heads need be, by some experts. Leonine, I'd say. Hair a blue-black, untouched by gray, although the dark, smooth-shaved face was that of a man at least forty years old.

Is there such a thing as black ice that is clear and sparkling—and cold below the point of any thermometer's gauging? I don't know whether there is or not, but such is the impression I received when Shipp's eyes were raised to mine, on a dead level, after I had quietly told him my name, occupation, and present mission. Black, glittering ice.

I had a very good reason for telling him just who and what I was. I wanted to see how he would react. I saw.

"May I ask," he said, after we had stared at each other for a full moment, "why you have seen fit to pay me a call?"

"You may," I told him. "But it is unnecessary. I shall tell you exactly why I am here."

"Ah! I am greatly interested, and shall be obliged—"

"Pass that!" I interjected. "When did you last receive a letter from Orlando Seton?"

He gave me a cold stare. "Is it at all certain that I ever received a communication from such a source?" he asked.

"Absolutely certain. If you do not choose to reply to my first question, perhaps you will to this: When did you last write to him?"

"Norton—er—I believe that is the name, is it not? Well, Norton, just why are you nosing into private business affairs of mine—affairs which cannot possibly be of use to you in clearing up this case?"

"Why do you beat about the bush, when you are asked to lend your aid in tracking down a murderer? Do you think that is acting the part of a good citizen? Have you something to hide, or is your present attitude just your snobbish way of resenting what you no doubt tell yourself is an unwarranted intrusion?"

Shipp's dark face turned an angry red, and he half rose from his chair. I motioned him back.

"You did write to Orlando Seton," I accused sternly. "I have your own words, over your own signature, to prove it. You did receive letters from him—several. Now, tell me this: Why did you not inform the police about your appointment with Seton, to meet him at his camp—the camp which proved to be the last he will ever make on this earth?

"Why, when the authorities were digging everywhere for information which might lead to a clue, did you keep silent? Perhaps you will answer that?"

Shipp's handsome face suddenly became grave. "Is it so serious as all that?" he asked, his tone considerably less caustic. "Frankly," he went on, "when I heard of Seton's death—which news reached me shortly after breakfast that morning—I knew that my cake was all dough. No hope of handling the Renne's Mill property then.

"Now, Mr. Norton, I am a very busy man, and I did not want to be vexed with a long and tedious conference with the police—perhaps more than one. Had I possessed knowledge of the least bit of value to them I should have gone before the police without delay. But I knew nothing which could throw the least bit of light upon the matter.

"Therefore, I considered I was within my rights, and said nothing. In fact, I dismissed Seton from my mind, along with the Renne's Mill project, which died with him."

I nodded. "Permit me to say, Mr. Shipp, that your explanation is plausible, defining an attitude which is not unnatural under the circumstances. Do you know a man named Tannello Seton?"

"Oh, yes," he replied. "Seton is quite a figure in the mining life of Joplin and the district. Do you, like our police, hold that young Seton is a party to this crime?"

"I haven't gone far enough to form an opinion concerning him," I replied. "His seeming flight looks bad—but it may not have been a flight. He may turn up any time now, and with an iron-clad alibi. By the way, Mr. Shipp," I requested, rising, "may I have a glance through your letter-file—the current 'S'?

"It may be that in some of Seton's correspondence there is a thread which, followed out, will lead to something. By your leave?"

I stepped quickly to a cabinet which occupied one corner of the room, abstracted the "S" drawer and placed it on the desk. Shipp's face was a picture of fury—fury which he strove to mask, with indifferent success.

"I—my girl is new," he informed me in words which seemed to hurt him. "She may or may not have filed the letters from Seton in their proper place. She is very careless!"

I closed the file and returned it to its place. Then I faced the realtor, standing.

"You are clairvoyant this afternoon," I said. "The Seton letters are not in their appointed space—just as you felt sure they would not be. Talent, such as you have just displayed, has raised men to high and enviable places in this old world—and yours may so elevate you.

"Good afternoon, Mr. Shipp—and don't be too hard on that girl of yours! Really, she may not, after all, be to blame!"

Yes, I closed the door behind me as I passed out.

9

MYSTERIOUS LIGHTS

I LOST NO time getting in touch with Steele.

"Got a nursing job for you, Jim," I told him.

"Shipp?"

"Yeah. Put him to bed at night; and take him up in the morning. You'll need a local man to do the fine stuff—I'll arrange that with the chief—since you are not wise to the town. But you stick close around in order to tip me off if anything turns up."

"Got something on him?"

"No. He's under cover with valuable information, or I'm badly off. Just watch him, see that he doesn't duck out, and keep tabs on where he goes and what he does from now on."

"Right!"

Leaving Jim and Lakely, the latter assigned to duty in my behalf, on the job that night, I set out in a motor car alone, heading toward Renne's Mill. I did not mean to stop at the mill, since my destination lay two miles farther on.

To be specific, I was about to pay a visit to the Lorels, who, in company with a band of their people, were encamped at a spring in a grove near the highway.

True to their constant habit, they were dwelling in tents,

rather than in the hotels of the city—which they could easily have afforded to do. That's the gypsy, though, all over.

I wanted to see the Lorels, and for several reasons. Chiefly, however, I desired to know if by any chance they might have had some contact with Vincent Shipp.

I knew, or thought I knew, why none of Seton's letters appeared in Shipp's files. My explanation, offered to myself only, involved the realtor in the crime, clear over his head. It might or might not be correct.

Shipp, having prior knowledge, whether as principal or merely an accessory, of the fate awaiting Orlando there beside the mill, had destroyed all correspondence in his office from the gypsy king.

He had little, if any, fear that the old man would keep letters sent to him. His roving habits precluded not even a pretense at preserving such things, save only in cases of very important papers.

Shipp had only to destroy Orlando's letters to him, and thus get rid of any visible connection between himself and the gypsy. It was, needless to say, highly desirable that no one should suspect that he and Orlando were acquainted.

Orlando had kept a letter from Shipp, though. Probably he had received it just before setting out on his journey, and had thrust it into a pocket for closer perusal. Whatever caused him to retain the letter, the point is that he did.

Somebody robbed the body of the king, and the letter may have been discarded or accidentally dropped on the scene of the crime. Had Shipp—granting my theory proved correct—foreseen that a letter from him to Orlando would turn up, you can bet those missing letters would not have been missing.

They would have been in his file—right where they should be. Furthermore, he would have gone before the police without loss of time.

So much for Shipp. I'd know a lot more about him soon. Of that I was persuaded.

The Romany encampment was in a grove a quarter of a mile north of the highway, and two miles east of the mill. I crossed the bridge over Shoal River and drew up in front of the roadside store where Lakely had bought the peanuts that morning. Gas was needed, and I honked my horn.

A woman came out in answer to my summons—an old, white-haired woman. She wore clothing, rings and hair ornaments which caught my attention and held it. Her appearance was wild, barbaric, glitteringly splendid. The extravagant splendor characteristic of the gypsy.

"Gas, sir?" she inquired, and if her attire, and color, had not already identified her race in my mind, her voice would have. A certain soft slurring of words, a laziness of tone, noticeable in persons born in the southern part of the United States, and very pronouncedly evident in the speech of a Rom.

"Yes," I replied.

"There is a large encampment of your people to the west about two miles, is there not?" I asked, watching her as well as I could in the dim light of the store front.

The old woman was bending over the gas tank at the rear of the car, nor did she change her position until she had raised the hose and drained the last particle of gas out of it. Replacing the hose then, she informed me that I owed her one dollar and fifteen cents.

I paid it. "About that encampment of your people—" I began.

"Sir, I have no people," the old woman interrupted. "Do you wish for anything else?"

Dignity? More, I thought, than the occasion called for.

I departed—or rather started to do so. The driveway leading from the slab road to the store was in the shape of a half circle, passing under a portico, thence to the slab again.

As I made the turn and approached the road I had the mill on my right, and when my front tires were just onto the edge of the slab I clamped my brake down hard.

For an instant only, one of the windows on the third floor of the old mill had stood outlined in a yellow glow which faded before I had time in which to make certain that the light was not just a reflection of the lamps of a car which was approaching from the east. It might have been.

I felt my nerves jump just a trifle, an instant later, and before my watch had time to tick again I had wheeled my car westward and was driving back toward the mill. Fifty feet from it I drove off the slab and parked in the brush.

Another flash had shone briefly behind a window of the mill—this time on the first floor. And, even while I looked at it, the window on the third floor, which had first caught my attention, sprang again into yellow relief.

"Two persons, at least!" I thought, as I ran swiftly through the darkness toward the unlocked door of the place. "Hunting about up there, with flash lights! Shipp?"

It flashed into my mind that the realtor was probably one of those persons. The next instant I dismissed him as a possibility. Steele and Lakely were watching him, and had he come to the mill one or both the shadows would have been in evidence.

But—maybe they were! Perhaps the flash of light on the lower floor was from a torch in the hands of Steele or Lakely!

Maybe so—but when I crept inside that dark lower room I carried my flash light in my left hand, and my right was prepared to deal sudden death to anybody who invited it!

10

PISTOL SHOTS—AND A CRASH

I STOOD IN the inky darkness, scarcely breathing, listening intently. Not a sound broke the black silence of the old ruin.

Yet human beings were there. I could not have been mistaken. Should I flood the room with light, discovering the prowler and forcing him into action, or wait for him to make the next move?

I decided to wait. My entrance had been silently made, and I believed my presence unknown.

A board in the warped and broken floor of the room above me creaked sharply—then all was still again. The man who had been on the first floor, and whose light I had seen, had now mounted to the second, was my conclusion. Was he following some one who had preceded him into the mill? He whose flash had illumined the window at the top of the building?

Steele and Lakely, tracking Shipp?

There was no way in which I could settle that question. Nothing to do save await developments.

They were not long in materializing.

A shaft of light suddenly shot down the stairway into the room where I stood, missing the top steps and flooding the bottom ones with silver. Evidently its source was not in the room directly above, but must have come from a flash held at the top of the stairs on the third floor.

In the shadowed area near the head of the stairs, left so by the overshooting shaft of light, something moved. I caught it only dimly. Then came a terrific explosion, the old ruin seemed to tremble and rock on its foundations, and the shaft of light suddenly concentrated upon the steps at the top of the stairs.

B-o-o-o-m-m-m!

A sheet of flame burst upward from the stairhead, and again the old mill shook. What had, an instant before, been but a shadowy shape, stood revealed into the form of a man—a man with a smoking pistol in his hand.

The instant that second shot sounded the place was plunged into impenetrable blackness. I heard the man on the stairway descending swiftly—then, with a crash which dwarfed into nothingness, anything that had gone before, the stairway collapsed, piling its wreckage on the floor below.

I leaped backward, snapped on my current and flooded the place with light.

Pinned down by a mass of broken boards and scantlings, squirming in an effort to retrieve his revolver, which lay just too far away from him to reach, was the black-clothed form of a man.

It was neither Steele, Lakely nor Shipp.

Bardo Lorel was the man who struggled under the wreckage on the floor!

"I'd be sorry to do it, Bardo," I called, "but if you do

succeed in reaching that gun I'll drill a hole through your head!"

Bardo's eyes, two huge black pools of ferocity a moment before, closed abruptly at sound of my voice, and his jaws clamped rigidly. Then:

"Mr. Norton, *rye*," his voice came quietly, a note of pain in it, "I'd be pleased to have you lift this thing off my legs. I fear I am much broken!"

"Who is the man on the other floor?" I demanded, making no move to relieve him. "The chap you were chasing—shooting at?"

"I'm coming down to answer that!"

The words came from the black opening above, where the top of the stairway had been—and I snapped off my light instantly.

"No! No!" came the voice from above, in protest. "Light up again, so I can see to drop! You can cover me with your gun—but there is no need! I mean no harm to any one who means no harm to me!"

I took a chance, and the next instant a tall, dark, athletic young man dropped lightly to the floor from above, his black eyes blinking in the full flood of my flash light.

"You are a new one on me!" I told him, after a swift inspection. "A Rom, though, I'll bet my shield. Name?"

"Tannello Seton," he replied, bowing slightly—self-possession sticking out all over him. "And you are, I presume, Mr. Tug Norton, the detective from Kansas City?"

"Well," I almost shouted, when I got back my wind after that jolt, "I'll be damned!"

It was all I could think of at the moment.

11

A PAIR OF KINGS

Bardo Lord's voice had cast out its erstwhile plaintiveness, and become imperative.

"I'm still here, Bardo," I told him. "What's your trouble?"

"Please to rescue me! Have I not said that my legs appear to be much broken?"

"Quite so, Bardo. We shall attend to you directly!"

I spoke to Tannello.

"I'm giving this to you straight," I said, my eyes just as steady as his own, which stared straight at me without the slightest shadow of uneasiness in them. "I'm on strange ground, and among strange people—but I reckon this old howitzer of mine is just as capable of sending a gypsy down the last, long *patteran,* as it is the ordinary type of crook. I'm telling you this, and it's for your own good.

"Now," I went on, "lift that wreck off Bardo, and find out just how badly he is hurt—after first dropping your hardware on the floor where I can get it!"

I already had Lorel's lost gun in my possession, and meant to take no chances on Tannello.

"I am unarmed, Mr. Norton," the handsome Rom

assured me. "Bardo, there, shot fairly well. Well enough to knock the thing out of my hand—and give me this."

He held his right hand where the light shone full upon it. His index finger was only a bloody stump!

I've known crooks to break down completely because of a mere scratch from a bullet. But this chap, half of whose index finger had been shot off, never so much as batted an eye, or in any way betrayed that he was in pain!

"You've got guts, Tannello!" I said admiringly. "When Bardo has been attended to I'll do something for that hand!"

"Thank you, Mr. Norton. It is nothing."

He turned toward where Bardo lay—to be greeted with a flow of words, in pure *kalo ratt,* that had the sound of bullets hot from a machine gun.

I gathered, from the heat and noise of the explosion, that Bardo much preferred to lie there forever rather than be touched by Tannello Seton's vile hands. Tannello, himself, corroborated my thought.

"He prefers that you relieve him," he said quietly, facing me.

I strode a step or two forward, and gave Bardo the benefit of the full glare of my flash. "Look here," I said harshly, "I'm running this show—and you, for the present at least, are just one of the animals.

"I have just had a vision—a vision of that carpet you spoke of in my office, as it disappeared in the far horizon. But I don't give a damn about that. I'm going to treat you just as though I wasn't carrying your money in my pocket right now.

"Until you show up before me in a lot more favorable

role than that you are in at the moment, I'm running on my own! Get that? Well, that's good!

"Seton," I ordered, "untangle this bird, and find out what is wrong with him!"

Bardo suffered in silence the degrading touch of his kinsman's hands—though his black eyes glared murderously all the while.

"I am sorry, Bardo," Tannello told him, a moment or so after he had been withdrawn from beneath the stairs, "but you'll have to do with just a few minor bruises. Not even a tiny fracture. The weight on your legs had the effect of temporarily paralyzing them. You'll be all right as soon as circulation is free again."

"I also am sorry, Tannello!" Bardo spat. "Sorry it is your finger rather than one of your eyes, my bullet hit!"

"Cut it!" I snapped. "Those little pleasantries you fellows are exchanging can be saved till some future date! Maybe they'll help to pass the time for you when you are loafing in jail.

"At the present moment, I've got some questions to ask—and both of you have some tall explaining to do. Sit down on one of those busted stair-treads, Lorel, and you, Seton, sit on another—and not too close together!"

I was instantly obeyed. Bardo, strange to say, seemed to have no anger toward me: perhaps he had so much for Tannello there was not room for any more. At any rate, he sat down, and did so with good grace.

Tannello—well, I don't believe anything could disturb him greatly. Even his feeling toward his kinsman struck me as being a mixture of vexation and ridicule. I don't think he hated the chap at all. He sat down as directed, and lit a cigarette from a package he took from a pocket of his coat.

"Where have you been, Seton, the past two weeks?" was my first question.

"Boston," was the answer.

"What made you sneak away from Joplin?"

"I didn't. I know that such a construction was placed upon my departure by the police. The papers informed me of that. It is not correct, however."

"Explain," I directed.

There was a moment of silence while Tannello considered the grim and scowling face of his kinsman. Then, directing his fine eyes toward me again, he spoke:

"Since you, Mr. Norton, have been employed in this case by the Lorels," he said, "you are doubtless in possession of all the details which they could furnish you. I have no hesitancy, therefore, in touching a subject of rare delicacy.

"Zelena Lorel—Seton, now—was coming to Joplin with her husband, my uncle. Coming on her wedding journey. I loved Zelena Lorel then, and I love her now. Love her with a depth and heat of passion none save a Rom may know.

"I left Joplin the day before she was to arrive, and I left because I could not bear to be that near her—since she was never to be mine. Also, I could not trust myself.

"It seemed like my tortured brain was on the verge of betraying me into acts of madness such as are possible only to one insane with disappointment—frustrated love. So, Mr. Norton, I left the city."

I nodded. "Sounds reasonable," I said. "But why sneak away?"

"I did not. I planned to leave on the Kansas City Southern's morning train, rather than drive my car that long distance alone. When, after reaching the depot, I learned that the train was reported five hours late, I went by bus to Springfield, and began my journey from there, over the Frisco Lines."

"Right in the center of the plausibility target again," I commented. Tannello was either a mighty smooth article, or else innocent of evil. I didn't know which. "When did you get back, and what brought you?"

"I returned in a fast car, which I bought directly after at Boston. Sunday paper informed me, through a feature story, of what had happened here. I came without regard to speed laws, or the rights of fellow motorists—driven by my desire to reach the spot and find what had become of Zelena.

"I reached the outskirts of Joplin just before day this morning, put my car in a garage where I am unknown, and hid in the woods of the island below the bridge—you know the place, perhaps—until tonight.

"Then I started out in an attempt to learn the fate of the woman I love—though it may be the will of fate that I have lost her."

Darned if I didn't feel sorry for Tannello. I haven't had much experience in that sort of thing, but I could well imagine that a chap would get one whale of a kick out of such a love as his, even if he did lose the girl in the end. Tannello sounded true. I couldn't get around it.

Neither could I forget this:

He was next in line for the Romany crown. He had only to go back to his people with clean hands—or with the dirt on them fairly well covered up—to be acknowledged as their sovereign. At least, that is the way I had it doped out.

So, if Zelena was in a deal with him, and should reappear at a later date, claiming that she had been abducted and all that sort of thing, what was to hinder the pair from living happily ever after, and kinging and queening it around to their heart's content?

No. I didn't forget that.

"Didn't expect to find the little queen up here in the mill, did you?" was the next question I put.

"No," Tannello answered. "I entered the mill for a very good reason, though. I saw Bardo coming along the road from the bridge, and I went inside in order to avoid him."

"I see. But Bardo proved to be unavoidable. Now, Lorel," I commanded, turning on him, "your side of it! What were you prowling around here for?"

"The mill, and its immediate surroundings, has been watched closely ever since the crime was committed," was the quiet answer. Bardo seemed to have got control of himself. "Sometimes I have watched. Sometimes another—Danjefo. To-night it was my turn."

"What was your purpose? What did you expect to find?"

Bardo merely pointed—pointed toward Tannello.

"Ah, I see! You expected Cousin Tannello on the scene!"

"And he came—did he not?"

"You saw Tannello enter the mill, and followed him?"

"Yes."

"Why did you shoot at Bardo?" I asked Seton.

"I didn't," he denied. "I shot above him, intending it as a warning not to come higher."

"I didn't have any such friendly thought in my mind when I shot at you!" Bardo blazed. "I wanted—"

"Never mind what you wanted!" I broke in. "Answer a question! From what place have you been watching the mill?"

Bardo gave me a steady look from his smoldering eyes. "I shall not answer that," he said.

"I'll tell you where then," I retorted. "You've been hiding out in the little store where I got gas to-night—the Rom store. Going to deny it?"

He neither affirmed nor denied. He merely looked at me steadily, and said nothing.

"Who gets the kingship, now that Orlando has checked out?" I then asked.

"I have been called an apostate gypsy," Tannello stated in seeming irrelevancy. "And those who have applied that term to me may or may not believe it. I am, however, as much a Rom as I have ever been—as good a one as any in whom the blood of Romany flows.

"I left my people because of a deep wound in the heart which would not cease to burn and bleed. For that I am called an apostate!"

He arose suddenly—and I'd like, right now, to own a picture of him as he stood there in the light of my flash, his delicate nostrils distended, his fine face aglow with strong feeling. His voice rang when next he spoke:

"I am no apostate! I am a Rom! The King of the Roms!"

By the eternal, I could well believe it! He surely looked a king—every inch of him!

"What about Zelena?" I asked a bit later, and after Tannello, his emotion subsiding or else under strong restraint, resumed his seat. "What about her queenship, should she return?"

"America is ruled by man," Tannello answered. "So also is Romany. Zelena is queen now, if alive, but she would exercise her sovereign right only until a king could be crowned."

"So. Now, Tannello, in the event you should see fit to pass up the king business, who is next in line?"

Tannello was silent, seeming to give way to some one else.

"Who? Answer!" I commanded.

"He is here," Tannello replied quietly. "Why does he not speak for himself?"

Bardo!

"Preparations are even now being made for the ceremony of my crowning," came the soft, even voice of Bardo Lorel. "I shall, within a very short time, be acknowledged King of the Roms!"

12

I LOSE A MAN—AND GAIN ONE

STUNNED?

Yes—somewhat!

But I did not reach over and snap the cuffs on Bardo's wrists. For one thing, I disliked the thought of treating royalty in such a manner. For another, and much weightier reason, he had committed no crime that I could prove, even had I suspected him. Then, too, this stood in the way:

Bardo Lorel was Zelena's brother. I couldn't get around that. He certainly was not, to my mind, the type of man who would slay the husband of his own sister, and the sister also, in order to win a crown, or anything else.

There was, however, real food for thought in the disclosure that had just been made. Bardo loomed large as a possible chief actor in the drama.

Tannello. Zelena. Shipp. Bardo.

Tannello, Zelena and Shipp might be together in the thing, or Bardo, Zelena and Shipp might be working in cahoots.

And, finally, any one of the four might be working singly.

"How did you happen to recognize me so easily?" I asked Tannello, recalling the circumstance of his knowing me right off the reel.

"Perhaps you have not seen the evening paper?"

"Hadn't time to look at it."

"There's a front page news story about your arrival in Joplin, seeking to solve the mystery of Orlando Seton's murder," Tannello went on to say. "I ventured, after dark, to get a copy of the paper. Bardo called your name, after he tumbled with the stairway, and there you have your answer."

I had—and I was boiling hot! I could, I felt sure, account for the leak which resulted in that news item. We'll call it a manifestation of professional jealousy—and let it go at that.

After all, a bit of advertising was not likely to work any hardship on me.

"I've got to do something with you two fellows," I told the Roms. "If you, Tannello, show up in the city you will be promptly jugged. I don't want that to happen—at least, not yet. Bardo, I'm going to ask you to go to your encampment and stay there. At any rate, don't come prowling about the mill again.

"I'm frank to say that since you have been revealed as a potential king of Romany, you are just as much under suspicion as Tannello is. A motive is quite clearly defined. At that, I don't seem able to view you in the light of a murderer. If I could I would pinch you right now.

"Go home, then, and I will communicate with you at the earliest moment there is anything to say. Have I made myself clear? And have I your word to obey?"

Bardo arose. "Mr. Norton," he said, "I do not blame you for your change in attitude toward me—wrong though it is. I shall still consider myself bound to deliver that—er—

carpet, should you fulfill your part of the contract. I begin to think you will.

"As for Tannello Seton, I shall settle matters with him later—when there is no one present to protect him. He need have no fear that I will inform the *gorgio* officers of his return.

"In Romany, as he well knows, men do not leave such things to outsiders—they settle them, man to man. Good evening, Mr. Norton. I shall return to my *tan,* where I will be available to you from this time on."

He bowed with simple dignity, and departed without so much as a glance toward Tannello.

"A queer bird, that," I remarked to the latter, when Bardo had vanished into the night. "Tell me, do you believe him capable of such an act of atrocity as the murder of his brother-in-law, and the forced expulsion of his sister from the country—possibly her death, also?"

Tannello shook his head in an emphatic negative. "Dismiss all such suspicion from your mind," he replied. "Bardo had no hand in the crime. He couldn't have done it.

"Our rather strained relations arise out of the fact that he was chiefly instrumental in arranging the marriage of his sister to the king, and his harboring the thought that I am guilty of murdering Orlando and carrying off Zelena.

"I could almost find it in my heart to hate him for that— if I had not a real affection for the fellow."

"Mighty white of you, Seton—alibiing for a man who has just tried to kill you, and who hopes to usurp your place in Romany."

"Bardo believes he should be king," the Rom returned. "He believes me to be unfit, and he is next in line. He may have it—perhaps. I cannot say just now what I shall do in the matter. It depends largely upon whether I ever find Zelena—alive."

I said nothing to that, not wishing to get on the subject of Zelena's possible aliveness just yet. Instead, I asked:

"Can you prove your whereabouts, the night of the killing?"

"Without the slightest difficulty," was the prompt answer. "I was at the Great Northern Hotel, in Chicago—and that settles the question of an alibi."

"Why hide out in the woods then?"

"I wanted my liberty to-night," he told me. "I had the perhaps foolish thought that my eyes—the eyes of love—might succeed in following a *patteran* other eyes would be unable to see. That is why."

That chap was measuring up to the full stature of a king, in every act and word, since the ruckus in the mill began. My idea of one, at any rate.

I'm not one of those all-wise hombres who never makes a mistake in judging a man: who is able to look once at the cut of a stranger's jib and decide on the instant whether he's sound or not.

I'll admit that I have made a few mistakes in judging character, and that more than one of those mistakes cost me dear. But I was satisfied that Tannello Seton's hands were clean.

Maybe I was making another mistake in reading character, right then and there, but I took a chance on being right.

"Tannello," I said, "I have a feeling that you and I ought to join forces from now on. How do you react to that?"

"I decided on that, half an hour ago!" declared the Rom

with the friendliest grin imaginable. "What's the first job we tackle?"

Before I could answer that a police whistle broke the night-time silence of the out-of-doors, and, shutting off my light, I stepped outside.

"Hello!" came a hail from the roadway in the well known tones of my old buddy, the chief. "That's you over there, Tug?"

"Yeah!" I answered, hastening toward where he sat in his car.

"Saw a light, and figured it was you prowling around when you ought to be sleeping!" he said, as I approached.

"What's wanted?"

"Oh, nothing, I guess—only you and I each have a man in the hospital, and I thought you'd like to know."

"The devil!" I cried. "Steele?"

"Yeah. Steele and Lakely. The one with a fractured knee, and the other with a broken arm—to say nothing of scratches and bruises too numerous to mention!"

"How did it happen?" I demanded.

"A motor car came right up on the walk, then went on its way again—leaving Steele and Lakely squirming on the concrete like two worms on a hot griddle.

"Now don't ask me anything more, because that's all I know—only, I'll add, Steele says the man who drove up and got them was a gyp. A middle-aged one, with a scar across his cheek, and eyes that would make a mad rattler's seem dim!"

"Good night, chief," I bade him hastily. "Thanks for coming out. Promises to be a fine night to-night—don't you think? Don't hurry—but come again when you have longer to stay!" I yelled after his departing car.

Then I hurried back to the mill.

13

TRYING THE IMPOSSIBLE

THE EVENTS TAKING place in the mill had consumed a good bit of time, and it was nearing twelve o'clock when I dropped Tannello at a small hotel on the outskirts of Joplin. He would spend the night there, registering under an assumed name, and I would pick him up again about daylight the following morning.

When I parked in front of the City Hospital, a few minutes later, I could smell the rubber in my tires burning. I got immediate admittance to Steele's room, and found him suffering considerable pain from the fracture. The game chap had refused all narcotics, in order to keep his senses alert pending my arrival.

"Tug," he greeted, "you are right—Shipp is queer. Lakely and I trailed him from his office to his apartment, thence to a downtown café, where he dined. Next, he spent an hour at his club—The Ozark—and from there he sauntered leisurely along Fourth Street, turned north on Main and made his way toward the Kansas City Southern depot.

"On North Main the buildings are somewhat scattered, and the sidewalks were comparatively free of pedestrians. We dropped well back, and strolled along after him.

"Then it happened. A big touring car, coming from the

north and at a slow speed, suddenly sped up, swerved over the curb and onto the walk. So quickly and unexpectedly did it happen, Lakely and I had no time to dodge. The car got us, swerved back into the street and went on.

"I had a fair look at the face of the driver. He was a Rom, if I know the breed when I see it. Middle-aged, with a scar on his left cheek—very noticeable, and extending, as near as I remember, straight across the cheek from near the lobe of his ear to the corner of his mouth.

"Now, do you see the fine Creolish hand of Shipp in the thing, or don't you?"

"Yes. He dropped to you and Lakely, and tolled you off down North Main, after arranging the motor car stunt over the phone from his club. That's the way it looks. If so, then Shipp is mighty anxious to go somewhere, and decidedly did not want you chaps tagging along.

"I purposely threw a scare into him yesterday," I went on. "You have hunted quail, Jim. I used the same tactics a quail-hunter employs. Satisfied that Shipp was hiding in the tall grass, I made a noise calculated to flush him. If he failed to 'flush,' it would be a mighty hard chore, getting him in the grass.

"But, quail-like, he has risen from cover—and ought to be easily bagged. Lots easier to get 'em on the wing, Jim.

"Well," I concluded, rising, "I'll be getting along. Sorry you are laid up. Things are happening—the circle is narrowing. I'm going to try and locate Shipp—though I won't find him, I am fairly certain. Maybe get a wink or two of sleep, for to-morrow is going to be a busy day. Take a shot of dope, now, and go to sleep. I'll see you again soon."

Shipp had indeed made himself scarce. At his apartment

I was told that he had been called out of town on a deal, and had driven his car north on Highway Number One, for Kansas City. The night man at the garage where he kept the car corroborated that.

I turned in about two o'clock, but didn't sleep. Lying there in the dark, my mind got to turning over and prowling among the intricacies of a detective story plot which I had read years ago. A chap by the name of Dupin, a French top-notcher, found a letter in an impossible place.

Impossible because the entire force of Paris cops had declared the letter could not be in a certain house; they had searched it from top to bottom—almost tore the place down—and the thing simply was not on the premises.

Yet—and get the incongruity of this—the letter had not been destroyed, since to do that would be to defeat the purpose in stealing it in the first place, and it was absolutely unbelievable that it was anywhere but in the house!

Impossible for it to be in the house, and equally as impossible that it could be elsewhere.

Dupin got the letter. It was, of course, in the house. He picked it up right from under the eyes of the investigators. They had not found it, because it was in an impossible hiding place. Impossible, in the opinion of the Paris cops, that is.

I was searching for a motor van, in order to get on the trail of the gypsy queen. The van had done the impossible. It had got out of a place from which it was absolutely impossible for it to be removed without leaving unmistakable traces of its going. Impossible—absolutely so.

Yet the van was not anywhere to be seen. There was no cavern or other secret hiding place into which it could have been put. If the theory of the Joplin police was correct, then the van, logically, was still there in the brush—invisible, in some unaccountable manner, to the eyes of mortal man.

If I could have burned the memory of that Dupin yarn out of my mind, as one might have burned a book, I could have slept. No sleep for me, though.

Daybreak found me standing at a window looking north over the house tops of the city. In the distance could be seen the interminable mountains of chat; mountains which hemmed Joplin in, and would some day, I found myself thinking, tumble over and bury the whole place. Joplin would, I thought gloomily, become a second Pompeii.

Then my gloom was suddenly spent. I felt I was rising in the air, or had just had a shot of gas. My breath came in one great gasp—and the next moment I was beating it for the elevator, hell-bent for Renne's Mill!

14

SHOOTING AT THE MOON

"TANNELLO!" I EXCLAIMED, when the tall Rom was in the seat beside me, "we are, I believe, about to dive head-foremost into the forbidden realm of which Old Man Impossible is king—an impossible stunt in itself! You are a game man, I know, and you will have need to be, I'm telling you, before the sun shines on another day!"

The Rom's reply was made quietly. "It is impossible to believe in the impossible, Norton," he said. "The impossible doesn't exist, so far as I am concerned. You lead, and I'll follow. Hell would not be too hot for me, if it should be necessary to charge through it to find Zelena!"

"You've hit it square!" I told him. "The little queen's *patteran* follows a course smack through hell—but this hell is frozen instead of hot!"

I drove into the brush beside the mill, and made for the place itself, followed by the Rom. Directly we were within, we proceeded to pile up enough old tables and other articles to enable us to mount to the second floor, the stairway no longer being available.

Reaching the fourth floor of the mill, I stood once more at the north window and looked out upon those monster mountains of chat—cold, ghostly, indescribably forbidding.

This time, though, I had a pair of powerful field glasses, and with them I proceeded to scan that bleak waste inch by inch. Tannello stood beside me, outwardly calm and at ease, but with eyes which shone with the light of excitement.

I covered the slope of the mountain nearest the mill, noting the upright stakes which stood in ragged lines about thirty to forty feet apart. There were two lines, or groups, of such stakes. One along the extreme left of the mound, and another following along the edge of a shallow valley where two cones joined.

Now and then my glasses would focus upon a stake from which a bit of rope fluttered. The effect was startling; so like a show of life in a place where all seemed dead—and should, by rights, be dead.

The fourth floor of the mill was high enough for me to see above the mounds in the foreground, and get a bit of the south slope of a huge gray bank just beyond. The valley between the two was not exposed.

What was I looking for? Anything at all. Anything that might serve as a marker indicating the course the little queen's *patteran* had followed over there. For, impossible though it appeared that she could have gone in that direction, I expected to find trace of her there.

It was, remember, impossible for the motor van to have traveled either north, south, east or west. To travel at all, in fact. Certainly it could not have been driven into that great waste of chat, even had the river presented no insurmountable barrier.

I knew that. Knew that the van could never have climbed

those mountains—yet I knew that it could not have disappeared in any direction other than there. Where the van
had gone, so also had gone the queen.

An hour's eye-straining scouring of the waste left me
no wiser than I had been before. Was it possible that the
delay of a week had afforded time for the wind and rain to
obliterate all traces?

My glasses traveled once more up the line of stakes
beside the shallow valley, touched the one at the peak, the
tallest of the lot, wavered, came back—and held.

Held, while for a full minute I did not get my breath!

"Tannello," I said, turning to the Rom, striving to speak
in a natural tone, "tonight we shoot at the moon! Nobody
has ever yet succeeded in sending a slug into that impossible target—but we are ambitious, and are going to try!"

"Meaning?" the Rom queried in unconsciously lowered
tones. That terrible chat, I could see, had impressed its
eeriness upon him.

"That we are going to enter that hell—that frozen hell
over yonder to the north," I replied. "It's a long chance,
with the odds almost all against us. But we've got to do it.
Take the glasses."

He held them to his eyes, focusing them on the mounds.

"Now, find the row of stakes near the valley between the
two peaks in the foreground."

"Got it!"

"Do you see the ones that have short lengths of rope
attached?"

"Yes!"

"Old, weathered, rotten bits of rope, are they not? Left
there for years?"

"Quite right. They appear black."

"Now focus on the tall stake at the top. Got it?"

"Yes."

"See a long length of rope there?"

"Yes—I see!"

"Any difference in it and those attached to the other—"

"Hell's bells!" the Rom exclaimed as he swung suddenly about, his calm gone—swept away into that smothering, ghastly field of chat. "It is new! That piece of rope is new—yellow as gold!"

"Ah, my friend," I said, "now you know why it is so very necessary for us to take that long shot at the moon!"

15

A DROP IN THE DARK

I DON'T KNOW whether Tannello prayed during the draggy hours of the balance of that day or not, but I freely admit I did. And the sole burden of my prayers was that we'd have a moon when night came on. It looked as though I was going to get what I asked for, too—but I guess my spiritual voice, weak through lack of use, wasn't powerful enough after all.

Six o'clock came, and with it came rain. It came in a half-hearted drizzle at first—like the slow motion of a lazy man going to work. By eight it had increased in volume, and at eight thirty sharp, the malignant clouds quit dallying along, called on their reserve supply, and sent the deluge down.

To shoot at the moon when it is in plain sight is a mad thing to do, but to send a slug skyward on a mere guess at its position back of the clouds is far worse. Yet we had to fire the shot that night—rain or fair. There are some things which may not be delayed.

As for going about the business during the hours of daylight, that was out of the question. Daylight would have enabled us to see, of course—but it plays no favorites. Others would be able to see, also.

At nine o'clock, having quit hoping for a let-up in the

downpour, I set out in my rented car, a closed one, from my hotel. I had that day laid in a plentiful supply of extra batteries for our flash lights, of which each of us were to carry two. I had also bought two sixty-foot lengths of one-inch grass rope, the most pliable I could find.

I picked Tannello up at the hotel, and we drove directly to the west end of the bridge over Shoal River. Instead of crossing the bridge and parking beside the mill, I turned off across a flat and drove to a position in the brush north of the mill and across the river from it.

The extra batteries were stored in the pockets of our leather jackets, which jackets we calculated would turn the rain, and both of us very carefully examined the mechanism of the pair of revolvers each carried.

Then, with one coil of rope secured about me, and the other in hand, we left the car and struggled through the sheets of falling water until we came to where the slope of chat began.

As Lakely had said, this slope was not a precipitous one, but rose gradually to its peak. Because of that the particles of chat which composed it had lain where they fell, undisturbed by the slides common to the steep slants. Action of the weather had fused them into a crusted mass. How deep that crust was, and how capable of bearing our weight, we were about to determine.

"The flash now, Tannello!" I requested.

The Rom directed its rays about the slope until he located the first of the stakes which formed the line along the shallow valley between the cones heretofore mentioned.

"Hold it!"

Somewhere, in the history of some case of mine which

I have related in print, I have set down the fact that my early days were spent as a cow-hand in the West. Such is my recollection. At any rate, I had so toiled, and, as it happened, had become an expert with a rope. Most cow-hands are capable in that particular. My skill stood me in hand that night.

It was not much of a trick to throw my loop over the first of those stakes, since I had level ground upon which to stand. I did so, then hauled myself up the slick plane until safely braced against it.

Then Tannello followed. He held his flash on the stake next above, and, after one abortive effort, I looped it.

No use following, stake by stake, the progress of that night-climb up the chat-mountain. I, personally, desire to forget about it. We reached the top of the cone, after what seemed days of struggle, and sat against the stake while resting.

It was a black night, unrelieved even by lightning. The range of our flash lights was not great, but we could see far enough away to determine that the north slope of the mountain we had just climbed dropped gradually down—down into a pit of darkness.

What lay at the bottom? Water, most likely. If no lake had formed there, we were on the right course. If one had, then we must try another direction.

The top of the stake beside which we rested was fifteen feet above ground, and my flash revealed that what we had seen through the glasses was a loose end of grass rope which had been used to bind a blockpulley there. A new pulley. So far, we were headed right.

"While we rest, Tannello," I said, sitting as close to him

as possible in order that my voice might be heard above the patter of the rain and the drive of the wind, "I shall catch up a few threads for you.

"Shipp—we are going to assume that the man we are after is he—enticed Orlando here by holding out a golden offer for the Renne's Mill property. Warned in advance that the king would come on a given day, he made his preparations accordingly.

"I can only speak of the things which appear clear to me—the how of it all must develop later. The manner in which he first came to know of the existence of the tribal wealth, and how he was able to keep so well informed, does not appear, but those things will be known in time.

"With his confederates—how many I haven't the least idea—Shipp made ready. He, or some one acting for him, killed the old man while he lay asleep in his van and threw him later on the ground. Zelena, we will say, was bound and gagged before she could raise a cry. She was left in the van, and the van itself driven across the river.

The water is shallow, and by crossing over the ledge above where the masonry joins it, the thing could be done. Risky, but wholly possible to an expert at the wheel. The character of the strip lying between where the van stood and the river being solid rock, no traces were left.

"Having got on this side, a rope was then attached to the front axle of the van, and it was drawn up the slant it could not have negotiated under its own power. Drawn by means of that block-pulley above. You will say that the task required great power—more than the arms of many men could supply. Quite right. Men did not furnish the motive power.

"A small, portable electric hoist, such as are common in the district, used by mine operators to raise and lower mine-tubs in the shafts. Such a host could have done the work—and I have no doubt it did.

"Having got the van up here, it was lowered to the pit below us by the same means. The rope which threaded the pulley was then withdrawn, and, luckily for us, the pulley left to hang. Why not? Who would see it? It would be a waste of time to climb that timber and take it down.

"That is as far as I can see, at the moment, Tannello. More light, let us hope, will come soon."

"I follow you," the Rom replied. "But why bring the van up here, at the cost of so much labor? Why hide it at all?"

"To make it appear that you, who were being framed, had flown with Zelena in the van. They could not have known, of course, that you would conveniently absent yourself, as you did. Meant for the police to think that you had secreted both girl and vehicle somewhere in the district.

"They could not move the van far, it being so noticeable as to attract the attention of all who saw it. Traced, the police would have learned much from that van. Then, too, it had a secret compartment containing a large amount of money.

"In the event Zelena proved obdurate, the van would likely have to be broken up in order to find the secret. That would take time, and they could work at their leisure over in the chat heaps."

"Would they not have considered the matter of no returning wheel marks?"

"There are two points from which that may be viewed. One is that, having so much to think of and do, they failed to allow for that. Did not think of it, in fact. The other is that they were so thoroughly assured that the stunt they were pulling was an impossible one, or so considered by police and public alike, they had no fear of the car ever being found.

"Let the police explain the circumstance of no returning traces in any manner they could. Meanwhile they doubtless enjoyed the element of mystery with which their act had invested the case."

"And they are holding Zelena, you think, in order to get from her the secret of the hiding place of the tribal funds?"

"Absolutely."

"Now, there is another objection to what you say, and perhaps you will be able to wipe it away. This: How could Shipp have known about the van, the money in it, and the secret compartment? He could not have known where that compartment was located, since only three persons knew that—Orlando, Zelena, and the workman who built it.

"I know the latter, and answer for his silence. But it would be virtually impossible for Shipp to have known the thing existed at all!"

"Not if he had a spy in the camp," I answered. "Tell me, Tannello, who in the tribe might have worked hand in glove with Shipp?"

"There is no one!" was the positive answer.

"You are wrong!" was my equally as positive assertion. "Inside information came to Shipp—and from a member of the tribe! You can depend on that!"

Silence followed my words; silence dining which I knew my companion was thinking intently. Then:

"Norton," he said, "Romany has not been without its

traitors—though such have been few. Perhaps this generation has produced one. But if one exists—I would not be in his shoes for all the gold there is, let alone the stake he has played for! A terrible death awaits him—even though he were the king himself!"

As little as I knew about the gypsies, I could well believe it.

"Do you feel rested?" I inquired.

"Yes. Tell me, what do you expect to find down below?"

"The van—or its fragments. And from it I expect to trace the whereabouts of the little queen. Are you ready?"

"Yes!"

There were no stakes whereby we could lower ourselves down into the pit. No carrier had been necessary there, since the chat came from mills on the outer edge. All we could do was to drop over the edge, clinging to whatever chance offered. We did and arrived, somehow, at the bottom.

A desperate chance? Surely. But we were playing for stakes worth while—eminently so. If we landed in a lake, we would contrive to get out again. If we fetched up on dry chat, all would be well—notwithstanding a few scratches and bruises we might collect in the descent.

I eased myself carefully over the side of the cone, released my hold on the stake—and the next instant was sliding downward, gathering momentum as I went, toward the black pit below.

16

THE QUEEN'S PATTERAN

THAT WILD DROP down into the darkness of the unknown is something else I want to forget. Doubtless Tannello does, too.

That we landed high and dry is a circumstance due solely to the fact that the valley between those cones was on a higher level than the one next beyond, and the water falling there, seeking a lower level, had cut for itself a narrow channel between the neighboring peaks and found an outlet there.

Our clothing was almost literally torn from our bodies, and both of us were so badly shaken up we lay as we landed for a full ten minutes, recuperating. Then we took stock.

Something foreseen is something which may be guarded against, and we had so secured our flash lights and weapons as to protect them against loss or injury. The two coils of rope, one wound about my body and the other in Tannello's care, made the descent with us. Save for a few bruises and minor cuts, and the loss of nearly all our outer clothing, we were in good shape.

Coincident with our arrival on the bottom of the pit, the rain slacked off and, a few minutes later, played out altogether. It still was, however, as black as ink where we were.

Then began a slow, laborious search of the floor of the great inclosure. It was Tannello who made the discovery, and a shout from him brought me to his side.

He had caught his foot on something buried beneath the chat—and it proved to be part of the wreckage of the van. It had been broken up—doubtless to find the secret cache—and then its parts covered with chat.

Was the body of the little queen down under the particles of crushed rock, too?

That thought, I knew, was in both our minds. I decided not. Though there could be little doubt that her captors meant to slay her in the end, that would not occur until the gypsy hoard was safely in their hands.

Zelena still lived—provided she had the grit to keep her lips closed. If she had not—had, in fine, given up the information demanded, then she might well be dead.

I began casting around in the vicinity of the place in an effort to find what I had hoped to see in that valley. Two hundred feet away, I found it.

A concrete base upon which a zinc mill once had stood—and in the center of the base the open mouth of the shaft which had been the reason for its presence there.

The ends of two twisted electric light wires, showing at a corner of the shaft, explained where the current for the hoist had come from, and, incidentally, confirmed my opinion that a hoist had been used. Those wires surely led to the outside, and tapped a trunk-line there.

Nor was that all. Secured to an iron beam set in the concrete, and extending across the shaft, was the end of a grass-rope cable—brand new. I had expected to find it there. Else how could those above let themselves down into the shaft?

Once down, there would be no one left on top to release the thing. The rope, according to my calculations, had to be there—and it was.

I called Tannello to my side, just as the moon, threatening us from behind scudding clouds, broke through and gave us light.

The Rom came running, and looking back over his shoulder.

"In the name of God, Norton, look!" he cried, pointing toward the peaks of chat which hemmed us in.

I did—and my blood became like iced water in my veins! Those monster mountains of chat were moving—sliding inward! The terrific rain had done its work! As surely as we were standing there, petrified with horror, those towers of chat were tumbling down upon us—in the very act of burying us alive!

"Quick!" I shouted, galvanized into action by sheer terror. "Over the side, and down the rope! No! You first, damn you! Don't stand there—"

Tannello leaped, caught the rope and slid down into the shaft, and I was only one breadth behind him. Down we slid—one, two hundred feet, to land in the shaft's bottom, waist deep in water. My flash came out, revealing a wide opening above and just within reach, as the first shower of what was soon to be tons of chat came rattling down upon us.

I drew myself up and into the stope—for such it was— and Tannello followed.

An instant later a solid stream of chat crashed down

the shaft, and, in the twinkling of an eye, had blocked the mouth of the stope as solidly as concrete would have done. Blocked it forever!

"Norton," came Tannello's voice, after what seemed a long, long time, "do you know, we are securely sealed in this old mine for good, unless it has got some other exit?"

"Yes," I replied, as steadily as I could. "But there is another exit—the one Shipp and his gang use. The Lord only knows where it is, or how far away—but it's up to us to find it!"

17

ZELENA, QUEEN OF THE ROMS

WE IMMEDIATELY SET about it. Setting the catch on our flash lights, we followed the stope, the floor of which was a litter of broken stone, worn out picks and shovels, and other debris consequent to a mine's operation. There were many lateral stopes, for the most part ending a short distance away from the main one in pockets, or rooms, hollowed out by the picks of miners.

I looked at my watch, after it occurred to me that we had spent a lot of time and appeared to be making but little progress, and was amazed to see that it was three o'clock in the morning!

Tannello had taken the lead, for some time back, and was at the moment about to turn off down one of the numerous tunnels leading from the main trunk, when he stepped back, clutched my arm, and shut off his light. I followed suit instantly.

"There's a glimmer of light down there!" he whispered excitedly. "I think we've found them!"

I dropped on my hands and knees, crawled forward and thrust my head around a knob of jutting rock which flanked the short tunnel. It was as Tannello had said. A faint light showed farther down the lateral—evidently coming from a room at the end.

"Tannello," I whispered, drawing him to me, "we are going to investigate that light—and don't take any chances. If you have to shoot—shoot straight."

The Rom's body trembled. "Norton," he whispered in return, "I have a great favor to ask of you! If it is at all possible, leave this Shipp—or whoever the chief scoundrel may be—to me! Will you?"

"If I can," I told him. "Come on!"

We made our way without sound down the tunnel and to a position from which the interior of the room at the end lay before us.

The place is beyond me to describe. It was larger than any we had seen before, and from a shoring-timber of the ceiling depended a kerosene lantern. By its light we made out a number of bunks against the walls, and men sitting on them. I counted three.

One corner of the room had been cut off by means of a strip of old canvas drawn across it, and just in front of that strip, his black-clothed figure outlined against its whiteness, sat Vincent Shipp.

Back of the canvas—what?

Zelena, undoubtedly.

"Wait!" I cautioned the Rom in a whisper. "We've got to get Shipp from in front of the curtain! Zelena is back there, I think, and there's going to be some shooting. We've got to think of her!"

Shipp was speaking to his men, but his words were not loud enough to carry to our ears. We didn't mind that. We had found him—and that was enough!

"I have an idea!" Tannello whispered. "I'll cast one of these large stones into the room at his feet. Naturally, he will leap up and start to investigate. Then we can rush them!"

He picked a stone from the floor.

"Heave ahead!" I told him, drawing both my guns when I said it.

Wham!

The big rock, instead of falling at Shipp's feet, struck one of them. With a furious oath, he leaped to his feet.

"Who threw that?" he demanded.

"It—it came from outside!" one of the men on the bunks faltered.

"It couldn't!" Shipp snapped, starting for the exit. "There's nobody out there—"

"Except us, Shipp!"

I stepped forward into the light of the room as I uttered the words, Tannello close beside me.

"Hell!" Shipp's lips opened in a snarl of astonishment and rage. He leaped back, whipped out a gun and raised it.

My finger was on the trigger of one of my guns, and itching to press it. But I didn't.

Tannello's pistol spoke, the flame so close to my face I felt its heat, and Shipp's career ended then and there.

A man on a near-by bunk, a dark-skinned man with a scar on his cheek, the one who had sent Steele and Lakely to the hospital, leaped to his feet and swung a gun on me.

I got him, and then bedlam broke loose. When it was over, there were no prisoners to take above ground.

They wanted it that way, and so they got it.

Tannello dashed to the canvas curtain, swept it aside—

and right then I slipped out of the room. When I heard his voice calling me, a few minutes later, I returned to look for the first time upon the little Queen of Romany.

Well might Tannello's heart-wound have burned and bled for such a woman. I have never, before or since, feasted my eyes upon such loveliness as was hers. Pale, she was, and frightened.

But they had not used her roughly, though she had that night been informed by Shipp that she must reveal the hiding place of the gypsy hoard before the morning dawned, or die.

"From what he said," she told us in a voice sweet and musical, "I knew that some one was seeking for me diligently. He was very much alarmed, and seemed to realize that great danger threatened him. But how could I make him believe that there was no treasure that he could touch? Ah, Tannello, he would not believe me!"

"How's that?" I demanded. "No treasure? What the—"

Tannello laughed. "Oh, yes, Norton, my friend, there is much treasure," he said. "A million dollars of gypsy money is invested in the big building in which Shipp had his offices. There are other fine investments, too.

"Orlando long ago saw the light. He would not trust the *gorgio* banks, but there was nothing at all wrong with *gorgio* real estate! Being next in line for the crown, I knew all about it—advised him in many of his deals. Shipp, it appears, was badly misinformed!"

And that was that!

"What about that hundred thousand dollars?" I asked.

"He got it," Zelena answered. "Got it the night he killed Orlando with my dagger. They had to break the van up to find it. If we never see the money again, we shall not worry!"

"No, Zelena, we shall not worry!"

"Well," I told them, "since you two aren't going to worry, darned if I will either!"

18

BARDO DELIVERS THE CARPET

IT WAS NOT a difficult task to find our way above ground again. Zelena knew the general direction, and we finally came out into a cellar beneath a cottage on the western edge of the waste of chat. There the mill of a mine had once stood, and its workings had joined the one we entered from.

Shipp, in his character of realtor, had bought the cottage, after learning that the entrance to the shaft lay beneath, a circumstance but little known. For, be it said, his crooked operations had not been confined to his plunge after the treasure of Romany. Far from it.

The old mine had long been in use as a hideout for the gang of thieves which he headed. Much plunder was later brought out, along with the bodies Tannello and I had left behind us.

Tannello Seton returned to his people, and, I am proud to state, I was a guest of the tribe when he and the little queen were married.

I see them both, now and then, and expect to do so as long as all of us are alive. As to whether or not Shipp— who, it was definitely established later, was a half-breed Rom; his mother of that race and his father a French-

man—had a confederate in the gypsies' camp, I shall allow
you to judge.

I have said that I see Tannello and Zelena, King and
Queen in Romany, at intervals. Sometimes, almost always,
in fact, it is I who visit them at their St. Louis *tan*. I also see,
on those visits, the Lorels—mother, and also Bardo, who
became reconciled to his brother-in-law—and Danjefo—
but not Ricco, the third brother.

Never since the first time I beheld him have eyes of
mine seen him again. When I inquired after him, there
was nothing but silence.

Judge then, for yourself. Shipp had a confederate in the
camp. That is certain. Was it young Ricco? Ricco, in igno-
rance of how the tribal funds were invested, and hoping
for a crown? Only two brothers stood between him and
the throne. I have inquired for him, and there has always
been silence. Was it Ricco? I think it was.

Two days after I returned to Kansas City, I received a
call from Bardo.

"Here are the other strips for that carpet," he informed
me with an amiable grin, and thrust the material into my
hand.

But you won't tread on that carpet, should you chance to
come into my office. The old rug is still there. The new one
might shame my friends by its splendor, and so I decided
to keep it well concealed.

www.ingramcontent.com/pod-product-compliance
Lightning Source LLC
Chambersburg PA
CBHW022005050726
47499CB00002BA/460